WINGS OF FATE

A KINGDOMS OF FAERIE NOVEL

SKYE HORN

Printed in the United States of America
First Printed, 2020

Cover Design by Levierre at 99 Designs
Editing by Ella Medler
https://ellamedlerediting.yolasite.com
ISBN: 978-1-7345968-0-9

Published by Skye Horn
skyehorn.com

For my parents, who raised me to believe life could be magical.

This first one is for you.

TABLE OF CONTENTS

CHAPTER 1

STANDING DRENCHED IN THE RAIN OF A FOREIGN COUNTRY AFTER over twenty hours of travel definitely made Thea Gilbert's list of top-ten-worst days. She admitted it probably didn't rank as high as her parents' dying in a car accident or finding out she was adopted, but it definitely outranked breaking up with her high school sweetheart, Marcus, after his heartfelt proposal. Apparently, being eighteen and an orphan meant she needed a husband to take care of her. That was one reason she'd left Colorado and fled to Ireland, despite the guilty voice in her head patronizing her and slating her decisions.

"Are you here to see the Faeries too?" a little boy asked from beside her, startling Thea out of her thoughts. He stared at the unextraordinary green hillside with eager eyes.

Sure, Ireland was beautiful, but once she'd seen one rolling green plain, hadn't she seen them all?

Thea glanced at the boy briefly. He stood with his hands tucked into his red hoodie next to an elderly woman who wore a matching red raincoat. "Granny says they only come out at dusk."

"Don't bother the poor girl," his grandmother scolded,

tugging the little boy away from the hill. "Let's get inside before you catch your death."

Before Thea could formulate a response they pulled their hoods tight over their heads and hurried down the path to the village, leaving her alone in the rain. She knew this weather was normal in these parts, but by the ominous clouds forming overhead and the shortage of people willing to stand outside, she wondered if this would sooner grow from a sprinkle into a storm.

Regardless, she forced her feet toward the Hill of Knockainey, which was the entire reason she'd chosen Ireland as her destination to begin with. According to her adoption file, this was where her biological parents had abandoned her, wrapped in a purple silk blanket with no hint of who they were. She'd let herself sink into an aching numbness since her parents' deaths, but it never extinguished the loneliness that constantly plagued her. It resurfaced in the form of a stomachache, twisting her insides until she felt as if she might puke, but she swallowed back the bile, inhaling sharply. Just because she was now an orphan didn't mean she needed to fall apart at the seams.

Like the little boy who wished to see the Faeries, Thea wished she could see what her biological parents had thought when they left her in this cold, rainy country fifteen years ago. She was grateful for the loving and supportive parents who'd raised her. They'd put her through private school and intended to send her to art school in the fall, but the car accident had changed everything. Thea hadn't touched her sketchpad since.

The insurance money had made this trip possible, but she knew it wouldn't last forever. At some point in the near future, she'd have to face the fact that she was alone now. She had no idea how to be an adult, because they didn't teach you that between social studies and biology classes. Tax season was one of her biggest fears, as was trying to figure out how to pay the mortgage on her parents' house when she worked as a barista at a coffee shop for minimum wage. Perhaps that was why this trip was so important to her. She knew her parents were gone, but as heartbroken as that left her, she thought maybe finding her biological parents would fix the emptiness she felt.

They at least owed her an explanation, right?

The issue was that she had zero information on who her biological parents were—or had been. It took a few hours of googling to find out that the only real significant thing about the Hill of Knockainey was that in Celtic Mythology, the Goddess Ainé, who was Queen of the Faeries, lived within the hill. Until the late 1800s, the Irish people still held celebrations for the Faeries in the very spot Thea now stood. However, that told her nothing of realistic importance.

As the rain became more intense and her red locks began sticking to her skin, Thea wished irritably that she'd prepared more for this trip by at least packing an umbrella. She reached up and braided the unruly mess into a single braid that fell over her right shoulder. She pulled her hood up over her head and her jacket tighter around herself, but refused to turn back no matter how bad the weather persisted to be. The sun was setting, and Thea thought of the little boy who wanted to see the Faeries at dusk. She wished he were here to make this space a little less lonely, but his grandmother had been right. They'd both catch their death in this storm.

Thea rested the palms of her hands on the earth at the base of the hill, closing her eyes as she wondered what connection her biological parents could have had to this place.

Had they been Irish? Did they, like so many other of the locals in this area, believe in the mythology behind this plot of land and think leaving her here would bring her good fortune? She couldn't know the answer, but she could imagine their intentions had been good. She could pretend they hadn't just abandoned her like everyone else seemed to.

Thea knew it wasn't fair to think of her adoptive parents'

deaths as abandonment, but she also couldn't lie to herself and say that wasn't what it felt like. A single tear, mixed with rainwater on her face, trickled its way down her cheek, off her chin, and landed beside the place her hand still rested. Thunder exploded directly over her head and lightning struck the spot just in front of where she crouched. She shot backwards upon the impact, sliding across the damp grass into a shaking heap with the smell of burnt hair in her nostrils.

Despite its wetness, the earth was hard beneath her, and she swore profusely as it trembled too. Her entire body ached from the impact, but she wasn't reacting the way she should have been. Time moved in slow motion as she checked herself for injuries, whimpering at the sight of her blood-stained jeans.

I'm either dead or hallucinating, she thought, trying to pull herself back to her feet.

She figured that she must be dead, but if she weren't dead, then she definitely had serious brain damage to believe the earth shook at the very moment lightning struck her.

An ache filled her from head to toe as she struggled to pull herself to her feet, only managing to get to her knees. The place where she'd been crouched before had a soft glow to it now, as if a door had cracked open in the ground itself and light from somewhere else peeked out from behind the door. Thea frowned, crawling toward it as a whisper of noise met her ears.

We see you, Princess. We're coming, it said, and a prickle of dread clawed its way down Thea's spine. The whisper crawled across her skin, turning droplets of water to ice, and blinding light escaped the crack in the earth, opening wide enough for someone to step through: a man with wings like ravens'.

KIERAN FELT her presence before the Threshold opened, not that she could have opened it without guidance. Magic was complicated, and since she'd lived in a world without magic for fifteen years, he doubted she possessed the ability to open a door between realms.

"What is it?" Ethel asked from the log she sat perched on. She stopped playing with the daisies she'd picked miraculously from the snow, meeting his gaze. Flowers hardly grew in this region, but when they did, Ethel did not miss the chance to bring them home or turn them into hairpieces for the other girls in the village. However, whatever expression he'd made distracted her so much that she tilted her round face to follow his gaze toward the empty space between the two massive tree trunks.

It looked completely ordinary to a human eye, such as Ethel's, but to his trained Fae gaze, the space was ablaze with ancient magic. Kieran knew he shouldn't leave his post. His orders were to guard the Threshold so that none of King Malachi's soldiers crossed to the land without magic—to her. However, the pull he felt to cross it rippled beneath his skin, pulsing through his veins in chilling tendrils that tortured him. The little voice in his head that was supposed to help him make rational decisions was being silenced by another telling him she was right there within his reach.

This had never happened before. She'd never been this close to the Threshold, or at least, not while he'd stood guard. He wondered what had changed. Did the magic call to her as it had done to her ancestors, beckoning her to the home that craved her return?

He couldn't know the answer, but he could imagine in the same way he'd imagined their reunion so many times before. All across the land of Faerie, the people would cheer for the return of the missing Princess of Ivandor. He would stand at her side, a protector of his future queen, the way he'd promised to do since the day she was born. Against his better judgement, he pictured what she looked like after all these years apart, wondering if her gray eyes still mirrored her mother's, or if she still had a single dimple when she smiled. The last time Kieran had seen her, he'd carried her through the Threshold under her mother's orders. He'd been only ten years old, but he remembered.

It was likely the princess had no recollection of him, but the agony he experienced in her absence still haunted him daily, as did the regret he felt for leaving her alone that night.

"What *is* it?" Ethel repeated, now standing directly behind him. He barely heard her speak as his mind spun around the possibility of being reunited with the princess after all of this time. He forgot his duty and his post, he forgot everything he knew mattered about the reason he guarded the Threshold, because all that mattered was her. The pull across the Threshold captivated him, and the whisper he heard beyond its barrier clouded his once rational thoughts.

Come and find me, it sang across the wind to him.

"Do you hear that?" Kieran asked, taking an unstable step forward. His wings felt heavy on his back, as if trying to weigh him down. He ignored even that sign though, listening to her call out again and again. "I hear her."

"Hear *who*?" Ethel grabbed Kieran's arm, catching him off-guard. Some distant part of him realized that in his right mind a human girl would have never surprised him like that. His training prevented mistakes like that from happening, and yet, he continued to ignore the red flags. "Kieran, you need to get away from there."

She looked toward the Threshold, reminding Kieran of what he was about to do. He decided then, shaking Ethel's grip from his arm and settling his hand on the hilt of his sword. The wind rustled around his feathered wings, and he tasted the magic in the air. It carried a familiar, sweet scent to his nostrils, a mixture of daisies and pine, and he knew she was there waiting for him. The blinding sensation carried him forward, and his ravenous need to be near her caused his heart to pulse painfully against his chest. He couldn't leave her again. The regret would suffocate him, and surely, he would die, or rather deserve to die. He knew he was breaking the law by even considering it, but nothing else mattered any longer.

"Tell them I'm bringing the princess home," he said without looking at Ethel. The musical whisper on the wind became deafening in his ears as he approached the Threshold.

"Kieran, wait—" she said, but he didn't bother. She wasn't strong enough to stop him, nor did he believe she'd try. Ethel had grown up with stories of the princess; she idolized her like a sister she'd never had, despite the fact that they weren't actually related. She wanted her return as much as he did, so when she turned and ran toward the village, Kieran was not surprised. He knew she trusted him; she would do whatever was necessary to prepare for the princess' arrival. That first meant telling his Aunt Iris he was breaking the law, and he didn't envy her for that job.

Knowing Ethel was safely away from the Threshold, Kieran summoned the power required to open the pathway to the land without magic and the earth quaked beneath his feet. His wings unfurled behind him anxiously and then folded against his back. Within moments he felt the magic stirring in the air around him and beneath his skin. It throbbed like a life force begging to be released, but dormant until called upon. Her call to him was as clear as the magic in his blood, and as soon as the doorway opened, he stepped through with the reassuring thought that he would finally see her again, too distracted to notice the shadow following closely behind.

CHAPTER 2

When the unexpected chill subsided from Kieran's skin, his eyes adjusted to the new darkness surrounding him. He didn't remember crossing the Threshold being so uncomfortable, but it'd been many years. His training had covered adjusting his senses to this type of change, but by the frightened look on the face of the young woman in front of him, Kieran realized a moment too late that he'd made a terrible miscalculation. He tried to conceal his wings behind him, hoping he wouldn't frighten her any further, and extended his hand to help her to her feet.

"Hello, Princess."

Her features became clearer as the magic enhanced his sight, almost as if she were standing in direct sunlight. A long, wet braid of flaming red hair hung over her shoulder, but a few strands had fallen loose to frame her heart-shaped face. She'd grown out of the softness that often existed on children's faces, gaining a more defined chin and nose, much like her father's. He watched as her gray eyes stared at his extended hand with apprehension, but there was a sparkle of curiosity in those eyes.

"W-Where did you come from?" she asked. Her voice shook as she glanced at the space where the portal now lay concealed. Kieran took a moment to examine her, unable to wrap his mind around the fact that this young woman was the same as the toddler he'd left on this very spot fifteen years ago. She lacked any visible Faerie traits, which their species often developed as adolescents. He could only assume that was because of the absence of magic in her life. However, despite this, she'd grown to be as tall and beautiful as any Fae he'd ever met, if not more beautiful. The sun had trailed her skin with kisses along her cheeks and nose, and her eyebrows pulled upward in the same way they'd done as a child when he didn't respond immediately.

"You called for me," he replied, withdrawing his hand and letting it fall awkwardly to his side.

"Excuse me?"

Kieran watched her facial expression as it shifted between fear and confusion, frowning. This wasn't how he'd imagined their reunion. Her fingers curled into a fist instinctively and he held up his hands, taking a calculated step forward. Her untrained eyes would perceive him as a shadow in the darkness, putting her understandably on guard. He crouched low so that they were eye-level, hoping it might ease some of her tension. This was when he noticed her shiver, although he felt positive she'd attempted to conceal it from him. Without a second thought, he focused on the air around them and used the smallest amount of magic to warm it. Air was his specialty, but he didn't dare risk using too much magic.

"I've gone about this all wrong," he said, letting the gentle breeze carry his voice across the space between them. She'd clearly noticed the change in temperature, because she lowered her arms slowly from where they crossed over her stomach. Her eyes darted around, as if she could feel the magic surrounding her, but her confusion only increased. Doe-like fear reflected beneath the star light, twisting his insides into agonized knots. He was sworn to protect her, and yet, all he'd done so far was terrify her.

"I think I should go," she said, hardly above a whisper. She stood unsteadily and took a step away from him, her instincts driving her into the classic fight-or-flight response. It appeared she'd be choosing flight tonight.

"Please," he pleaded.

As the clouds shifted in the sky and the moonlight shone across his features, her expression transformed from fear to shock to recognition. The bile threatening to rise from his stomach settled at the sight. His soul lifted, and his lips stretched into a broad grin.

"You remember," he said without question; it was written all over her face.

"T-That's impossible. How do I know you?" she asked. The answer to her question was far more than Kieran could explain here and now, but the fact that she recognized him at all lifted a fifteen-year-old weight from his shoulders. He wanted to stretch his wings and lift her into his arms, but he controlled his urges carefully.

Kieran had spent so long dreaming of this moment. He'd wondered if she'd recognize him and desired that recognition more than anything in all the four Kingdoms of Faerie.

"I remember you, but it's like a dream," she said.

Her brows pulled together as she stared at him, and her fear melted away. She took a deliberate step in his direction, closing the distance, and her small pink mouth fell open into an *O* as his wings entered her vision.

"I thought I was imagining it," she said unafraid. "What are you?"

The sudden tremble of the ground beneath them cut Kieran's response short, for this time, it was not him stepping through the Threshold. The princess' eyes grew wide as she looked beyond him to where the doorway began reopening.

"Get behind me," he ordered, turning his back on her. He unfolded his wings, spreading them wide to form a wall between the princess and whoever was coming. She did as he said without question, but the warmth he'd surrounded her with snapped away so quickly that she started shivering again. As the surrounding air grew colder, the shadows crawled through the glowing crack in the earth, slinking like a disease into a new, unexplored place. He cursed and drew his sword from the baldric that was slung across his chest. A deep azure illuminated the blade as his hands wrapped around the hilt.

Shadows snaked in their direction, but Kieran whipped them away with a flick of his wings. A tiny gasp behind him alerted him of her fear, and he wanted nothing more than to get her out of here before it was too late, but there was no time to flee now.

He stood his ground.

"Do exactly as I say, do you understand?" he directed his command over his shoulder and heard a slight squeak of agreement just as a figure stepped across the Threshold. The shadows stretched out from her fingertips as extensions of her thin limbs, attempting to strike at Kieran's wings. She wore the seal of King Malachi upon her right shoulder, embroidered in deep crimson thread along her black leather sleeve. Her short blonde hair accentuated her pointed ears, but despite her obvious attempt to look older, the softness of her face gave away her youth.

"You appear to have finally slipped up, Kieran," she said with a wicked smile, stalking around him like a cat would a mouse. Her voice was melodic, as many Fae's voices were. Her eyes, however, were rimmed with red—a sign of the dark magic she wielded. "I never thought of you as foolish, but you left the way wide open for me. Following some silly voice in your head? *Come and find me...*"

Kieran's back stiffened at the repetition of the words he'd heard so clearly, the words he'd assumed came from the princess.

"You—" he started to say, but her annoying giggling cut him off.

"Oh, won't you ever learn not to trust the voices in your head?"

He felt foolish to have thought the princess had called to him, a pang of hurt even, but didn't let that hurt reflect on his face. Instead, he gripped the sword a little tighter and glared at the young Fae.

"Go back to your father, Amara," he said coldly. He lifted the sword, ready for the fight of his life. Despite her age, Kieran knew Amara was a skilled warrior, and after using magic to open the Threshold, he was no longer at full strength. The dark magic she commanded made her considerably more dangerous, but if he failed to keep Thea out of Amara's grasp there would be a far greater darkness to face.

"Now, now... you wouldn't keep me away from my dearly missed big sister, would you?" Amara cooed, attempting to peek behind his wings just as he lunged with his sword aimed directly for her heart.

THEA WATCHED in horror as Kieran unsheathed his sword, momentarily distracted from the massive black wings outstretched in front of her. She stood frozen, as if her limbs had completely forgotten how to move or react, while he lunged for Amara.

You've snapped, she told herself when the short-haired girl who'd literally just walked out of the earth announced herself as

Thea's sister. Despite the strange leather attire Amara wore, she seemed no older than fifteen or sixteen. Thea tried to look around Kieran's wings, but he all but growled at her to stay where she was. She didn't like him bossing her around, but regardless of any urges she had to run away, an invisible force physically held her ankles in place.

"You're not getting near her," Kieran said in the most animalistic tone Thea had ever heard outside of a movie screen. The hairs on the back of her neck prickled at the sound, while every instinct in her body urged her to run as fast and as far away from this situation as she could.

What was she doing? Why wasn't she screaming for help or calling the police? She recalled the old woman and her grandson who'd been standing at her side just minutes before this all began, wondering if they were still close enough to hear her yell.

Two lunatics were fighting with swords in front of her, her feet were magically glued to the ground beneath her, and one of those lunatics had wings—actual, raven-like WINGS. Why wasn't she running for her damn life?

Despite the wings on his back, Kieran's feet never left the ground. He positioned himself between Thea and Amara at all times, but it didn't work to his advantage. Amara's two blades sliced a clean line across the back of his calf and red liquid began to soak through his pant leg as he let out an outraged scream of pain.

Thea, who'd suddenly discovered her voice again, shrieked at Amara to stop. All thoughts of fleeing slipped from her mind as her heart raced at the sight of Kieran's blood pooling onto the ground beneath him. Waves of repulsion twisted her stomach into tight knots, rising into her throat as she thrashed against the invisible chains that seized her, trying desperately to reach out and help him. Reckless desire to protect him from Amara's blade overcame her, erasing all sense of logic and reason. She could practically see the invisible line connecting them, a line that she feared would shatter her if severed.

Kieran's pleading gaze met hers, begging her to remain where she was, but Thea ignored him. She wasn't a damsel in distress, despite the obvious difference in ability between them. She wouldn't allow him to die protecting her out of some misplaced sense of duty he appeared to possess. To Thea's horror, Kieran's distraction nearly got him impaled through the stomach.

"Please, stop!" she screamed.

Amara laughed.

"Look at this; *she's* worried about *you*, and *you're* supposed to be the one protecting *her*." Her laugh was hideous and cruel, but before Thea could think to respond, one of Amara's snakelike shadows twisted itself around Thea's legs. It inched icily up her body and cupped her chin as if it were caressing a lover.

Thea wanted to vomit.

Amara continued to smile from where she fought Kieran effortlessly a few yards away. He limped on his injured leg, and Thea realized that whatever magic Kieran was using, he was splitting it between keeping her out of harm's way and fighting against Amara. It was exhausting him and would cost him his life.

The tentacle-like shadows wrapped around Thea's neck like a boa constrictor, and she whimpered despite herself, watching Kieran's gaze flicker back toward her. She wanted to snap at him to stop looking at her and focus on Amara. It was clear that Kieran was outmatched, so the last thing he needed to be doing right now was worrying about her. However, she wouldn't be snapping at anyone because the shadow was swallowing her like prey. She choked on the suffocating darkness, slamming her eyes shut as her vision blurred. The last thing Thea heard before the magic completely consumed her was Kieran begging Amara for her freedom.

Fight it! A voice said in her head, but not the usual little voice that told her when things were right or wrong, nor the sinister tone she'd heard earlier saying they were coming. This voice was crystal clear and demanding, but not cruel. *Fight it or you'll both die tonight!*

How? Thea asked. She struggled to breathe as Kieran's screams grew farther and farther away.

You know how, said the woman's voice. The familiarity of the voice was just as unexplainable as Thea's familiarity with Kieran, but she ignored the insanity of the situation. Whatever was going on in her head would have to wait for a time when she wasn't about to die. Burying the panic, Thea didn't allow herself to overthink her next actions. Instead, she opened her hands from the fists they'd clenched into and willed herself to break free of the shadows drowning her.

She thought of Kieran, fighting alone to protect her against Amara. She thought of Amara's claim to be her sister, and the attempted murder of both Kieran and herself. And she thought of her parents' lies, which had placed her on this path to Ireland in the first place. All of these thoughts and emotions burned beneath the surface of her skin, threatening to explode like the monstrous thunder in the sky, but instead of letting them shatter her, she used them to power through whatever held her captive.

Magic, the voice explained, and the nonsensical word made absolute sense to Thea, even as she tried to rationalize another explanation.

Looking down, she saw the same glow that had illuminated Kieran's sword radiating from the palms of her hands. She didn't have time to understand what was happening, because whatever it was, she felt it draining her of every ounce of remaining energy. So, without hesitation, she held her hands up, palms out, and aimed in the general direction she'd seen Amara last. It was nearly impossible to see through the shadows that engulfed her, but as soon as her hands lifted, the tentacles of icy darkness recoiled, fleeing back to their source. Thea glimpsed Kieran diving out of the way just in time as the magic shot from her hands, hitting Amara square in the chest. The surrounding darkness disappeared, leaving only a wide-eyed adolescent staring at Thea from the ground.

Thea dropped her hands back to her sides, her strength crumpling from the inside out, and felt herself falling toward the earth, only to be caught by a powerful set of arms. Despite her drenched clothing, his skin felt warm against hers and the musky scent of earth on his shirt made her smile deliriously.

"You're welcome," she told him. She rested her head against his chest, listening closely to his racing heartbeat. His breathing was quick, and the way he looked at her was almost proud. He lifted her into his arms without a word, but she shook her head, still conscious enough to understand.

"Your leg is injured," she argued, her eyes fighting her in an endless battle for sleep. A distant part of her told her to be scared that Amara would attack again, but she had no energy left to do so.

"It's only a scratch," he lied as she recalled the amount of blood that had spilled from his leg. "We need to leave. She knows she can't fight us both, but she hasn't noticed how weak it has made you."

Thea felt offended by his comment. She'd just done something extraordinary and saved both of their lives, but he was calling her weak? She frowned, failing to hide the hurt on her face.

"I didn't mean it like that," Kieran commented, but did not appear in the mood to elaborate. His eyes darted around them as he limped toward the place she'd seen both him and Amara emerge from the earth. "You shouldn't have been able to do that without training. How did you know what to do?"

"She told me," Thea said. She yawned, nuzzling her head against him, unable to hold it up any longer.

"She?"

"Where are you taking me?" Thea asked, her eyes closing. A safer darkness took her into its arms as she finally gave into her fatigue. She felt Kieran kiss her head and wondered if it'd been her imagination as he mumbled a single word against her skin: home.

CHAPTER 3

THEA WALKED THROUGH A FIELD OF POPPIES IN A FLOWING WHITE dress that brushed the forest floor. Her fingertips touched the tops of the flowers, which grew larger than any poppy she'd ever seen. Trees encircled the massive meadow, and pinkish-purple reflections danced across the dawning sky. Thea recognized the dream by its vibrant color scheme and the hazy feeling of her thoughts, but she struggled to remember how she fell asleep in the first place. She racked her brain for any solid moment to grasp onto, gasping as the memories overwhelmed her.

"Kieran," she said aloud, spinning around as if she could run from the meadow to find him. Instead, she found herself face to face with a red mare who stood grazing among the poppies.

Human-like amusement sparkled behind the animal's golden eyes.

"Uh, hi..." Thea said. She figured in a dream she could control any outcome, but considering she wanted nothing more than to wake up, it seemed she had no control at all. The mare let out a soft whinny and returned to her grazing, while Thea tilted her head.

The horse's mane hung in beautiful auburn strands that nearly matched the color of Thea's own hair. Her tail flicked, swishing back and forth with the breeze, and her eyes continued to watch Thea. Those eyes were more intelligent than any typical horse's; Thea felt them staring directly through her, seeing everything that had happened to her over the past couple of months, exploring the loneliness and regret she'd buried. She felt each emotion being taken from her, each memory being replayed as if she were experiencing it all over again, and a tear trickled down her cheek.

"Stop," she said. Her voice cracked. "P-Please."

The memory of the life she'd left behind in Colorado flickered around her. She saw Marcus' heartbroken face as he read over her goodbye note long after she'd boarded a plane, the engagement ring glimmering painfully clear against his open palm. She'd been too scared to tell him in person—so sure he'd convince her to stay.

"Please," she begged again, not wanting to see anymore.

Thea saw the single tear that fell from the mare's eye as she lay in the grass, bowed low at Thea's feet, and although she did not speak, Thea understood her message.

Then she awoke.

AT FIRST, Thea didn't open her eyes. Instead, she allowed the dream to linger a moment longer behind her eyelids. The mare's kind gaze relieved a small part of her that had been clutching the pain and loss of the past few months. Sharing those difficult memories with someone, even in a dream, filled her lungs with a fresh breath of air. Air that tasted like pine trees and poppies on the soft pillow beneath her head.

"I think she's awake," said an unfamiliar voice. Someone else hurried loudly out of the room as Thea opened her eyes, blinking slowly against the fresh light. She was wrapped in cotton blankets on a particularly comfortable bed that practically filled the entire bedroom.

Thea shifted to untangle herself from the blankets as a curly-haired girl stared at her wide-eyed from across the room.

"Princess Claire, it's such an honor to finally meet you," the girl squeaked, actually squeaked with an embarrassed blush. She practically ran to Thea, throwing her arms around her in an awkward hug that made every muscle tense up in Thea's body, and then pulled away. Her face was flaming. "I'm sorry, that was completely inappropriate. It's just that we are so happy to have you home, and the village is already celebrating, and you've been asleep for three days, and I just can't believe I'm actually meeting you, milady. You're so beautiful and I just can't—" Thea could hardly keep up with how quickly she spoke, but responding didn't matter because suddenly the girl burst into tears, knocking Thea completely speechless.

She reached out to rest her hand on the girl's shoulder and tried to think of something to say. The problem was, she had no idea why the girl was crying, or even more importantly, why she'd called her Claire.

"It's okay," Thea consoled. "My name is Thea though, not Claire."

"Oh," the girl rubbed her eyes and sniffled as her tears slowed. Thea withdrew her hand but feared she might scare the poor girl into another emotional breakdown. "But Kieran said—"

"Perhaps we should let Kieran explain things to her when he gets back, Ethel."

The words had come from the doorway of the bedroom where a woman in a dark-green dress who appeared around the same age as Thea's mother stood. She had a heart-shaped face and emerald eyes that looked as if someone had painted them on, and the neatly braided crown of blonde hair around her head reminded Thea of a fairytale. The woman's natural beauty stunned Thea as she sat beside her.

"My name is Iris," she said, patting Thea's hand with a kind smile. "I'm Kieran's aunt, and this is my home."

She handed Thea a glass full of crystalline water, which Thea took a drink of without hesitation. The cool liquid soothed her parched tongue almost immediately.

"I'm Thea," was all Thea could think to respond as she stared at Iris.

"Ethel, would you please go prepare lunch for our guest?" Iris said, and the girl nodded happily. Her cheeks were still streaked from tears as she ran from the room. "You'll have to excuse her; sometimes the young get overly emotional."

"Where is Kieran?" Thea asked, glancing around what she could only assume was his bedroom. There were no pictures on the walls or decorations in the room, but the scent on the pillow when she'd woken up had been the same as when he'd carried her. Aside from the bed, there was a desk in the corner of the room that had two daggers lying across it, a fireplace casting light and warmth around them, and a small bedside table with a candle on it. Someone had drawn the curtains open, allowing sunlight to fill the bedroom.

"He'll be back soon. He's gone to alert King Aragon of your arrival."

"King Aragon?"

"Kieran will explain when he returns. I'm sure this is a lot to take in."

"Why did Ethel call me Claire?" Thea asked, feeling dissatisfied with the short answers she was receiving from Iris.

"It's your birth name."

Thea thought about this, and despite her argumentative nature prodding her to say that a pre-teen girl couldn't possibly know anything about her birth name, she controlled her response.

Thea craved an explanation, but Iris obviously didn't plan to give it to her, so she would just have to wait for Kieran to return.

She was beginning to question her sanity during this entire situation.

"What happened to my clothes?" she asked, her voice rising an uncomfortable octave as she realized she was half-naked beneath the blanket. "Kieran didn't…" She couldn't even finish her sentence; her cheeks burned furiously.

"No, no." Iris laughed for the first time, and Thea's mortification melted into relief. "Your clothes were coated in blood. Ethel and I undressed you, but unfortunately, the clothes weren't recoverable."

"Oh, well, thanks."

Thea couldn't help but frown. Those had been her favorite jeans, and they weren't cheap.

What was she even thinking right now? She'd just woken up in a stranger's house after being attacked, but she was worried about her favorite pair of jeans?

Insane. You've completely gone insane. That's all.

"We think those will fit you." Iris nodded toward a pile of neatly folded clothing at the end of the bed.

"Those look like dresses," Thea said, her voice growing smaller. She tried and failed at not sounding ungrateful.

"And?" Iris raised an eyebrow. It was a look much like the one her mother would have given her when she had no choice but to do something. She looked away from the aching reminder. The numbness had worn off during the adrenaline of nearly dying. She wanted nothing more than her mother or father's embrace now to comfort her.

But she reminded herself that she'd never experience that comfort again. She needed to grow up before she got herself killed waiting for someone else to protect her.

"Nothing. I'll try them on. Thank you," she replied, her voice tight with gratitude. "Will Kieran be back soon?"

"I hope so." Iris headed for the door of the bedroom, glancing over her shoulder at Thea once more. "I'm sorry that I can't answer your questions yet, but I promise that everything will make sense soon."

Without another word, Iris left the room, leaving Thea alone to dress.

What am I doing here? she wondered with a growing panic. If everything she remembered about the night before was true, then shouldn't she be running? And why had Kieran just left her with a bunch of strangers? Even if they didn't *seem* dangerous, how could Thea know they weren't just lying to her?

She reached for the pile of dresses with a fresh sense of dread. Whatever awaited her outside of this bedroom couldn't be confronted in her underwear, and since her own clothing was long gone, she had no choice but to make do with what they had given to her.

Her stomach growled as she sorted through the array of garments, but she settled on the simplest dress she could find. It was black velvet and just brushed the floor when she pulled it over her head.

She slipped on a pair of plain leather flats she found at the foot of the bed, hoping she would not trip over the bottom hem of the dress when she walked, and tugged on the sleeves a little to straighten the clingy material. The neckline of the dress dropped lower than Thea would have liked, scooping just across the top of her breasts, and to her horror, the midsection of the dress was a corset that needed to be laced up the back.

After a few minutes, she managed to pull the strings tight on her own, nearly falling over in the process. She hated the feel of it, but it did give her a place to tuck one of Kieran's daggers discreetly away—just in case.

"Oh," Ethel said when Thea finally found her way to the

kitchen. She'd followed the smell of freshly baked bread down the hallway after finding the front door of the cottage. Thea intended to escape out that door, but she couldn't do that until she had something in her stomach—not if she wanted to survive. "Princess Cl—I mean Thea, you look beautiful."

Iris nodded her head in agreement and handed Thea a bowl of stew with a torn-off piece of bread balanced on the side of it.

Thea went to sit on a stool at the kitchen counter, but found herself twisting around uncomfortably because of her cinched waistline as she tried to eat.

The kitchen wasn't like anything she'd ever seen before. The hand-cut countertops were a beautiful marble with buffed edges; shelves full of ingredient jars, some of which Thea recognized and others that she didn't, lined the walls; and a stone oven that brought warmth to the entire room had a large pot dangling over the fire, which Ethel scooped a ladleful of steaming stew out of for herself.

Thea tried to wrap her mind around finding herself in a place that lacked so much modern technology. There was no refrigerator, nor sink, but a bucket of soapy water that appeared to be used for dirty dishes sat in the corner by a low stool and a pile of dishcloths.

She tried to weave tales of logical explanation for everything she saw, but no matter what she told herself, none of this made any sense. Where was she? And how in the world was she going to get home?

"You should eat," Ethel said. Thea's stomach growled again as she eyed the stew in front of her. Everything in it looked familiar. There were carrots and potatoes, as well as green beans and corn. Her mouth watered at the smell of the freshly baked bread, but Thea hesitated anyway. Should she really be eating food from strangers after someone had just tried to kill her? It seemed like a red flag, but nothing about the stew screamed "poison" or "danger."

Slowly, Thea took a bite off the corner of the soft bread. It seemed like the safest option. The taste of flour and salt exploded across her tongue as she chewed.

Iris watched her as she dunked the bread into the stew, and Thea decided that if these people really wanted to hurt her they could have done so when she was unconscious. So, what exactly did they want from her?

"Where am I?" Thea asked as she neared the bottom of her bowl of stew. Her stomach felt stretched from how quickly she'd scarfed the food down, but it thanked her regardless as the pains of hunger subsided. She licked her fingers and her spoon, realizing she really must have been out for days if she were this hungry, and then downed another glass of water. She needed whatever nutrients she could get if she meant to leave this place, but she also needed to know exactly where this place was.

Surely they must still be in Ireland, perhaps in some Quaker-style village that existed without interference from the modern world. That was the only logical explanation her brain could conjure.

"The Kingdom of Grimwalde," Ethel said as she finished her own lunch and reached to pick up Thea's empty bowl, still smiling.

"Grimwalde?" Thea repeated the strange word. She'd never heard of it before, but she didn't claim to be the most knowledgeable person on the topic of geography. There were probably many places she was unfamiliar with.

"One of the four kingdoms," Ethel continued, dropping her bowl into the bucket of soapy water. She seemed oblivious to the look of confusion on Thea's face, but Iris saw it.

"Ethel," Iris warned, meeting the young girl's gaze with warning.

"What?" she asked, incredulous.

"How far from Knockainey am I?" Thea asked. She desperately wanted to get out of this house. Nothing about anything that these two women were telling her made sense. Even if Ethel was only a child, that Amara girl hadn't been much older, and she had most definitely been dangerous.

Thea's heart sped up in anticipation while the two women stared at her.

"I don't know of a Knockainey," Ethel said, her face full of honesty, but Iris' eyes had darkened, so Thea focused her attention there.

"How far?" she demanded of the older women.

"You are no longer in Ireland, Thea."

Thea heard the words, but again, they made little sense. She just stared at Iris, her head shaking from side to side. That wasn't possible. She had to be in Ireland because Kieran had been injured. The amount of blood she'd seen him lose was enough to convince her that there was absolutely no way he would have been able to take her far without medical attention. She wasn't a doctor, but she knew that. Thea stood, trying to hide her trembling hands.

"Wait—" Ethel took a step toward her but Thea had been ready for that. She snatched the dagger out of her corset, holding it up in the most threatening way possible toward the two women. She saw a look of hurt flash across Ethel's face, but Iris' emotions remained masked.

"Clever girl," Iris said with a nod of approval at the dagger.

"T-thank you for the food, but I think I should be going now." Thea backed away toward the kitchen door, her eyes darting between Iris and Ethel.

She didn't want to hurt either of them, but they clearly were not sane. Maybe she'd stumbled into a cult—yes, that was a possibility. This was some Irish cult that still existed, but they didn't associate themselves with Ireland.

You know there is more to it than that, the little voice in her head said, but she silenced it. She couldn't handle feeling any more crazy than she already did.

Once the kitchen door had closed, she ran for the front door, dagger still clutched in the sweating palm of her hand. She didn't hear anyone following her, but she also didn't look back. There was too much at stake. She needed to find a phone, call the police, and get home to Colorado.

Coming to Ireland had been a mistake.

Her heart pounded as she swung the front door open, but the sight that met her made her stumble to a halt.

The ground was snow-covered, but that was impossible. Even if she'd been asleep for longer than three days, it had been summer when she arrived in Ireland. How in the world could there be snow on the ground here?

She felt as if her eyes might bulge out of her head, but she slammed the door shut behind her, bracing herself for the frosty air. There was no choice. Even if it made little to no sense, she needed to get out of here.

Thea took only a moment to examine her surroundings. She saw a few distinct paths that she could take. There was a path that led directly into the forest that surrounded the small cottage; a path that ended in gardens of dead flowerbeds; and a path to what looked like a large stable.

The irrational part of her wanted to run as fast and as far away as possible, realizing she should have done that the night Kieran had shown up. However, it was unlikely she could survive this winter weather on foot without some sort of supplies. So, she sent a silent prayer to whatever power listened and sprinted down the third path, hoping it would increase the probability that she lived.

Thea's shivering subsided as she entered the warmth of the stables. Light slipped through the cracks in the roof, revealing about six stalls with curious eyes glowing inside each of them as she passed. She didn't know why she wasn't just taking the first horse she saw and getting out of there, but something called her deeper into the stable. It pulled her toward the last stall, but unlike the others, she found nothing peeking out of the darkness. It appeared, from the distance, to be empty.

What are you doing? she asked herself even as she neared the stall door. She needed to leave, and yet, she couldn't stop her fingertips from closing around the cool steel clasp that sealed the stall shut. Regardless of her desperate desire to run, something was forcing her in this direction, something she had no control over.

It was then that the large shape inside the stall stirred. Her hand froze, warming the metal beneath her fingertips, as his amber-eyes opened to meet hers. Thea wasn't sure how she knew the creature's sex, but she did. He was larger than any horse she'd seen before, and as he stepped into the soft sunlight trickling through the cracks in his stall walls, she gasped.

A silver horn protruded from the creature's head, centered in the middle of his forehead between his eyes.

Thea was staring at a Unicorn.

CHAPTER 4

THE UNICORN'S GAZE WAS FIERCE AS HE STARED AT HER. HE
stomped his hoof into the hay, and Thea stumbled backwards as
her shock morphed quickly into panic.

"Easy, boy." Thea held up both her hands, but realized that
the stall door was now unlocked as the creature pushed it open
and came toward her.

She didn't know what to do. If she ran, he could spear her
through the back, but if she didn't run, could he not just as
easily spear her through the front? She frowned, keeping her
hands raised as she lowered herself to the ground, hoping to
show him she was not a threat.

Her body trembled as she felt a waft of his fiery breath
against her neck. Her heart raced as the hairs on his dampened
nostrils tickled her skin, and then the fear disappeared as
quickly as it had come—replaced by an unexplainable sense of
calmness.

I am Faylon. The new voice in her ever-chaotic mind was
deep and melodic.

"Faylon," Thea repeated, her eyes snapping up to meet his
once more. She didn't know how she could hear him, but she

didn't feel as if she were going crazy anymore. This voice, unlike the female one in her head, had a body associated with it, and as crazy as it sounded to hear voices in her head, it felt no crazier than standing in the presence of a mythical creature.

The Unicorn gave a soft snort of approval, and Thea could see a smile sparkling in his eyes. He no longer looked fierce, or dangerous, but something else lurked beneath the surface of his amber gaze—something magical.

"B-but how?" she asked. "How can I hear you? How do you even exist?"

Amusement replaced the smile. He nudged her with his warm nose as she pulled herself to her feet, staring at him. She had so many more questions rising, but she heard something then that stopped her.

"Thea?" Ethel called out from beyond the stable door. Her voice trembled from the cold. "Are you in there?"

Thea frowned. She felt some guilt for how she'd treated Ethel, despite the young girl's kindness toward her.

"Can you help me get out of here?" Thea pleaded to Faylon. Her guilt was not enough to keep her in this place. She wanted to go home. She *needed* to go home.

The Unicorn lowered himself as if to say "Climb on" but Thea just stared at him warily. She'd ridden horses before, but something about riding this giant creature seemed far more dangerous.

You can trust me, he told her, and despite her uncertainty over climbing up onto his back, she believed him. A sense of knowing had replaced her fear. It pulsed inside of her with an absolute trust she'd never experienced before. She'd recognized Kieran, and trusted him to an extent, but this was different. The bond between Faylon and her felt ancient, as if it had always existed.

Her heart thumped against the drums of her ears as she tucked the dagger back into her corset and pulled herself up onto his back, twisting her fingers into his mane to keep her balance when he rose. Somehow, Thea knew that Faylon would protect her from whatever danger she faced. She didn't know where the feeling came from, but she trusted it as much as she trusted him.

Hold on, he said in a more gentle tone. They walked toward the stable door that Thea had failed to lock.

Faylon pushed the door open and Thea had barely glimpsed Ethel's surprised face outside when the Unicorn lurched forward. Ethel stumbled backward to avoid being trampled and fell to the ground.

"Sorry!" Thea cried out, but her hands didn't leave Faylon's mane. She hung on for dear life while he broke into a gallop that left Ethel and the cottage far behind as the surrounding forest swallowed them whole.

Riding a horse, Thea decided, was nothing like riding a bike. Her entire body felt awkward as it bounced unevenly atop Faylon's back. She clutched at him with her legs to keep from slipping right off his side and twisted her fingers so roughly into his mane that she thought she might actually begin pulling strands out.

Apologetic gasps escaped her drying lips as she clutched at him, but he never complained. Instead, he just continued onward, moving deeper and deeper into the forest. Thea had no idea where he was taking her, but her body shivered from the intense cold as the heavy canopy of trees shaded them from the warmth of the sun.

She was thankful for the long sleeves of the dress, but it did nothing to protect her face or hands from the icy wind that Faylon's steady gallop forced her to endure. Her teeth chattered furiously, but there was no turning back now—not that she would have known how to get back anyway.

"Where are we going?" she asked Faylon as she dodged yet another low-hanging branch. The grace of his gallop amazed

Thea. His breathing had grown heavier the farther they went, but his hooves fell onto the snow-covered earth rhythmically. Eventually, Thea's body adjusted to that rhythm, allowing for a more stabilized ride. She doubted she'd be walking properly for the next few days though.

You'll see, he replied cryptically, causing Thea's eyebrow to lift.

They continued until the trees thinned and warm sunlight touched her skin. The forest had felt like night, but all she saw past the end of the tree line was bright rays of vitamin D. A flood of relief washed over her at the sight, and Faylon slowed to a trot.

"Wow," Thea gasped as they left the forest for the snow-covered plains outstretched in front of them. The powdered white glittered under the sun's rays, nearly blinding her with its brightness. Strands of Thea's once-neatly braided hair whipped wildly around her face. Without the windshield of tree trunks around her, the wind stung, but even that couldn't deter her from the blissful feelings of freedom.

I'm really not in Ireland anymore, she thought and to her surprise, Faylon answered her thoughts.

Welcome to the land of Faerie.

Thea didn't know what was harder to believe: the fact that she wasn't in Ireland anymore or the fact that a Unicorn was telling her she'd stumbled into a land of magic. How could she keep denying it though? All the signs were there.

First, there was Kieran—her winged savior.

Then there was Faylon—her unicorn companion.

And last, there was the entire world around her. This winter buzzed with something deeper than a natural weather occurrence. There was magic pulsing through the air—magic that buzzed directly through her core.

How could she continue to deny the insane facts laid out in front of her?

Hold on, he told her, surprising her out of her thoughts as he climbed one of the larger hillsides.

Thea's eyes widened as they neared the top. Miles of forests and plains stretched out around them, separated by what looked like villages of buildings, but the most magnificent beauty of it all was that the entire landscape was blanketed in white.

This is Grimwalde, Faylon explained to her as she closed her slightly parted lips. *To the Northwest you will find Gimmerwich, and to the Southeast you'll find Blackmire.*

"Ethel said there were four Kingdoms," Thea commented, looking toward the Castle of Grimwalde, which she could just glimpse beyond the village. She'd seen the ruins of many castles on her journey through Ireland, and yet this one appeared whole. Even from a distance, Thea could tell that this castle wasn't abandoned, but rather inhabited—probably by the king of whom Iris had spoken.

The fourth kingdom, Ivandor, lies Northeast of us, Faylon's voice was gentle as his eyes turned fiercely toward the Northeast. Thea followed his gaze. *That is where you were born.*

"How do you know that?" Thea asked, unable to hide her shock.

Because I was born there as well.

That explanation told Thea all she needed to know about his troubled look. She slipped from his back, praying for grace, but stumbled as her feet hit the ground. A cold breeze teased Thea's bare legs where her dress had torn during their journey, but she ignored the chill and leaned her head against Faylon's neck, listening to the steady beat of his heart.

"Why did they send me away?"

She didn't expect an answer from her companion. Just because he'd been born there didn't mean he really knew anything about her past. The answers to her questions remained at the cottage where Kieran abandoned her. If she'd only stayed, maybe he could have told her about her birth parents, but she'd run, just as she always did.

A sigh escaped Thea's lips as she stroked Faylon's muzzle, shivering. She wouldn't survive nightfall in these conditions. It was too cold, too wet, and she was too human. Kieran had warmed her back in Ireland, but she had no idea how he'd done it. He'd taken care of her, kept her safe, and she'd run away from him.

"What am I supposed to do?" she said more to herself as a fear of the unknown crept over her. Her rash decision-making had consequences she would now suffer. If she were lucky, Faylon would know the way back to the cottage and Iris would allow her to stay, but what did that mean about her life back home?

What life? a cruel version of herself asked. *Your parents are dead. Marcus will never forgive you for what you did to him, and even if he did, you don't want to marry him.*

It was the brutal candor she'd been avoiding. She'd left Colorado in search of answers, but what happy ending had she really expected? Crawling back to Marcus was the worst imaginable thing Thea could imagine. Regardless of how sweet he'd been to her during her grief, she needed to find out who she was without him and without her old life. How could she go back now and pretend none of this had ever happened?

You can't, Faylon said, listening to her inner turmoil. She didn't mind his ability to know what she thought. In fact, she found it semi-comforting to have someone else in the chaos of her mind. *I'm sorry that this is how you found out the truth, but nothing will make this go away. King Malachi knows where you are now. It is only a matter of time before he comes after you again. You'd be putting everyone you love in danger if you returned.*

Thea didn't know who King Malachi was, or why he wanted her, but the seriousness of Faylon's tone made a sense of absolute dread pull at her already tight muscles.

Why does he even want me? To kill me? Use me? What have I done to deserve any of this? Desperation seeped through her thoughts, but how was she supposed to wrap her mind around putting everyone in danger, if no one would even tell her the reason *she* was in danger?

"Princess Thea," came a tense whisper of her name across the wind. A soft thump echoed behind them, interrupting their conversation, and Thea spun around to meet the source of the familiar voice.

Kieran stood a few feet away, folding his wings back against himself as he glared at her, clearly furious. This was the first time that Thea had really seen Kieran. At the Hill of Knockainey, he'd been little more than a tall shadow, but now every detail she'd missed before became crystal clear, and her mouth had become as dry as cotton.

His tousled brown hair reached the tops of his shoulders, and although it was partially pulled back, a few strands fell against his stubble shadowed chin, framing his face. Her hand twitched at her side, wanting to brush the tousled hair away from his endless green eyes. However, she kept her feet planted and her face composed, mentally scolding herself for the incredibly embarrassing thoughts that left her feeling completely exposed to him. Her eyes shifted slowly to the silky black wings he no longer hid from her, and she noticed the feathers twitch beneath her gaze.

"Hello, Kieran," she finally replied in a small voice that didn't sound like her own. Her fingers clenched into fists as another wave of trembling cold overcame her. Her toes felt frozen in the simple leather flats, and her dress fluttered against the wind while his eyes drifted down to see the bare skin peeking out from beneath.

It brought a flush of color to Thea's cheeks and she pulled the dress back over her legs, attempting to keep it in place, as their gazes finally met.

37

She could still see the anger on his face, but if she wasn't mistaken, she'd also glimpsed a flash of desire that he'd quickly hidden away. The silence was deafening, and yet, she didn't know what to say.

She couldn't say she was sorry for running away, because she wasn't. Her instincts had told her to run, so she'd done so. She also couldn't say she was ready to go back, because what would that mean for her life?

"How did you find me?" she ended up asking him.

"Why did you run?" he retorted, and a flash of anger sizzled through her.

These people can't just answer a question, can they? She thought with annoyance. Instead of answering him, she crossed her arms over her chest and stared at the snowy ground, pressing her lips into a straight line. She would just refuse to talk until he gave her answers, as childish as that made her feel.

The crunch of snow beneath boots told her he was walking toward her, but she didn't dare look up. Thea felt the same pull she had felt the night that he found her in Ireland. It called her to him, begging her to meet his gaze, but if she did that, she was sure she would crumble right back into trusting him.

"You could have been killed," he said, his voice softening. Thea thought he almost sounded guilty, and she nearly looked up. "What if Malachi had been here?"

This captured her attention. It was the second time she'd heard the name Malachi in less than an hour, and now she was sure that was who had sent Amara to kill her. But if that were the case... The thought stung.

"Who is Malachi?" Thea asked, finally meeting Kieran's eyes.

An agonizing guilt that stunned Thea had replaced the look of anger in Kieran's eyes. She hadn't expected to see such an emotion on his face. Kieran seemed like the type of person who would always have his emotions under control, but here he was, an open book for her to read. Her arms uncrossed slowly and he reached out to touch her cheek with his hand, surprising her further.

"I think you already know who Malachi is," he said. Thea thought he sounded sad as he spoke the words—his face most definitely reflected that sadness—but she didn't want to admit the thoughts she'd been piecing together in her mind. His callused hand warmed her cheek, rough against her soft skin, and yet, it was as gentle as someone who was stroking a timid animal.

He believes you might run again, she thought, searching his eyes for the answers she desperately wanted. Her eyelids lowered to hide the fear that threatened to bubble up to the surface. She didn't want to believe what she was about to say, but she needed to know for sure. So she spoke slowly, her voice dropping to a monotone.

"He's my father."

There was no question at the end of her sentence. She'd put the pieces together. Amara had tried to kill her; Kieran had demanded Amara return to her father; Amara had claimed to be Thea's sister, which meant Thea's father was trying to kill her, or at least capture her.

But, why?

"Yes," Kieran responded.

He placed two fingers beneath her chin and lifted her head to meet his gaze once more. Thea saw him studying her face, taking in every aspect of her appearance in the light, but she didn't hide herself away from him. Instead, she watched the way his skin tightened across his squared jaw, and the rise and fall of his Adam's apple. He wore a long-sleeved tunic shirt tucked into a pair of black leather pants and a weapons baldric strapped across his chest with a variety of blades attached to it. Her eyes flickered across each one, remembering the dagger she'd tucked away in her corset, but she didn't fear his swords or daggers.

"You scared me," he said, eyes darkening with an agony that made Thea's breath catch. "I thought..."

Thea reached up to take his hand from beneath her chin and gave it a gentle squeeze, not knowing where her courage was coming from, but needing to make that darkened look in his eyes disappear. It hurt to see him look at her like that.

"I'm sorry that I ran."

She'd been so sure that running away was the right thing to do, but now, seeing the torture she'd brought to him, she wondered if she'd been wrong. Should she have turned around as soon as she realized Ethel and Iris weren't lying about her not being in Ireland anymore? Should she have waited for his return? She knew she couldn't change the past, but she wished she could make at least one right decision today.

"When Ethel told me you left, I went looking for you, but I didn't see you until he brought you onto the hilltop. If you hadn't come up here, I probably never would have found you." His voice trembled over each word, as if the very thought of never finding her might tear him to pieces. It broke Thea's heart, although she was unsure why he felt such a deep need to keep her safe.

"You knew," she mumbled, directing her gaze to Faylon. He stood picking leaves off the branches of a dying tree nearby, but he glanced at her as she spoke, lowering his head as if in apology. "That's why you brought me here—not to show me the kingdoms."

"It's his job to protect you," Kieran said, stroking his thumb over the back of Thea's hand.

"What? Why?" Thea asked, looking back at Kieran, but his eyes lingered on the goosebumps that decorated her skin. It was mid-afternoon, but her ruined dress and wet feet sent a chill through her entire body.

"I'll explain that later," he said and his wings spread wide, wrapping around them both. Before she could gape or react at all, he pulled her against his chest and a flood of warm air surrounded her. His wings shielded her from the cold, and his chin rested against her hair. A slow tremble overcame her as the warmth spread from the tips of her toes to the top of her head, but she welcomed it happily, letting her eyelids flutter closed as the magic kissed her skin.

Magic, she repeated in her head, trying to make sense of the word. She'd seen so much of it lately. Between Kieran's arrival and what had happed with Faylon, she couldn't keep denying its existence. So, she embraced it as she lifted her head to look at Kieran once more.

"I can't keep running away," she whispered, her voice no longer trembling with fear, but rather with a desperate need for answers about the past. Every rational part of her screamed that none of this was possible, but she refused to deny what was right in front of her any longer. She wanted the truth. She *needed* the truth.

Time felt slow as Kieran studied her face. Perhaps he wasn't sure if she could handle it yet. Perhaps he was still angry that she'd run away. Thea wasn't sure, but she didn't look away.

"What do you want to know?" he finally asked and anxious relief rolled over her, releasing the tension between her shoulder blades.

"Tell me everything."

CHAPTER 5

Kieran realized that telling her everything wasn't an option. They'd be sitting on this hillside long past nightfall if he started down that path. However, she deserved an explanation if he hoped for her to stay. Having her in his arms was distracting his thoughts, though. She'd been in his embrace before, but the situation had been different then. For one, she'd been half-unconscious. For two, their lives had been in mortal danger. Now, there were no real distractions from the feelings that stirred within him as she pressed closer for warmth, nor from the softness of her small mouth just inches from his own.

"I don't know where to start," he admitted. Her slight tremble didn't go unnoticed by him as the feathers of his wings brushed against the bare skin of her leg. Her dress had ripped almost completely up her thigh during the ride, and he spent an impressive deal of time forcing himself not to glance at the exposed skin. However, when his feathers brushed against her, his control felt like it might shatter. There could have been explosions in the sky or war on the plains below, but Kieran wouldn't have noticed or cared. He wanted to stay in this moment forever. He wanted to hold her in his arms for an entire lifetime. He wanted—and that was the problem, because he couldn't have what he wanted if it was her.

Her lips parted slightly as she prepared to answer him, exhaling a breath of sweet air into the space between them. The temptation to taste that sweetness tortured him, but that was why he needed to stop before that same dangerous desire reflected any further on her face. Kieran needed to take control of the situation, because if he didn't, they'd both walk away broken. His body was not as rational as his mind, though. He imagined pressing his lips to hers or raising his fingers across her exposed skin, but he suppressed that longing.

Her braid had loosened during the ride, and he wanted to release it so that her hair would fall untamed around her shoulders. However, he settled for tucking a silky strand behind her ear instead.

"What are you?" Thea asked for the second time since he'd found her. Her eyes looked away from his now, but they examined his wings. She reached her hand toward them, then looked at him for approval. Swallowing hard, he nodded his head as her fingertips traced along the veins of his feathers with deliberate gentleness. He was thankful the feel of his wings distracted her, because he didn't trust his face to hide the torturing desire he felt at her touch. He'd allowed no one to touch his wings before. Sensitive nerve endings lined them to help him navigate the skies, but beneath her fingertips they had an entirely new purpose.

"I'm a Fae," Kieran finally choked out, regaining Thea's full attention. Whatever look she saw on his face made her eyes widen in surprise, but it didn't deter her from continuing her gentle caress as Kieran fought to regain his control. "And so are you."

"Like Tinkerbell?" Thea asked, but Kieran had no idea what she was talking about. He reached out and took her hand, unable to undergo any more of her unbearable teasing. His breath caught, and he swore he saw her smile at his sudden reaction to her touch. He wanted to let her continue, as well as do far more, but the consequences were too great.

"The Fae are a species born from the love between a Goddess and a human," Kieran explained, but he didn't let go of her hand. "The legend says that Aimé, The Goddess of Life, had a human lover. When they bore children they created the Fae."

"I read about her in Ireland," Thea said. "The Celtic call her the Queen of the Faeries."

"Well, they aren't wrong," Kieran replied, stroking his thumb across the back of her small hand. "She's the reason we exist. Without her, we wouldn't have access to the elements—to magic."

"So, is she here too?" Thea asked, seeming at least momentarily distracted. "And why did my parents send me to a land with no magic if I'm a Fae?"

Kieran watched as she tried to put the pieces together, but her brow was only furrowing with deeper frustration. This story was so much more than just a mother sending her daughter away. This was the story of an ancient war between Goddesses, a battle between good and evil, but how was he supposed to tell her centuries of legends without overwhelming her?

"Aimé isn't the only Goddess in these lands. She has a sister who goes by the name of Morrigan, but our people call her the Goddess of Death.

"The legend says that Morrigan was angry when Aimé brought humans into their lands through the magical doorway we now call the Threshold. Morrigan believed that humans would bring death and destruction to nature, but it was Morrigan who turned into a monster. Her jealousy over her sister's affection for the humans drove her to do horrible things. She started wars, murdered villages of innocent humans, and eventually, built up her own following of Fae."

"But if she eliminated the humans, then wouldn't there be no Fae at all?" Thea asked.

"No, it actually turned out that the offspring of two Fae were always magical, but the offspring of a Fae and human could be either species.

"When Morrigan realized this, she built an army of Fae who believed we should keep the species pure and they sought to eradicate humans from the Land of Faerie. Morrigan started a war that rages on until this day between the elitist Fae and the humans, but more importantly, she made an enemy out of her sister."

"What did she do?" Thea asked, her face paling. Kieran had heard this story so many times that telling it was like a second nature. All Fae children grew up hearing about the two Goddesses. The Fae raised in the west Kingdoms, like Gimmer-wich and Grimwalde, knew that the Goddess Ainé would always win, that light would always overpower darkness, but those raised in the Eastern Kingdom of Blackmire still prayed to the Goddess of Death for deliverance. The northern king-dom, Ivandor, was the original kingdom in Faerie, founded by Ainé herself, but King Malachi had brought death to its lands at the start of the Dark War fifteen years ago, ultimately separating the land of Faerie into two feuding sides.

"She killed Ainé's human lover," Kieran said, his eyes staring down at their intertwined fingers. Thea's knuckles whitened as she gripped his hand, and a single tear trickled down her cheek. "After his death, Ainé trapped her sister in a prison of sorts, although no one really knows where it is. The stories say that Ainé herself is the key to that prison, but magic always has a loophole, Thea—*you* are the loophole."

THEA'S HEAD was spinning beneath all the information Kieran

had unloaded on her. She wasn't human—something about that made absolute sense, and yet, how could it? How could she be anything but an ordinary human girl? She'd experienced no strange occurrences as a child, never made things happen that she couldn't explain. At least, she hadn't until she met Kieran. The memory of blue light shooting out of her hands flashed through her mind without invitation.

Magic, she reminded herself, as if saying the word more often would make it more believable.

The Fae weren't sparkly winged creatures with pixie dust to make you fly. Nor did they appear to be cruel animals that feasted on human hearts. So, what were they? What was she?

Kieran had mentioned a connection between the elements and magic, so Thea thought more of the Celtic versions of the Fae. That was where the story of Ainé originated, so she figured there must be some truth in those legends. Ainé had crossed the Threshold who knows how long ago and taken a human lover that started an entirely new species, that made Thea's existence possible... She didn't know how to wrap her mind around that information yet, so she moved onto her next question.

"How am I the loophole?" Thea asked. If she was a key to opening a prison that held the Goddess of Death, then why in the world had Kieran brought her back? Why had he risked it all just to see her again?

"Are you sure that you're ready to hear this?" Kieran asked. His free hand reached up to cradle her chin, tilting her head so that she stared up at him. She noticed the way his skin pulled tight across his jawline beneath the tension. Golden specks glistened within the irises of his green eyes, and now that she was looking more closely, a quiet blue undertone created a sea-green color in their depths, rather than the forest-green she'd first noticed. The arms that held her were hardened by muscles, and with the quietness of the hill they stood atop, she heard and felt his heartbeat quickening against his chest.

Thea allowed herself to really see him and knew without a doubt that he saw her too. The intensity of his gaze made everything else in her life feel trivial, as if her subconscious was telling her she was missing this, missing him. Being with him let her temporarily ignore the pain of losing the people she'd loved most. It allowed her to forgive herself for the pain she'd caused others, and it even allowed her to escape the pressures of everyone thinking she was a princess—a key to a prison world that held the Goddess of Death, she reminded herself miserably.

She felt trapped by his gaze, but she didn't want it to end. She wanted to steal this moment with him and never return from it. Although it made zero sense, every one of Thea's deepest desires felt linked to Kieran, and for the briefest moment, she allowed herself to imagine closing the space between them before he could answer her question.

Their quickening breaths seemed to flow in sync now, and a soft flush tinted Kieran's cheeks. His eyes lowered to where his wings had touched her leg, and he slowly let them brush over it again, this time more deliberately. It sent a shiver across Thea's skin, although she no longer felt the crisp winter air. Instead, a fire she feared could never be extinguished burned through her veins. Thea could see Kieran arguing with himself over something, but she refused to move away from him unless he said he wanted her to, no matter how unbelievable this all felt.

"We can't do this." Kieran's voice trembled as he spoke, but Thea just stared at him in confusion. She'd seen the desire on his face moments before, but now a wall had snapped up, masking any further emotions from her.

He didn't move away from her, but the palm of his hand brushed her cheek and then dropped back to his side. "You want me to tell you about your parents, right?"

Thea felt torn between her desire to know what internal struggle he faced and her desire for more information about her parents. She was both impressed that he knew exactly what to say to distract her and disturbed by how easily he shut his emotions down against her. That would be a conversation for another day though, she decided, realizing suddenly that she didn't intend to run away again.

"I do, but *this*," she squeezed the hand that still held her own, "you're not getting out of forever."

Kieran turned her so that her back was pressed against him with a quiet agreement. It was yet another wall between them that Thea wished to pull down, but she didn't fight against it right now. She wanted to know what made her the key to the prison that held Morrigan, and her desire for more information about her biological parents had been the entire reason she'd begun this journey. She wouldn't shy away from that now.

"I've explained to you that there are Fae who follow Morrigan—Fae who believe they are a superior species to humans." Kieran's voice was a murmur against her hair, but she heard him and nodded her head. "Well, your father comes from a lengthy line of Fae who share those same beliefs about humans."

"And my mother?" Thea asked. Her tongue felt stuck to the top of her mouth as she spoke.

"Your mother was one of the bravest women I have ever had the pleasure of meeting."

"Then why would she marry a man with such horrible beliefs?" Anger trembled beneath Thea's voice. "And if my father turned out to be such a shitty man, why didn't my mother just leave him? A lot of children grow up with terrible parents, but why get rid of me instead of him?"

"I don't know exactly how things work where you grew up, Thea, but a queen can't just leave a king here.

"Your father was from Blackmire and your grandfather arranged the marriage to bring peace between two kingdoms that had been at war for years. Your mother kept your father from turning Ivandor into another Blackmire for many years..."

"So, what happened then?" Thea asked, trying to control the pleading in her voice. She hated not knowing. She knew there were four kingdoms; Kieran had now told her that Blackmire and Ivandor were at war, so her mother had married to end a war, but what did any of that have to do with her or with Morrigan's prison? Why had she been thrown out of Faerie when she had done nothing wrong?

Kieran seemed to sense the agony beneath the surface of Thea's exterior because he tightened his arms around her. She felt herself being pressed against his hard chest while she stared out in the direction that Faylon had told her both Ivandor and Blackmire existed. They were too far away for her to see, but she imagined them in the distance, constantly fighting each other, constantly reeking of death and destruction, at least until her mother agreed to marry a monster.

"Fifteen years ago, your father murdered your mother, Thea," Kieran said, and a chilling numbness crept over Thea. She'd prepared herself for this news, despite her constant hope that it wasn't true. "But not before she could do everything in her power to keep you safe."

Thea turned herself around to look back at Kieran. She needed to see his face, needed to see the truth in his eyes as he told her the story, but all she saw was a man who looked completely haunted by his past. When he met her gaze sorrow trickled past the walls of protection he hid behind.

"I know it's hard to understand, but your mother had her reasons for sending you away, Thea. I was too young at the time to understand it, but my mother was the Queen's best friend, her handmaiden, and a seer—a Faerie with a gift of prophecy, whom the goddess speaks with.

"I was in the village when the attacks began. Creatures crept out of the forest and attacked both humans and Fae, dark magic made the air taste like burnt metal, and the screams as they slaughtered people..." His voice trailed off and Thea felt a shudder go through her. She reached up, placing her hand against his cheek. The stubble of his beard tickled her soft skin, but she didn't let go as he trembled beneath her touch.

How long had he kept these memories locked away? How long had they haunted him as she now saw they did?

His eyes closed at the memory and shook his head back and forth, as if trying to make it disappear. Thea pictured Kieran fifteen years younger, just a boy fearing for his life in a village of death. The image made her want to scream.

"I managed to get back to the castle, back to you and both of our mothers. I found out that my mother'd had a vision... a vision that your father would use you to set the Goddess of Death free from her prison."

He paused and seemed to be gathering his thoughts.

"Visions come from Ainé herself, but my mother used to say no vision was set in stone. Your mother told me to take you to the Threshold. She said it was the only way to keep the prophecy from coming true."

Thea absorbed the information Kieran gave to her slowly. She'd asked him to tell her everything, but she'd never imagined her story would have started like this. When she found out she was adopted, she'd thought her biological parents had abandoned her. Now she tried to wrap her mind around the fact that her mother had sent her away to protect her from some terrible future that involved her father and the Goddess of Death. Her stomach twisted into knots at the images that flooded her brain.

"How old were you?" she asked. She knew it wasn't the most important question to ask, and yet, she needed to know.

"I was ten." His eyes reopened, and she felt like her heart might be physically breaking into pieces. Ten. He'd been only ten years old and her mother had asked him to risk his life for her as if it were more important than his own. "I know what you're thinking, but it was the only way. Your father is predictable when it comes to whom he would suspect took his daughter. He never would have suspected the boy who entertained her with books and music, especially not the son of a handmaiden he only noticed when demanding things of her. I was the only one your mother believed could get out of the castle with you without being noticed."

Thea was unconvinced. She tried putting herself in her mother's shoes but couldn't imagine any scenario where she would have risked another child's life just to save her own child. Then, she thought of what might have happened if she hadn't made that choice.

I wouldn't be standing here with Kieran and the Goddess of Death would be free, murdering all the humans in Faerie, she thought miserably.

How could Thea judge her mother's decisions knowing that they had saved so many people?

"I'll never forget the look on your mother's face that night, Thea. If you hear nothing else I say to you, if you decide you want nothing to do with our world, please just remember this: your mother loved you. She loved you with every fiber of her being, and if there had been any other way, she would have never sent you away."

Thea's throat tightened. She needed to know what happened next, and as Kieran searched her face, she wondered if he was asking himself the same thing she'd been asking since his story began.

Could she handle the truth?

"I managed to get you through the Threshold that night. The queen had told me that under no circumstances was I to stay with you, because if I did, the king would discover I was the one who'd taken you away and search for me." Kieran sighed heavily, the story seeming to exhaust him. "I remember I kissed you on the forehead to tell you goodbye that night. You opened your eyes like I'd broken whatever spell kept you asleep, and when I told you everything would be okay, you looked at me with such complete trust.

"And then I left you there alone," Kieran paused, finally meeting Thea's eyes. She thought she saw tears forming behind his lids, but if they were there, he didn't let them fall. "Iris found me as I tried to return home, but we never went back to Ivandor after that night. My mother had remained by your mother's side when your father realized you were gone. He'd demanded she tell him where you'd been taken, but neither of them would do that. You didn't die that night, but our mothers died to protect us both at the hand of your father."

Unlike Kieran, tears flowed freely down Thea's face. She'd been expecting this. She knew her mother was no longer alive. She'd pieced together the facts to know that her mother had given her life for her, but she hadn't expected Kieran's mother to have died for her as well. Her heart broke looking at the man in front of her, who'd suffered because of her. Her hands shook at the thought of the shadowy-faced man in her mind who'd murdered a mother she wished desperately to remember. The anger overwhelmed her when she thought of Kieran's mother, dying to protect not only Kieran, but Thea as well.

"Why did you bring me back to Faerie?" Thea asked through her tears.

"At first, it was pure selfishness," Kieran admitted. "I have lived so many years regretting leaving you there, wishing I had stayed with you. I didn't care about the consequences—I just wanted to see you again."

Thea's tears slowed as she saw the regret he spoke. He'd spent fifteen years beating himself up over something he'd had no control over and it had taken its toll on him, hardened him somehow against the rest of the world.

"But Amara would have found you no matter what I did," Kieran continued. "She obviously knew about the Threshold already and knew about my connection with you. I don't know how or when they figured it out, but they were coming for you, Thea. When I saw Amara was there, I couldn't just leave you again. I have to protect you."

Thea saw then for the first time that Kieran felt responsible for her. She imagined that ten-year-old boy again carrying the weight of the world on his shoulders alone, only to return and find out they had murdered his mother while he followed the orders of his queen.

Had he ever blamed himself? Or her? Had he thought of what might have been different if he hadn't done what he was told that night?

"I felt you," he interrupted her self-doubt. "I felt you on the other side of the Threshold and knew that if I just reached out, I could see you again. The pull was irresistible, but my foolishness nearly got us both killed."

"Nearly," she said. "And yet, here we are."

"And yet, here we are."

"I don't know what my mother would have said," Thea's voice trembled slightly at the word mother, "but I was searching for the truth when you found me. I didn't expect this to be my truth, but I'm glad you came to find me."

Kieran rested his forehead against Thea's and both of them closed their eyes. She felt him pull her tighter against his chest once more, his wings keeping her safe from the cold. She didn't need to open her eyes to understand whatever was happening between them had consequences. His hesitation, his warning, and his guarded nature told her well enough that he was still trying to protect her. She didn't care, though; she didn't want his protection if it meant she couldn't have this moment in his arms.

He'd answered her questions enough for the time being, although she was sure there was more to hear. The answers hadn't been what she'd expected, but she felt lighter knowing them regardless. She could think of her adoptive parents without the anger she'd had before. She thought instead of the kindness and love they'd shown to her, even though she was not their own. She also thought of her biological mother and hoped she could prove herself to be as brave as she'd been. The thought of her father made her angry, but even he had a part in her story that she couldn't deny. She had a journey ahead of her, that much she knew, but she hoped with all her heart that Kieran would remain at her side for that journey. He shifted to kiss her forehead, just as he'd done the night he'd left her in Ireland and the night fate had reunited them.

His next five words did not waver.

"I will always find you."

CHAPTER 6

When they pulled apart, a piece of Kieran remained with Thea. The last time he'd spoken about his mother's death had been the night his aunt Iris found him in the woods. That night had changed his life forever, but he'd never been comfortable enough with anyone to actually talk about it, not even Ethel, despite her kind, understanding nature. Now, he had Thea, whose tragedy intertwined so closely with his own, looking at him with understanding. Despite their time apart, he felt no uncertainty with her, nor any distrust; it was as if she'd always been a part of his life.

"I won't run away again," Thea said with a note of apology in her voice as she tucked her hand into her corset and pulled out the dagger. She held it out to him with an embarrassed flush that amazed him.

"Keep it," he told her, closing her fingers around its hilt. "If you're really staying, then you will need to learn to protect yourself. It won't be long before your father sends someone else after you."

She watched him with a childlike innocence that made his heartache. It was his fault she was back in this mess, no matter how much he tried to convince himself that Malachi would have found her regardless. She'd gotten lucky with Amara the first time, but they no longer had the element of surprise. That meant that anything that happened to her was on him, but most Fae spent their entire lives training to use magic. Thea had what? Days? Maybe a week, before another attack happened? The thought twisted his stomach into knots.

"Hold it like this," he told her, adjusting her fingers so they could grip the dagger more naturally. "And aim for the soft spot between the ribs."

He pulled her hand forward to press the tip of the dagger against the very spot he'd mentioned, showing her.

"Okay," she said in a small voice, visibly swallowing back her fear. Her hands shook around the dagger, so Kieran wrapped his own hand around hers to steady the blade.

"I will protect you, Thea," he murmured, never looking away from her face. "I promise."

"You never called me Claire," Thea said with a sudden look of surprise. "Ethel called me Claire."

"Iris told me that you go by Thea before I left to find you. She thought it might calm you down if you heard the name you know." He gave her a small smile and then tucked the dagger back into its hiding spot for her as she blushed.

"So I'm Thea, not Princess Claire?" she asked.

"You are Princess Thea," Kieran responded. "Claire was the name given to you by your mother and father, but you had more than one mother and father. It's part of your identity. You'll always be a princess though."

He watched as Thea thought about his words, eventually nodding in agreement. She repeated "Princess Thea" aloud, as if it would help her adjust to being called by it. He lifted her hand to his lips, kissing the back of it, and lowered himself into a kneeling position in front of her. Her eyes widened in surprise, and her cheeks flushed the deep red of fresh roses. He felt nervous himself, but tried not to show it as he looked up at her from his kneeling position. He let go of her hand and unsheathed the sword he kept constantly at his side, inserting it into the ground between them, as was customary.

"Princess Thea, I pledge myself to you as the first of your faithful guard. If you will have me, I promise to protect you with my life." He lowered his eyes to the ground, staring at the place where his blade met the earth. He realized she wasn't familiar with their customs, but he needed this to happen before anything else did. He needed to know that she wanted him to remain at her side, and that he could protect her from the journey ahead. He couldn't fight her battles for her, but he could stand at her side until he took his last breath if she would allow it.

"Kieran—"

"I need this, Thea."

Silence passed between them as Kieran met her eyes. She looked beautiful with the sunshine kissing her freckled skin. The snow on the surrounding ground glistened beneath her. He could think of no better place than here to ask her to have him.

"Okay," she said finally, "on one condition."

Her eyes sparkled like the icicles hanging from the tree branches as she raised him up from his kneeling position.

"You are my equal, and I will treat you as such. If you wish to stand by my side and protect me with your life, then you understand I will stand by your side and protect you with mine. I won't have you being a marauder, but I will have you."

Kieran considered her words. Her newness to their lands and their traditions was clear, and yet he longed for what she said to be true. He longed to be her equal in every way, shape, and form. However, she would eventually discover their laws would never allow that.

"I'll do my best to remember that, Princess Thea, but you'll soon find that few will agree with those terms throughout the kingdoms."

"Good thing a queen doesn't have to be agreed with then," she said, sounding like her mother. She looked around, her eyes troubled, and he followed her gaze. "Faylon left me," she said with a pout so familiar to him that he couldn't help but smile.

Kieran roared with laughter as he lifted Thea into his arms, a teasing smile playing across his lips. It had been ages since he'd laughed or smiled so much, but it felt good, like stretching a muscle he'd nearly forgotten how to use. Thea's torn dress fell away from her leg, but he tried not to let his eyes linger for too long on the spot, focusing on the way she looked at him when he cradled her against his chest. He hoped she would never stop looking at him that way. Behind her gray eyes he saw the same trust he'd seen the night he left her in Ireland when he'd told her everything would be okay.

This time, he intended to make sure of it.

"I suppose that means we're flying home." He grinned. Her hands tightened suddenly into his shirt, and he pressed his feet into the ground as he ran toward a spot where the hillside's elevation dropped. Kieran smiled as Thea squealed when he launched himself over the drop and into the air.

"I don't think this is protecting me with your life," she gasped, peeking around his arms to look down as they soared high into the sky.

"Trust me," he replied loud enough for her to hear him over the sound of the wind. When she nodded, obviously having heard him, he spun through the open air, his laughter booming as she screamed in shock before he dove toward the ground.

"I do, but—"

He swooped across the snowy floor, just inches from its surface, and smiled at her. Her hair was almost completely undone now, and he admitted to himself that she looked stunning with it falling freely around her shoulders, just as he'd imagined she would. He had to look away.

He forced his wings to carry them higher once more, holding her tightly against his chest before falling into a gentle glide across the sky.

"Admit it," he spoke without looking at her, "flying is the most fantastic and freeing thing you've ever experienced!"

Kieran caught her staring up at him. Her lips were slightly parted, the same way they'd been earlier, and her breath came more quickly than usual. He wondered what thoughts were crossing her mind, because the ones within his own head were driving him to the edge of the control he fought so hard for. He desperately wanted to close the small space between them by pressing his lips to hers. He wanted to fly her far away from the kingdoms to live a simple, happy life together, but if he did that, if they left now, Malachi would win and, eventually, so would the Goddess of Death. He knew fate had brought Thea home for a reason, and yet all he wanted was to rationalize taking her away from that reason. All he wanted was to protect her.

"What are you thinking about?" Thea asked as they flew over the village and neared his aunt's cottage.

"Fate," Kieran replied. Fate had brought Thea to Ireland. Fate had made sure he was stationed on guard duty that day. Fate haunted him with undeniable feelings for Thea. Fate both brought them together and kept them apart.

Thea raised an eyebrow at him and said, "Fate can be changed."

Kieran didn't have a response for that. He wasn't sure he believed that fate could be changed, but thankfully, Ethel and Faylon stood waiting for them when they landed, saving him from the argument.

"You have a familiar!" Ethel said. She clearly didn't sense the tension between Kieran and Thea. Instead, she stood stroking Faylon affectionately as he grazed.

"A what?" Thea asked as Kieran set her down on the ground and took a step away. She glanced at him with a raised eyebrow and then looked back at Ethel.

"A familiar is a bonded creature," Kieran explained, glancing between Faylon and Thea. "I guess it isn't surprising that yours is the offspring of the very one that saved our lives fifteen years ago."

"What?" Thea asked.

"That's a story for another day, Thea. For now, just know that not all Fae have a familiar. Most of the time, they show up when a Fae desperately needs comfort and they are almost always creatures of light, such as your Unicorn here."

He smiled over at Faylon, who was enjoying the soft strokes of Ethel's hands. Thea just rubbed at her temples, clearly over-whelmed with all the information Kieran had given her.

"Do you have one?" Thea asked Kieran.

"No, but Iris does. I'm actually surprised you didn't see Gwendolyn in the stables."

"Gwendolyn?" Thea lifted an eyebrow at him.

"She's a Pegasus."

"You're lying to me... First Unicorns, and now Pegasi? What's next? Mermaids?" Thea's hands were on her hips now as she stared at him in utter disbelief.

"Ah, I wouldn't go looking for the merrow—they're nasty little creatures."

"Oh!" Ethel gasped suddenly, staring at Thea's leg. "What happed to your dress?"

"I guess I'm not used to wearing dresses," Thea replied glancing down at the torn fabric. "You don't think it's possible for me to get some type of, I don't know, pants?"

"Pants? But you're a princess..." said Ethel, bewildered and oblivious to Thea's blushing face.

"I'll talk to my aunt," Kieran assured her.

"I don't know, Kieran. She might get a lot farther if we give her pants," Ethel said with a hint of anger in her tone as she glanced at Thea. It appeared her pleasant surprise about the familiar was being replaced with hurt over Thea's departure.

"I'm sorry that I ran away," Thea mumbled, shuffling her feet in the snow.

"Thea, you probably should go change before we meet the king."

"I'm sorry, what?" She glanced at him in surprise. However, Ethel's face lit up, just as Kieran had known it would. She never stayed mad very long.

"You're meeting the king?" Ethel grabbed Thea's hand, dragging her through the front door of the cottage. Thea looked absolutely panicked, and Kieran gave her an apologetic smile as she disappeared. The smile faded into a sigh though as the door shut between them.

What am I getting myself into? he wondered, looking up at the clouds above him. He found the clouds comforting when he faced impossible choices.

"You look very much like your father when you do that," aunt Iris said, appearing from inside the house. She smiled at Kieran, but a veil of sadness lurked beneath that smile at the mention of her brother. "He used to stand outside and contemplate the cruelty of the Universe too."

"I was contemplating the cruelty of fate, but I guess that could be the Universe," Kieran replied.

"Wouldn't Ainé be fate?"

"I suppose." Kieran shrugged his shoulders, kicking the snow beneath his feet. Iris often saw right through him, but at this moment he wished she wouldn't. "I know what you're thinking."

"Do you now?" she raised her eyebrow at him and for a second it was she who reminded him of his father. "Tell me."

"My emotions are clouding my judgements with Thea. I'm being reckless and foolish. I'm digging my own heart's grave because fate has brought us to each other but will never allow us to be together."

"I didn't realize you'd become a mind-reader since you met her," she said. Her voice carried a dangerous tone that told him he'd crossed a line, but he didn't really care. For a moment, he wanted to be self-pitying and tell someone how terrible he felt. She came to stand beside him and mimicked him, looking up at the clouds. "I'll never tell you who you should or should not love. I'll also never tell you that love won't break your heart."

Kieran looked at her and frowned.

"I'm sorry," he said, realizing the exact line he'd crossed. Iris' eyes were far away, remembering something she rarely spoke of. "I'm beyond selfish."

"You're in love." She smiled sadly at him. "Love makes you say and do things you normally wouldn't do. That's why people call it dangerous."

"Would you do it all again?" he asked. He felt like a child asking her for advice. "Would you love her, even though you know the cost?"

"I'll love her for the rest of my life," she replied. "And yes, I would do it all again because our love was real. That is what you have to ask yourself—is your love real enough to risk it all?"

She rested her hand on his shoulder, gently squeezing it, and he knew the conversation was over. The ghosts of her past lurked behind her eyes when she walked toward the forest as she often did when memories threatened her control. Kieran watched her disappear through the tree line, repeating her advice to himself.

Is your love real enough to risk it all?

He knew the answer to the question, but feared the consequences.

∿

THE STRUGGLE TO decide which dress was most appropriate to meet the King of Grimwalde felt endless. Thea stood half-naked in the middle of Kieran's bedroom while Ethel held up each dress to her, mumbling about her skin tone, her hair color, and the way her freckles showed or did not show as much with certain styles. Thea's frown deepened with every passing scrutiny from the pre-teen girl who apparently knew much more about high-court fashion than she did.

"How old are you exactly?" Thea asked as they settled on a midnight-blue gown that cut uncomfortably low at the neck. A piece of sheer blue material had been sewn into the V-line to make it slightly more modest, but it did nothing for Thea's discomfort when she looked in the mirror Ethel had hauled into Kieran's bedroom from her own.

"Thirteen." Ethel beamed, tugging at the bottom of the dress so that it would fall straight. "But I'm quite mature for my age."

Thirteen, Thea thought, feeling ashamed of how she'd nearly run the poor girl down with Faylon earlier. Of course, every thirteen-year-old thought they were mature for their age, but Ethel seemed to have forgiven Thea and moved on to focusing on dressing her up like a doll.

Thea admitted the dress was gorgeous to herself but never aloud. It was floor-length and hung perfectly over her curves, accenting only the places she wished to have accented. Like the black dress, Thea felt self-conscious, but even through her self-criticism she admitted the dress made her look more elegant.

"One last thing," Ethel said and took Thea's hair in her hands without so much as a warning. Thea protested, but the girl was relentless. She combed through the mess that hung halfway down Thea's back. Her hair had a fair number of flow waves for Ethel to work with, and it amazed Thea how easily she untangled the knots that had formed during her afternoon adventures.

"There is no magic that makes this easier?" Thea asked with

an uncomfortable laugh. Ethel glanced at her in the mirror with a shy smile.

"There may be, milady, but I'm human."

Thea's mouth fell open. It was true that Thea hadn't noticed wings or pointed ears on the girl, nor any other Fae feature, but she'd assumed Ethel was a Fae because she lived with Kieran and Iris.

"Don't worry," Ethel said, her cheerful smile never faltering. "Kieran taught me how to fight so that one day I can stand by your side without magic."

The idea of this small-framed girl in any sort of fight made Thea frown. She disliked anyone standing to protect her, and yet that seemed to be all anyone wanted to do today. Ethel's hand was on Thea's shoulder as she combed, but Thea placed her hand on top of it.

"I would be honored to have someone like you at my side," Thea said. She squeezed Ethel's hand, and the girl grinned at her much like Kieran did when he approved of something she'd said. Thea thought of her own world and how Ethel would thrive in a land where humans weren't looked down upon like they seemed to be here, but this was her home. As Ethel continued to work happily on Thea's hair, she hoped she could be the change they all believed she was. She wanted that change for her.

"You're all set!" Ethel said, pulling her out of her own thoughts. Thea glanced in the mirror and saw Ethel had braided some of her hair into a crown around her head, like Iris', but left most of the hair to fall into loose curls down her back. Tiny flowers decorated the crown, drawing attention to it, and for the first time since arriving, Thea saw herself as a Fae. Sure, she missed her jeans desperately, but she couldn't deny the effect that the dress and the hair had on her. Ethel had dressed her to look like a princess, and she no longer felt like an imposter.

"Thank you, Ethel." Thea rose and pulled Ethel into a tight

hug. When they broke away, she saw the tears that filled the young girl's eyes. "You're a wonderful friend."

Ethel sniffled, still smiling, and bobbled her head up and down as she wiped her tears. Thea smiled back at her. She'd had no siblings, but she wondered if this was how older sisters felt for their little sisters or brothers. She'd hardly spent any time with Ethel at all, and yet she already felt the need to protect her.

"Are you ready, milady?"

Thea took a deep breath and straightened her gown out one more time before nodding her head.

"As I'll ever be."

Ethel led her from the house, insisting that, as a princess, they should announce her arrival. Thea tried to argue that it was only Kieran waiting for her, but Ethel rolled her eyes to say that was exactly why she wanted to announce her. Ethel handed Thea a shawl made of the softest fur she'd ever touched to drape over her shoulders, and after Thea's wary gaze, assured her it was not made from any animal. She accepted it, immediately grateful for the warmth it brought to her shoulders.

Ethel opened the front door and cleared her throat. Kieran was standing a good distance away, facing the opposite direction as he stared out at the forest. His dark outline looked painted against the snow with wings folded handsomely against his back. A fresh powder settled on the ground as snowflakes fell from the darkening sky. It made Thea long for a piece of paper to sketch the irresistible image.

"May I present Princess Thea of Ivandor." Ethel's smile radiated as Kieran turned to look at them both. He cocked his head to the side, looking Thea over with an appreciative smile before walking toward them. Thea's heart raced at his approach, and Ethel murmured, "I can hear that from here!"

Thea resisted the urge to kick her beneath her gown. Maybe this actually *was* how it felt to have a sibling.

Kieran reached them and bowed low to the ground with all seriousness.

"My future queen," he said, sending a shiver down Thea's spine. While Kieran's eyes were lowered, Ethel moved to show Thea she should extend her hand for him; she did so clumsily.

He chuckled, taking her hand and pressing his lips gently against the back of it before rising.

"You look magnificent."

Thea lowered her head in a semi-bow as she said thank you. She wished she had makeup on to hide the red tint that burned her face, but hoped the dress' blue tone against her skin would do the trick.

"You two had better get going," Iris said, returning from the woods with a bundle of wood tucked in her arms. "The king expects you for dinner."

Faylon appeared then, bowing low for Thea to mount. Kieran extended his hands for Thea to place her foot in, helping her up onto the unicorn.

"Try not to tear your dress this time, Princess," he whispered just low enough for her to hear.

Thea rolled her eyes, but smiled.

"Don't pretend you didn't enjoy the improved style," she replied, tilting her chin a little tighter. She pulled the dress up so that it sat high on her thighs and would hopefully be less likely to tear. Kieran's eyes widened at the sight, making Thea smirk.

Ethel covered her mouth, attempting to hide her giggle, and Thea swore she saw Iris' eyes roll as she ushered the younger girl inside.

"I'll never pretend." Kieran laughed and then, after one last look at the bare skin of Thea's legs, took off at a run, his wings extending wide behind him. "Try to keep up this time."

Thea gave Faylon a light nudge, just enough to tell him to get going, and they took off after Kieran's disappearing shape. She watched him soar across the sky and laughed as the falling snow kissed her skin.

She enjoyed the freedom she felt when riding Faylon, and as they leveled themselves beneath Kieran, she admitted for the first time that she felt like she belonged.

CHAPTER 7

A MAN DRESSED IN ARMOR GREETED THEM WHEN THEY ARRIVED AT the castle gates. Thea dismounted from Faylon's back as gracefully as she could manage while Kieran landed beside her in silence. She straightened her thankfully undamaged dress and tucked a few of the loose strands of hair behind her ear. The soldier bowed before Thea without meeting her eyes and placed a fist over the left side of his chest in salute. Thea looked at Kieran, unsure of the proper reaction, but just like on the hilltop, he was calculating their surroundings and not paying attention to her. She knew he was in full soldier mode now and wouldn't be helping her with her questions on etiquette.

"Welcome to the castle of Grimwalde, milady," the soldier said, finally lifting his eyes to meet hers. "The king awaits you in the throne room. If you will both follow me..."

He turned without waiting for a response, and Kieran offered his arm to Thea, apparently satisfied with her safety for now. She looped her arm through his with a grateful smile and allowed him to lead her through the large entryway as the gate lowered down behind them, sealing them in.

"It is a p-pleasure to have been invited." Thea felt this was the proper response to what the soldier had said, but she couldn't control the slight shake in her voice as she spoke. She cleared her throat, as if that might make it disappear, while they walked across a courtyard toward a set of double doors. Curious whispers echoed around the courtyard from many onlookers. Most of them were dressed like Thea, in fancier clothing, some were soldiers, and others looked like ordinary humans.

Thea noticed several humans and Fae who dressed more casually. These individuals worked around the courtyard, managing flowers, assisting the more nicely dressed inhabitants, and staring at Thea, just like everyone else.

"Are they slaves?" Thea whispered to Kieran.

"No, but they work for the king," he replied, glancing at her. "Like your mother, King Aragon believes in fair treatment of all beings in his kingdom."

As the soldier opened the double doors, they were led into a corridor of magnificent paintings. There were many portraits, but one Fae appeared to have been painted multiple times. She had flowing waves of flaming red hair, much like Thea's, and was often pictured beside a red mare. Thea recognized her without ever having seen her before. It was the Goddess Ainé. Alongside her portraits and paintings were bloodier murals of a female Fae dressed in a soldier's armor. Death and destruction often surrounded this Fae, flocks of ravens, and remnants of war—except in one painting where she stood as a child on a lakeside with a much younger-looking Ainé.

Thea realized the other Fae must be Morrigan, the Goddess of Death, and shivered. The murals raised the hair on the back of her neck, so she tried not to look at them for too long.

When they reached another set of double doors at the end of the hall, the soldier slipped inside to inform the king of their arrival. He returned a moment later, holding the door open for them to pass through. Kieran unhooked his arm from Thea's and motioned for her to go first. She nodded, desperately wishing she still had his support, and then entered the large, brightly lit room.

It took a moment for Thea's eyes to adjust from the darkness of the candlelit hallway to the brightness of the throne room. Skylights lined the ceiling above them, allowing natural rays of sun to warm the room and brighten it. An enormous crimson rug lay upon the floor in front of them, and sparkling gold adorned the walls. She'd never been somewhere so beautiful before, and for a moment, all she could do was stare with her mouth open.

"Breathtaking, isn't it?" someone said from the other side of the room. Thea stopped examining the ceiling to look toward the elderly man who'd spoken. He sat upon a stone throne.

"May I proudly introduce milord, King Aragon of Grimwalde," the soldier said, bowing low to this king.

Thea quickly lowered herself into a curtsy of sorts, and Kieran's face morphed into a soldier's mask.

"T-thank you for inviting me to your magnificent home," Thea said, furious with the unescapable tremble in her throat.

You are a princess, she reminded herself, but it didn't help. She felt beyond nervous.

The king rose from his throne, walking forward to meet them. He used a golden staff to keep his balance, but despite his age, he didn't appear weak to Thea.

"Just wait until you see your own kingdom, my dear." King Aragon reached them, and Kieran bowed low, but Thea remained standing as he held out a hand to her. She placed her hand in his, just as Ethel had motioned her to do with Kieran, and watched as he lifted it to his lips carefully. It was not an uncomfortable moment, but a respectful greeting between two new acquaintances. She understood the meaning behind it, but when she met the king's gaze all the reminders she'd given

73

herself about being a princess and having manners went out the double doors she'd entered through.

"Oh!" she gasped before she could stop herself, and King Aragon smiled as Kieran stiffened. "I'm so sorry, I didn't mean to—"

The king waved her off and patted the back of her hand assuredly. His eyes were glossed over with clouds of white— endless as the depths of glass.

"Although my sight has long abandoned me, I still see you, child." He led her toward the middle of the room and called for someone to bring in a place for them sit. Within seconds, a few men carried in a table with three comfy-looking leather chairs, as if this were a normal occurrence. Adolescents then replaced the men, setting the table with an array of cheeses and meats. Thea's mouth nearly watered at the smell of coffee being carried out from the kitchens. She'd thought coming to this land meant she'd never have another cup of warm, caffeinated crack, as her mom had once called it, in her life.

Never having coffee again seemed to be an unreasonably cruel addition to the rest of the changes she was experiencing.

"Sit, please." The king motioned them toward the three chairs and Kieran hesitated. "You as well, my boy."

"Coffee? Tea?" asked one of the young men serving them. Thea nodded energetically at the cup of coffee and sighed happily as soon as the hot liquid touched her lips, despite the fact that it definitely burned her mouth. Kieran lifted an eyebrow at her, looking as if he were trying not to laugh, before accepting a cup of tea for himself.

"I've heard you wish to be called by your human-given name, Thea." King Aragon took a sip of coffee, coughing a little afterward into a white handkerchief. Thea wondered how in the world he would have heard that, since Kieran hadn't known she went by Thea until returning from his visit with the king.

"It's the only name I've ever known," Thea said, taking a

74

nibble at a piece of cheese she didn't recognize. It tasted like heaven on her tongue.

"Well, then Princess Thea you shall be," said the king. He tapped his staff on the ground like a judge's gavel and smiled brightly at no one in particular. Thea snapped a cracker in half to follow her cheese and wondered if she should say something else to the king.

Thankfully, before she could worry too much about it, he spoke again.

"Ivandor has been in the shadows for far too long," he said. "But are you sure you wish to be queen? I imagine you have many questions about our culture, our world, and having grown up among humans—"

"Humans are no different to Fae." Thea set her coffee cup down with a soft thud, frowning. She realized she was being defensive, but after her conversation with Ethel, she felt a little on edge about the Faerie-human class difference that seemed to exist here.

She thought of her parents and all they'd done to make sure she'd had a happy life, despite her not even being their own daughter. They'd been the nicest people she had ever known, and they had been human. After their deaths, her boyfriend, Marcus, had also been amazing. He'd taken care of her even when things had ended between them. And then there was Ethel, who, despite being told she was less of a being than the magical creatures around her, strived to please them and fight for what she believed in. "I mean no offense, milord."

Thea didn't know if she was using the proper terms for addressing the king, but she felt angry at him for even insinuating that being raised by humans made her any less capable of becoming queen. She also didn't like the smirk that was forming on Kieran's face as she spoke.

"I told you she was feisty," he said to the king as if she was not there.

"You were right, of course." The king laughed in response, and Thea felt her face growing pink. She obviously was being excluded from whatever conversation the boys were having. "She's just like her mother."

"I'm sitting right here, you know?" she said, with slightly more venom than she'd meant to. The king struck his staff against the ground once more with a booming laugh that made her jump.

"*Just* like her mother!"

Thea took another sip of her coffee and realized the king hadn't meant to insult her at all. He'd been testing her.

But had she passed?

"I know I didn't grow up here, but I'm here now," she said, for the first time truly picturing herself as the queen they all hoped she'd be. "I have a long way to go before I can be queen, but I believe in bringing equality to our kingdoms. We need to be united." Thea didn't realize until after speaking the words that they hadn't been her own.

She felt Ainé's presence within her mind, the same way she'd felt it before at the hillside in Ireland. It wasn't as clear this time, but it was definitely there.

Thea could feel the Goddess' belief in her as clearly as she felt herself inhaling for breath. Ainé wanted her to unite the four kingdoms, and who was she to refuse? She saw the corruption, she saw the suffering; who would she be if she didn't at least try to change it?

"Spoken like a true ruler," King Aragon said. "Your mother would've been very proud of the woman you've grown into, and I must say, your human parents must have raised you well."

The compliment brought tears to her eyes, and she was glad the king couldn't see. However, he reached into his pocket and handed her a handkerchief regardless.

"How did you..." Thea took the handkerchief gratefully and wiped her eyes and nose.

"King Aragon is a seer," Kieran explained.

"Of sorts." The king laughed, folding his hands into his lap. "I lost my physical sight many years ago, but the Goddess enhanced my other senses to make up for it. The visions are never as life-changing as your mother's were."

"So, you knew both of our mothers, then?" Thea said, unable to contain her curiosity.

"Yes. As your mother was my god-daughter, I would say I knew her quite well." The king smiled, but his nostalgic tone led Thea to reach her hand out to touch his. The guards by the door became tense, taking a few steps towards them, but King Aragon lifted his hand and placed it on top of Thea's. "I don't know if this will come as pleasant news to you, but your mother did also name me as your great-godfather, my dearest Thea."

Thea sniffled but did not cry again as she looked at the old man. She no longer saw only a king. She saw a man who'd been changed by war and age, a man who'd loved and lost. She'd lost so much family that she allowed herself a single moment of happiness at discovering she was not so completely alone in the world. Even if they weren't related by blood, this man was the closest thing to family she had left, and he was just as closely related to her as her adoptive parents had been.

"Would you tell me about her?" Thea asked, never letting her hand leave the warmth of King Aragon's.

"In time, yes, but first I must ask you what you know of your father."

Thea frowned, not wanting to talk about her father. From everything she'd heard so far, she didn't care if he was her father, she wanted nothing to do with the man.

Kieran reached over and placed his hand on her knee, catching her by surprise. Despite her desire to hear more now, Thea reminded herself that if she was to be queen, she needed to understand the way the Royal Fae worked behind castle doors. There would be time to discuss her mother later, but this was her first glimpse at her future in the Royal Court, whether she liked it or not.

"I only know what Kieran has told me," Thea said. "My father is a monster. He murdered both our mothers in cold blood. My mother sent me away to protect me from him."

Kieran nodded his head in agreement, but the king only looked thoughtful, waiting for her to continue.

"He wants to free Morrigan from her prison so that she can purge this realm of humans." The words tasted like bile on her lips, but Thea continued on anyway. "My mother knew something—I don't know what— but somehow, I am the key to releasing the Goddess of Death."

Thea didn't know what else to say, so she just fell back into her chair with a sigh. Her father was a monster, but despite that, she felt an ache at knowing her own flesh and blood had betrayed her, when his job was to protect her.

"There is a lot more to your father's history than you have been told, Thea. His upbringing was crueler than many could even begin to imagine, let alone endure." The king spoke slowly, as if recalling memories from long ago. "Your mother had a kind heart that pitied him because of it."

"I will not make the same mistakes that my mother did." Thea frowned. She hated to think of her mother as making any mistakes, but that was exactly what it had been. She had let a monster into their kingdom and it had gotten her killed. Thea would not allow that fate for herself. She would stop her father from releasing the Goddess of Death and she would make it possible for Kieran and anyone else who'd been forced to flee to return home.

Surprisingly, it was Kieran who spoke next.

"A cruel upbringing is no excuse." He slammed his fist on the table and Thea jumped in surprise. "Some of us grew up without parents at all, and we aren't out trying to massacre innocent people!"

Thea took Kieran's hand off the table and wrapped her fingers through his. Something about his words told her that there was far more to the story than he'd originally told. She didn't care though, because he was right. A cruel upbringing was no excuse for turning into a monster. She didn't know what had happened to Kieran's father, but seeing the fury on his face, she believed that it must have had something to do with her father as well. He was rigid all over, ravenous for a revenge that Thea feared could never be quenched.

How can he even stand to be around me? she wondered. *Don't I remind him of the very people who ruined his life?*

The questions broke her inside, but she continued to squeeze his hand soothingly, hoping his anger would fade.

"Aren't you just as determined to kill Malachi?" the king asked. Thea held her breath, waiting for Kieran to explode with whatever emotion haunted him, but it didn't come. He seemed to be considering the king's words carefully, trying to understand what he meant.

"I don't wish him dead," Thea said, her voice steady once more. "He'll pay for his crimes, but I am not a judge, nor an executioner."

Kieran's entire body was shaking, and Thea feared the darkness that filled him. The kind man she'd seen just hours earlier was fading behind a wall of shadows. She remembered the darkness that had surrounded her when Amara came and feared it now tempted Kieran's soul.

"That's what makes us different from Malachi," the king finally said. "We won't risk our souls for the sake of revenge."

Kieran didn't reply, and Thea's fear only increased. She squeezed his hand, but he shrunk away from her touch, standing and walking out of the room without another word. She stared after him, her lips slightly parted with words left unspoken. The door slammed shut behind him, and she winced as if it had physically hit her.

Perhaps she'd been right. Perhaps he couldn't stand being around her.

"He suffered a great deal under Malachi's rule. His father went after Malachi after his mother's death."

"What?" Thea looked back at the king with wide-eyed shock. "Ivandor was under my father's rule though—that would have been a suicide mission!"

"Exactly..." King Aragon's voice sounded much older. "His father had no intention of returning. He left his sister with the responsibility of caring for his only son."

Thea fought the anger within her. Kieran hadn't told her this part of the story, but why should he have? They were just starting to get to know each other and this darkness he kept locked away, this sense of abandonment—Thea didn't know how to help with that.

"If his father sought revenge, why doesn't he understand there is a better way?" Thea asked, glancing back toward the door with a desperate hope to see him return, but he didn't.

"Hate clouds his mind. We must always remember that anger is a well-trodden path to hate, and hate is what Morrigan feeds on."

"How do I help him?"

"You already have." The king's smile was genuine, and with the help of his staff, he stood. "There's a light in his eyes since your return."

Thea didn't know what that meant, nor how he'd even know that Kieran had "light in his eyes," but it appeared their visit was ending, so she rose as well. She wished to ask him more questions about her mother and about Kieran, but knew that she needed to respect the time he'd given her.

"We'll speak again, but I'm an old man in need of rest," he said. "Kieran needs you, Thea. He needs you as much as he needs the air he breathes. You have something that many others only dream of; let that guide you on your journey."

Thea walked around the table and hugged the king, despite the guards' obvious disapproval. They shifted uncomfortably near the door, looking at each other with confusion.

"Thank you, King Aragon." She rested her head against his rumbling chest as he embraced her with a throaty chuckle.

"You may call me great-godfather if you like." His voice no longer sounded like a king's. In fact, Thea believed he almost sounded nervous.

"Thank you, Great-Godfather." She stepped away, smiling up at him, and knew he could see her happiness, even without his sight. His guards came to his side then and Thea bowed low to him. "It has been my greatest pleasure to meet you."

"And mine to meet you, dear child. Now go find what you are searching for. There is much work to be done."

Thea allowed the guards to escort her from the throne room and found Kieran waiting for her in the hallway. He leaned against the wall looking moody.

"I thought you left me here," she said with a nervous smile.

A moment passed as they looked at each other. Whatever thoughts of revenge and hatred Kieran had still haunted his eyes, but something else was there as well, something that Thea clung to: hope.

She walked up to him, this time extending her own arm for him to loop his through, just as they'd done when they'd arrived. He linked his arm with hers and let out a heavy breath.

"I'll never leave you," he said, and they left the castle arm in arm.

CHAPTER 8

THE NEXT FEW DAYS PASSED IN AN ANXIOUS BLUR OF TENSION. King Aragon had requested Kieran return to his guard duty, at least part time, to ensure the village remained protected from any unwelcome visitors, but when he wasn't in the village, Kieran was teaching Thea how to wield the dagger, which she constantly kept hidden in her dress, or his sword. Iris seemed to avoid Thea at all costs, but Ethel always sat watching the two of them spar in the yard with an amused smile.

"Ouch!" Thea cried out as Kieran dropped her to the ground yet again, pinning her arms down with his feet as he stood over her.

"You left yourself wide open," he scolded for about the millionth time. "You'd be dead—"

"If this were an actual fight, I know." Thea jerked her arms out from under his boots painfully and rubbed the dirt from her skin.

"This isn't a joke, Thea." Kieran reached out a hand to help her up, which she accepted with bitter gratitude. They'd been at this for days. Every moment that Kieran was at the cottage he had Thea running some sort of training exercise. First, he wanted her to run—run until her Jell-O legs could no longer hold her upright anymore. Then it had been controlling the dagger and sword, and now he was trying and failing at teaching her how to dodge attacks. Bruises covered her entire body, and muscles that she hadn't even known existed seemed to never stop aching. It didn't help that she was having to learn to do all of this fighting in a dress either. "We don't know when Malachi will make his next move. Amara knows you are with me. It's only a matter of time before they find out where I am in Grimwalde. Iris' cottage has remained off the king's maps for years, but he is capable of anything at this point."

His worry diffused a bit of Thea's anger.

"I think she's looking better," Ethel called out from her perch on a pile of hay that Faylon was trying to take from beneath her. She shooed him away and held out a sugar cube instead.

"It's okay, Ethel." Thea wiped her forehead and sighed. Despite the frigid winter air, sweat dripped from her skin during these exercises. She desperately missed indoor plumbing and showers because of it. "Kieran is right."

He seemed surprised by this, but Thea just reached for the cup of water beside Ethel, downing the cold liquid as her lungs burned with over-exertion.

"We don't know when my sister will make her next move." Thea frowned. She'd started calling Amara her sister for experimental purposes, but it still felt wrong on her tongue. The girl had tried to kill her, but if everything Kieran had told her over the past couple of days was true, she'd also been raised by a monster. Would Thea have been any different in her shoes? She wasn't sure. "But what I don't understand is why you aren't teaching me to wield magic."

Apparently, Amara was only Thea's half-sister, but Thea knew nothing about her mother. Kieran had only shrugged in response when she'd asked.

However, the facts were that her father and her sister were

plotting to use her to release the Goddess of Death into Faerie, and while Kieran was trying to teach her how to defend herself against that happening, they were getting no closer to any answers about exactly how her family planned to use her, and Thea still had absolutely no clue how to use the magic that everyone claimed was in her blood.

"We've been over this, Thea," Kieran said sliding his sword back into the sheath at his hip. "Until you are physically stronger, your body won't be able to handle the magic."

They had, in fact, been over this, but Thea still didn't understand it. She remembered the exhaustion that had followed using magic in Ireland, but surely there was a way to train herself to control that, right? Kieran claimed it came with stamina—knowing how to balance physical exertion with magical exertion—but that just pissed her off. Thea had never played sports as a kid. She'd also never worked out. She'd been one of those girls who could stay in decent shape without ever really needing to do anything—or at least, she'd thought she was. Now that she was being forced to use foreign muscles in her body, she wondered just how fit she actually was.

"Ethel, I need you to go to village," Iris called from the cottage door, looking out at the three of them.

Ethel let out an audible groan that made Iris raise her eyebrow and place her hands on her hips.

"You'd better just go," Kieran warned, seeing the look on his aunt's face. "Plus, Mica is back. I saw him there this morning."

This changed Ethel's expression drastically. She jumped up off the hay and ran toward Iris, saying something about grabbing her cloak. Thea watched with a moment of amusement.

"Does Ethel have a boyfriend?" she asked, tilting her head.

"No, but she has a crush on a boy in the village." Kieran laughed and came to stand beside Thea. "You should go with her. It would be nice for you to meet some of the other villagers. They all know you are here, after all."

"I can leave?" Thea said, sounding more shocked than she'd meant to. Kieran glanced at her with a raised eyebrow and a frown.

"You're not a prisoner, Thea. I'm just trying to keep you safe."

"I didn't mean it like that," Thea said, but Ethel was coming back from the house, cloaked now and with a satchel of coins on her hip.

"Thea will go with you, Ethel," Kieran called out before the girl could disappear into the forest. She glanced over at Thea with a wide-eyed excitement.

"Just let me get changed," she said, motioning to her dirty clothing. "I will see you later then?"

She directed the question at Kieran, who nodded his head with a small, crooked smile.

WHEN THEA RETURNED a few minutes later she wore a clean dress with a warm winter cloak draped around her shoulders. She pulled the hood of the cloak over her head to block out the chilly winter breeze as she went to meet Ethel.

Kieran had already slipped inside with Iris, explaining that they had matters to discuss, which he would tell her about later. Thea was curious about what matters these were, but seeing the excited look on Ethel's face kept her to her original plan. They hadn't gotten to spend a lot of time together, just the two of them, and Thea thought it would be nice to get to know the younger girl a little better. Plus, as Kieran had said, she wanted to meet the other villagers.

"Kieran told me that our worlds are quite different," Ethel said as they entered the quiet forest cover. The village was not a far walk, so they left the horses and Faylon behind. Thea was secretly grateful for this, knowing that riding on Faylon's back would have only made her already sore legs worse. "Do you ever miss it?"

Thea thought about this for a moment. She hadn't thought of herself as being homesick before, but as Ethel said the words, her stomach twisted into a familiar aching knot. Her parents had died less than three months ago, and even though she'd had plenty of distractions, she missed them desperately. She wished for her mother especially, thinking of how she could always read the way Thea was feeling just by looking at her. She also wondered what her father would think of Kieran. Even though Kieran and Thea weren't anything more than friends, she knew her father would have seen right through her feelings.

Her father had never really liked Marcus. He'd told her she was made for a far greater life than what a small-town boy could bring her, but was that greater life one at Kieran's side?

"I'm sorry, milady." Ethel put her hand on Thea's with a sympathetic smile. "I don't remember me ma or pa, but I can't imagine losing Kieran or Iris, or even you."

Thea squeezed her hand, trying to escape the depressing thoughts in her head. At least she had memories to hold onto. Ethel was an orphan, but she constantly remained optimistic despite all the lemons life threw in her direction. Thea wished she was more like that.

"It's difficult to think of the parents that I lost or of those I left behind, but I know where I belong." Thea glanced over at the younger girl with a kind smile. "I spent my entire life wondering where I belonged, but I understand what was always missing. If anything, I was homesick before—and now, I'm home."

THEA'S FEET ached after the twenty-minute walk to town. The beautiful path distracted her along the way, but now that they'd reached the cobblestone roads, she felt the blisters inside her leather shoes. She didn't want to complain as Ethel continued the same cheerful chatter since their heartfelt conversation.

Thea found it easy to be around her. It amazed Thea how carefree Ethel was, despite the circumstances she'd grown up in, and Thea felt slightly ashamed of how she herself had acted at that age towards her own parents.

"We need to see Mirielle to pick up some herbs for Iris," Ethel said as they slowed down in front of a small wooden cart. It was full of many plants that Thea didn't recognize. A single mule stood attached to the cart, with his muzzle in a bucket of grain and a blanket over his back.

"Ethel!" A young man came running around the back of the cart, grinning ear to ear as he lifted Ethel's small body into his arms, spinning her in a playful circle. He looked only a couple of years older than Ethel, who squealed something about how she would be sick before the young man sat her feet firmly back on the ground. He tossed an arm around her shoulders.

"Liar," he teased, leading her toward the back of the cart where an older lady, with the same yellow eyes as the boy, sat smiling. "Ma, look who finally came to see me."

"Mica, dear. Let the poor girl go." The woman laughed and Ethel blushed as Mica removed his arm with an apologetic bow.

"And who is it that she's brought with her?" Mica's mother looked past Ethel at Thea, and her eyes widened.

"Goddess above, you look just like her." The woman placed a hand upon her heart and stood, walking over to Thea's frozen body. Ethel gave her an encouraging smile.

The woman bowed low in front of Thea, motioning for her confused boy to do the same.

"That's really unnecessary," Thea blurted, looking around with embarrassment as a few villagers glanced their way.

"This is Princess Claire, but she goes by Thea, so really, this is Princess Thea," Ethel whispered to Mica, who looked up with his mother's same wide eyes. "Thea, this is Mica and his mother, Mirielle."

"Please make them stop," Thea begged Ethel, who giggled in response.

"You really should get used to this type of behavior, milady."

Thea knew she never would.

She reached out to help Mica's mother back into a standing position, but when their hands touched, Mirielle shrieked as if Thea had burnt her.

Thea immediately dropped her hands, and Mica ran to his mother's side.

"I'm so sorry," Thea gasped, bewildered at what she'd done to the woman. "Did I hurt you? I meant to help…"

"Shh," Mica said, not looking at Thea. Ethel came to her side quickly, her face shining with excitement.

"She's having a vision!" Ethel whispered loudly.

"She's a seer?" Thea asked. She'd met only one other seer, King Aragon, but he hadn't acted like this when he touched her. He'd just seemed to know unexplainable things.

"Death is coming," Mirielle cried, grabbing Thea by the hands.

Thea felt like she was drowning beneath icy waters. Her breath caught, and the village faded away. A flock of black ravens swarmed around her, clawing at her skin and screeching so loudly that she thought her ears would bleed. When Thea resurfaced, a voice sang seductively from the middle of the flock.

We see you, Princess. We're coming.

Thea tried to find the source of the voice but all she saw was blackness as the ravens engulfed her.

The vision was gone as quickly as it came, and Thea stumbled backwards, nearly tripping over the uneven cobblestone ground. Mirielle's crystalline eyes, which had looked identical to King Aragon's for a moment, returned to their soft yellow tone.

The color returned to her cheeks, but she fell against Mica's chest and sobbed horribly. Thea stood frozen, trying to steady her breathing as Ethel approached Mirielle. Concern replaced her excitement as she knelt.

"Mirielle," Ethel clutched the woman's other hand tightly, "what did you see?"

"Malachi's daughter is here."

"Yes, but we already knew that..." Mica said, glancing up at Thea, then back to his mother in confusion. Thea and Mirielle's eyes met. The woman was completely drained, that much was clear, but there was something else, something Thea was supposed to understand.

She was regaining control of her senses too slowly; she tried to wrap her mind around the vision, to recall why the words felt so familiar to her. Who was coming?

All at once, it hit her. She remembered the ravens painted in the murals of death in King Aragon's castle. The Fae associated Morrigan with ravens, and *she* was the one who kept taunting her, who kept saying she was coming. *Malachi's daughter...*

"Not me," Thea said abruptly and looked at both Mica and Ethel. "She's not talking about me! Ethel, you need to get Kieran." Panic was tearing at her, but she fought for control of her emotions.

Malachi's daughter is here.

Mirielle wasn't talking about Thea; she was talking about Amara. Amara had found a way into the village, undetected by King Aragon's guard. Mirielle had seen death coming, but Kieran had said the visions weren't always clear.

Thea hoped that was the case now.

"I don't have a horse..." Ethel said, looking pale. Thea cursed. It'd taken them nearly half an hour to get to the village by foot.

"I'll go," Mica said. "I'm half-Fae; I can run faster."

Ethel looked embarrassed, but nodded her head in agreement. He was gone before anyone could think of another option, and Mirielle's voice broke the silent panic as they watched him go.

"We need to hide you, Princess."

And then, the screaming began.

CHAPTER 9

KIERAN AND IRIS WERE SITTING IN THE PARLOR DISCUSSING Thea's upcoming training when they heard Mica screaming outside.

"Kieran! Kieran, come quickly!" The boy's face was bright red as he tried to catch his breath. He looked as if he might collapse, but Iris shouldered herself under his arm to keep him upright. Kieran's heart raced in anticipation as his eyes scouted the area for whatever danger Mica had come to warn him of, but he saw no immediate threat. Mica coughed, trying to breathe and speak, but he'd obviously overexerted himself with whatever magic he'd used to enhance his abilities in getting to them.

"What happened?" Kieran demanded. He knew he sounded cruel, but whatever had driven Mica to come find him loomed out of his reach.

"My ma," he said, coughing again. It was a rasping cough that tore at his throat. "She said—"

"Out with it, boy," Iris said, but her tone was kinder than Kieran's.

"Malachi's daughter is here."

"Well, yes, Thea is in town with Ethel..." Iris said, looking with clear relief toward Kieran. Mica was shaking his head frantically, though. His eyes were closing as exhaustion threatened to overtake him.

"Thea sent me—"

Kieran needed no further explanation, knowing Thea would have only sent Mica to warn Kieran if the danger was real.

"Take him inside to heal," Kieran said, not waiting for a response from his aunt. He ran toward the village with his wings outstretched behind him, and the earth disappeared from beneath his feet.

THEA AND ETHEL sat huddled together in a clothing shop. With all the forcefulness of a mother's voice, Mirielle had ushered them inside, demanding they remain quiet. The shop's clerk, whose name Thea had learned was Mr. Bloomington, had no objection once he heard who Thea was. Instead, he just continued to gape at her with wide, ogling eyes that made her want to throw one of the hard leather shoes from his shop window at his head.

"I shouldn't be hiding in here," Thea said to Ethel in a low whisper. "If my sister is out there, hurting people—"

"Then you are the one she is looking for," Ethel interrupted, clutching Thea's hand.

"Exactly!"

"Shh!" said the store clerk. The girls returned their gazes to the small crack in the curtains that showed them the street outside. People were running in all directions as a black mist crept across the ground, birthing shadows that whipped out at the fleeing villagers. Some Fae used magic to fight off the darkness that threatened them, but many were dragged away kicking and screaming by invisible hands. Thea could see

Mirielle a few feet beyond the shop door, fighting off the dark magic that threatened their hiding place with a barrier of water she'd summoned from the snow at her feet. Thea could see was the soft blue glow from Mirielle's slightly trembling hands and knew whatever magic she was performing protected them for the time being.

"Whoa," both Thea and Ethel said in unison, but Thea could see how much effort the magic took. Kieran had mentioned that each Fae specialized in a certain elemental magic, although Thea hadn't discovered what hers was yet, Mirielle's was obviously water. It didn't matter how long Mirielle fought though, dark magic overpowered elemental magic that the Fae typically wielded. Thea had discovered that the night she and Kieran had fought Amara. Sure, Thea had caught Amara off guard that night, but they'd lost the element of surprise; she had no idea how to wield her magic. Kieran had only focused on little else but her learning how to hold a sword or run away, and despite her fear, she refused to run now.

Where were King Aragon's soldiers? Thea wondered furiously. Kieran hadn't been on duty today, but they'd assigned other soldiers to the village to make sure none of Malachi's followers showed up. So, where were they now? Why weren't they protecting everyone?

Thea recalled the icy tentacles that had restrained her in Ireland, and a mixture of fear and anger made the muscles in her back tighten and twitch. If Amara was here because of her, then she couldn't just sit here and watch as the villagers ran terrified through the streets or were dragged away for whatever game Amara now wanted to play.

"Kieran will come," Ethel said, as if it was supposed to help her feel better.

"I don't need Kieran to save me. I need to help these people." The guilt of hiding away while people like Mirielle fought to protect her made her sick. She stood, ripping her hand out of

Ethel's, and ran out the door, ignoring the pleading she heard behind her from both Ethel and Mr. Bloomington.

"What are you doing?" Mirielle said, her eyes widening as Thea rushed past her magical water barrier, drenching her to the bone, and directly into the shadows. She didn't reply.

The sky above had darkened into a deep gray, and bile rose in Thea's throat at the sight of the bodies scattered on the ground. She hadn't been able to see them through the shop window, but now she did. Their limbs were twisted at odd angles and their lifeless eyes ripped at her guilt as her hands trembled. There were men, women, and children's bodies. Those who hadn't been fast enough or strong enough to get away were left in puddles of their own blood that stained the cobblestone streets.

My fault, she thought in horror as the shadows that had tormented and murdered parted, creating a path for her to follow, leading her exactly where Amara wanted her to go. She clenched her hands into fists as she passed more bodies, at least a dozen of them—dead because of her.

However, the screaming had stopped and a deathly silence chilled her to the bone. She hoped that meant the rest of the village had escaped.

"Amara!" Thea called out into the darkness for her sister, and heard a familiar wicked laugh, followed by something else, something that made Thea's anger falter into panic.

"Thea!" This was not a female's voice, but a man's, a man she'd already failed so many times before.

Marcus' voice called out for her desperately. She ran toward it, as fast as her blistered feet would take her, screaming for him. A prickle of dread formed between her shoulder blades as she reached the center of town—the eye of the magical storm. Amara leaned casually against a stone fountain in the middle of the courtyard, taunting Thea with a smile as she unfolded a piece of paper.

"Dear Marcus, I'm sorry that I can't say this to you in person." Amara read the paper aloud in an even more annoying tone than usual. She'd never missed a chance to mock Thea. "But by the time you get this, I'll already be gone. I loved you, but so much has changed. I've changed. *Blah. Blah. Blah.*"

Thea didn't look at Amara, although she heard her letter being read aloud. She'd slipped that letter under the door of his apartment in the middle of the night, too cowardly to face him before she'd left for Ireland. She couldn't escape facing him now, though. He stood directly in front of Amara as she crumpled the letter, dropping it onto the ground with an overdramatic *oops,* and pulled a dagger from her knee-high leather boot. One of his eyes was purple and swollen shut. Blood dripped from his nose and split lip, staining the snow at his feet.

"Marcus." Thea wanted to run to him, but as if reading her mind, Amara pressed the sharp edge of the dagger against the soft spot on his throat. The snow grew more crimson.

Marcus did not react, though. Instead, his single open eye stared at Thea like he wasn't really sure if she was there or not. He had a dreamer's gaze, and his words scratched against his throat when he tried to speak. "I thought you were dead." A single tear stained his cheek. "I came after you—"

Amara kicked the side of his leg, and with a hideous crack he crumpled into the snow, screaming. The leg was bent at an unnatural angle, and Thea could see the slivers of bone piercing his skin even from a distance. Amara laughed as Thea screamed and moved forward, only to be stopped by Marcus' bloodied blond hair being jerked backward so the dagger could more easily be seen against his throat. Thea's body trembled, and there was a painful clutching behind her sternum.

"Do you know how easy this was, sister?" Amara asked, faking a pout as Marcus let out a sob. Thea watched his Adam's apple rise and fall against the knife, but soon both of his eyes were closed and she wondered if he'd passed out from the pain.

There was so much blood spurting out of his leg now, creeping toward her through the quickly melting snow. It steamed, releasing the stench of metal into the air. "There I was, stranded on the other side of the portal until the next full moon, and your boyfriend comes wandering in with a picture of you, asking if anyone has seen you."

Marcus' mangled body made Thea want to puke. She tasted bile in her mouth, threatening to push its way past her lips, but her anger outweighed her nausea. She wanted to kill Amara for what she'd done to him. She wanted to run at her now and rip the dagger from her fingertips to shove it directly into her chest. Thea knew nothing about killing someone, let alone someone as powerful as Amara, but she didn't care at this point if she died trying.

Amara reveled in Thea's anger, as if it were a reward for her behavior. She giggled as she continued her story, stroking a finger along Marcus' cheek. Her hand was the only thing that kept him from crumpling into the lake of blood beneath him.

"I told him I knew where to find you and he followed me like a pathetic, lovesick puppy. Humans are quite stupid, you know." She glanced up and Thea noticed, to her horror, that Ethel had followed her. Mirielle now stood, gripping the younger girl by the forearms—holding her back from joining Thea. "Of course, I still needed to wait for the full moon to recharge my magic, so I had a little fun with your human toy." She smirked now, winking at Thea as she leaned down and pressed her lips against Marcus'. He whimpered, and when she pulled away, Thea felt the magic sparking at her fingertips, itching to be released. She was losing control.

"Don't do anything silly, sister," Amara said, eyeing Thea. "I'm here to make a deal with you, but first, satisfy my curiosity. Does Kieran know you have a boyfriend? Or are you just shutting it up with two men? No judgements here, but I think Kieran might not like the idea of sharing you."

Thea knew Amara was baiting her and was glad Marcus appeared to be unconscious for this conversation.

"Let. Him. Go."

"I'll take that as a no." She laughed. "No bother, then. Marcus here shouldn't feel bad about all the *naughty* things we did since you've moved on with another man. Not that he had any choice in the matter."

Thea couldn't take any more of the banter. She raised her arms, ready to blast Amara with magic the same way she had before, but instead, she was pinned painfully to the ground by dark magic. The surrounding mist twisted into shadows and seized her arms and legs like strong icy hands, bringing her into a kneel with no effort at all.

"You didn't actually think I'd let you do that again, did you?"

Thea spat as she tried to break free of the vicious grip, tasting blood on her bitten lip. None of this would have happened if Kieran had just taught her how to do more than run away. If she knew how to control her magic then maybe she could have done more to fight Amara—but instead, she was trapped like prey being forced to watch the predators approach. It infuriated her, but that anger wasn't only directed at Kieran. She'd spent so much time worrying about her feelings for him— worrying about fitting into this new world she'd discovered. She should have been more demanding of learning magic.

It didn't matter how many scenarios she played in her head, though. She couldn't think of a way out of this without more death. The people in the village had died because Amara wanted her, so the only choice she had, the only way she could stop more death, would be to do whatever Amara asked.

"Now, I would make you a fair deal," Amara continued, but Thea doubted that her sister had ever planned to do such a thing. "But I can't let you go unpunished for disobeying King Malachi. You are, after all, one of his subjects, and therefore, by law, required to do as his soldiers command."

Amara smiled cruelly as Thea's half-frozen flesh trembled under the snow-soaked dress. Her eyes watered when Amara's dark magic forced her chin up.

She strode toward Thea, practically dragging Marcus with her through the snow. Thea tried to cry out to him but felt as if she were choking on the mist around her. Ethel stared at Thea with a brightening red face. She was shrieking for Thea, but Mirielle was holding the thrashing girl back.

If circumstances had been better, Thea would have thought it was funny to see the older woman restraining Ethel like she was a rabid cartoon character, but amusing or not, Thea knew Mirielle was saving Ethel's life.

"*This* is what happens when you disobey King Malachi and our queen, Morrigan!" Amara was enjoying the moment of spotlight in front of Thea. It fed her ego as if it were a starving animal. She stopped in front of Thea, holding Marcus' face just inches in front of hers. Thea fought as hard as she could against the icy grip of darkness, but she felt completely out of control. Her panic was taking over as she fought the growing shadows of her own soul, focusing on trying to conjure the magic Ainé had helped her use before.

Where was Ainé now, though? Where was the advice she'd so willingly given when it had been Kieran's life at risk? She prayed, for the first time in her entire life, and was met with nothing but silence. Tears stung her eyes as she looked up at Amara's cruel smile.

"Please," she all but whimpered. Tears flowed freely from her eyes now. She would result to begging if it meant saving Marcus' life. "We are sisters... PLEASE! I'll do whatever you ask—"

The word *sisters* brought an unusual look to Amara's eyes, as if she were hearing it for the first time, but it disappeared the second Thea noticed it. Amara looked around, her face shadowed in darkness.

"We're only sisters when you need something, right?" she said, sounding almost hysterical. A raven swooped through the veil of mist, landing on Amara's shoulder with a sinister caw. "Well, Morrigan's wrath is far worse than yours, dear sister."

All hope disappeared when Amara met Thea's eyes again. The raven's talons sank into her shoulder, causing a thin trickle of her own blood to mix with Marcus'. Amara no longer showed any amusement with the situation; in fact, suddenly her eyes were no longer her own. They were an endless black.

"You will discover what it means to defy me," Amara said, but the voice no longer belonged to her. Thea recoiled at the sound of it; it was the sound of death itself.

Morrigan.

Amara, or Morrigan, leaned down and whispered something into Marcus' ear that made his uninjured eye reopen. He looked at Thea for help, begging her without a word to save him, but she could do nothing. Her tongue felt like sandpaper in her mouth, and she choked out a sob, begging Ainé to set her free.

"My sister is preoccupied at the moment," Morrigan said through Amara.

"I love—" Marcus said, but as Amara's dagger cut a thin red line across the base of his neck, his words were strangled by a gurgle of sounds that would never leave Thea's nightmares. Blood spurted out from the wound like a sprinkler, splattering against Thea's face and clothes. It left the taste of metal and rust on her lips.

For a moment, Thea remained frozen. She told herself it couldn't be real as Amara dropped Marcus' body in front of her. It thrashed unnaturally as the thing that must have been Marcus gasped for air. Thea fell forward into the crimson snow as the magic finally released her. The warm blood mixed with powdery snow on the palms of her trembling hands.

She reached him just in time to watch the life disappear from his eye like the flick of a light switch. Her own body was going into shock, she knew that, but there was something else. Something that boiled beneath the surface dangerously as she heard Amara laugh and watched the raven fly away. Marcus continued to stare at her, his body spasming against the cold earth, and when he finally stilled, her world exploded into darkness.

～

KIERAN KNEW he was too late when he heard her scream. It pierced his heart, and fear drudged its claws down his spine as he landed within the village square. Dark magic instantly surrounded him.

"Kieran!" Ethel screamed from Mirielle's death-locked grip around her. He allowed himself one moment of gratitude that the agony in Thea's scream had not been because of something terrible happening to Ethel. However, then he wondered what worse could've happened. His eyes searched for her through hate growing darkness. Ethel pointed toward the middle of the square; she looked terrified. "You have to stop her."

"Now, sister…" he heard Amara say with a note of panic. "Morrigan did that, not me. You should blame our father for this, for all of it."

"He isn't my father." Thea's voice was as cold as ice, almost unrecognizable. Kieran cleared a path through the eye of the magic-induced storm and found the two girls in a standoff. Amara was backing away slowly, and to his surprise, Thea stood over the mangled body of a man, enveloped by darkness. His blood ran cold as he realized the dark magic was not attacking her, but being controlled by her.

"Thea…" His voice shook as he called to her, but she did not hear him. Instead, as he approached her, the angry shadows lashed out at him, fighting him away. He felt their cold slicing into his skin, leaving large gashes, but he couldn't fight them without possibly hurting her.

"You murdered him!" Thea stepped over the body in front of her, towards Amara. Kieran glanced only momentarily at the dead man's form before deciding on how to stop Thea. He lunged toward her, tackling her onto the blood-soaked cobblestone.

Amara, seizing her chance, fled through the village in the forest's direction as Kieran and Thea rolled painfully into the stone fountain. He groaned as a few of his feathers bent in the wrong direction.

"How dare you!" she screamed, pressing the palms of her hands against his chest. A rush of powerful magic tossed him away from her like a feather on the wind. He recovered quickly enough to place himself on the path between her and Amara, fighting the shadows away with one wing as the other attempted to pull Thea to a position where he could look at her. When he finally did, he saw the red tint around her black pupils.

"Thea, *please*." Kieran pressed his hands against both sides of her face, trying to stop her from lashing out at him again. The darkness was feeding on her soul, erasing the woman he knew and turning her into the very person she hated most. She was almost gone.

Whoever the man in the snow had been, something inside Thea had snapped when he died. She was fueling the dark magic with hatred and grief. It would take a lot more than words to bring her back now. He wrapped his wings around her, hiding her from Ethel's terrified gaze. He saw the pain and anger in her, and despite the way the dark magic stung his skin, he used all of his strength to pin her arms to her side and pull her body against his. If he didn't get her back soon, he never would.

"She deserves death for what she did to him!" As Thea met his eyes, she withdrew the shadows that had so desperately clawed at him for freedom. She didn't want to hurt him, but she wasn't about to let Amara leave either. "Let me go, or I will make you."

"I'll never leave you," he told her, and in a last hope to attempt breaking her connection to the darkness, he pressed his lips against hers, tasting the blood and salt that her tears had brought to her tongue. Thea's body tensed up, but her lips reacted instinctively to his before she began pushing him away again. This time, though, she only used her hands. She looked up at him with tear-filled eyes, the red tint slowly fading away. "I will *never* leave you," he repeated, holding her gaze.

As the shadows disappeared from around her, Kieran was grateful for the privacy his wings provided. He stared at her, watching a million emotions play behind her eyes, until finally she settled on looking angry with him and smacked him across the face with a loud crack. He tried desperately hard not to stagger backwards from the force of it. Her face was once again full of agony, but the shadows were nearly gone. He hesitantly reached out to cradle her chin so that he could see her beautiful gray eyes, not caring that she'd hit him. He'd likely deserved it after tackling her. He couldn't blame her for the adrenaline rush she was feeling.

"You kissed me," she said. Her voice no longer terrified him.

"And it worked." He looked, thankful, into her untainted eyes. He'd shocked her enough to regain control of herself.

"I wanted to kill her," Thea said, collapsing against his chest in agonized sobs that rocked her entire body. "I couldn't stop it. I would have killed her."

"Who was he?" Kieran asked, so softly that he thought maybe she wouldn't hear him. He couldn't help himself. He'd just kissed her, and felt like his world might explode into happiness, but a man lay dead just a few feet away from them. A man she'd apparently cared so much for that she would use dark magic to avenge his death.

It made his heart ache in a way it never had before.

"I would have killed her, Kieran, and it wasn't even her. Morrigan possessed her somehow. I think she wanted me to kill Amara so I'd be a murderer, just like my father."

The doors of shops and cellars were opening, revealing villagers who had been watching everything that had happened from the safety of their hiding spots. It infuriated him that no one helped the princess, but that was his job. That was the job of the soldiers assigned to protect the village today. What had Amara done to them to keep them away? He feared the worst for his comrades, but didn't let go of Thea.

He needed to protect her. He wrapped her more tightly within his wings, burying the questions he longed to ask. He didn't know how Morrigan could have gotten into Amara's head, but if she had, then they had a whole new set of problems to deal with.

Amara had fled, aware that she could not defeat her sister yet again, but he wanted nothing more than to go after her and kill her himself for the pain she'd caused Thea. He fought that darkness within himself, though, pressing his lips to the top of Thea's head as Ethel approached them tentatively.

"You and Mirielle get these people away from her."

Ethel nodded and then looked at the dead body with a pale face. The boy in the courtyard was not the only one dead today. As the dark magic cleared away, Kieran saw the destruction that Amara had left behind. Villagers wandered the streets, calling out for their loved ones and checking the bodies of the dead with grim faces of despair.

"Is the princess going to be okay?" Ethel asked, as if Thea were not right there, cradled against him.

Kieran didn't answer, because he didn't want to lie. Ethel seemed to understand and left them to tell the villagers who lingered to give them space. Thea was fading out of consciousness in his arms. She'd used magic far beyond her experience, and dark magic at that. He wondered how long it would take her to recover this time and regretted ever leaving her alone in the first place. He'd thought the village was safe under the King's Guard, but Amara had found a way in.

Now, people were dead because Kieran had underestimated Amara yet again, and Thea had nearly destroyed her soul by using dark magic. His guilt was nearly unbearable, but he had a job to do.

"Don't leave him there." Thea's voice was nearly inaudible. She no longer cried, but she stared at the body in the snow. Her face mirrored the snowy paleness before she fell into complete unconsciousness.

Kieran cradled her familiarly into his arms and walked over to the body of the man. He looked around and found Mirielle watching him. Her eyes were full of tears, and he knew that, just like him, she blamed herself.

"I'll prepare him for burial," she said to Kieran.

"She must have really loved him," he said to no one in particular, merely needing to get the thought off his chest. Mirielle heard him as she leaned down to close the man's open eye.

She reached to pick up a crumpled piece of paper from the snow, handing it to Kieran.

"We all had first loves," she breathed.

Kieran had never loved anyone, but he didn't argue with Mirielle. Instead, he slipped the paper into his pocket.

He held Thea more tightly, a single tear trickling down his cheek and into the princess' hair, before soaring into the sky with her tucked safely into his arms.

CHAPTER 10

Thea awoke violently from a terrible nightmare a few hours after the incident in the courtyard. In it, Marcus begged her not to leave him, while Kieran beckoned her from across the Threshold. Just as she turned to go to Kieran, Thea heard the terrible sound of skin being ripped and a gurgle of gasps for air, but she could not turn to see what had happened.

Instead, she awoke screaming.

"Thea." Kieran's voice was gentle as she bolted straight up from his bed, her eyes flying open. He sat at the edge, but no one else was in the room with her. She recalled with terrible certainty what had happened.

"Where is he?" she asked, and then noticed the crumpled letter beside a glass of water on the nightstand. She snatched it up as quickly as she could manage and looked at Kieran accusingly. "Did you read it?"

"Yes." He wouldn't meet her eyes. "Mirielle is preparing his body for burial."

Thea didn't reply and Kieran wouldn't look at her; he just continued to stare at his hands. Everything that had happened felt like a blur, a nightmare she wanted to forget, but she remembered enough.

"Why did you kiss me?" This caught his attention, and he looked up.

"I thought it would surprise you enough to remind you that you're not a murderer," he said, but Thea frowned.

"Afterwards—" She recalled the look on his face as she faded in and out of consciousness. That look didn't add up to his words.

"You were pretty out of it," he said with guarded eyes and stiffening shoulders. "I just wanted to protect you. I am your guard, after all."

The words stung, but Thea lifted her chin a little higher, refusing to look away from him.

"I see. And you read my letter, why? Because that was your guard duty as well?" His faced darkened, and he turned to face her, placing his hands on each side of her. She did not flinch at the closeness of his face to hers, nor the anger burning behind his eyes.

"You have a lover to bury, Princess Thea." His breath smelled like alcohol.

He stood up, but she reached out to stop him, wrapping her hand around his wrist.

"You're jealous that I mourn for a man I used to love?" The anger in her tone was unmistakable. There was no point in hiding it.

She'd just watched someone she'd once loved be tortured and murdered right in front of her, and now a man she had undeniable feelings for was going to be angry at her for being upset? She didn't have the energy to deal with such childish behavior, and yet she couldn't let him walk away.

"Did you even read the letter at all?"

Kieran seemed at a loss for words. He was still very obviously angry, but with his wrist in her grip, he looked like an animal caught in a trap. Even under the influence of alcohol, he wouldn't rip himself away from her. She tugged him back down to the bed, scooting over so that he could sit beside her.

"If I was in love with him, would I have stayed here for so long?" she asked.

Kieran wouldn't meet her eyes, but she no longer cared. The guilt consumed her once more as she thought of herself and Amara. For a single moment, she pictured what she might have done if it had been Kieran broken in the snow, and not Marcus. She felt as if she were betraying Marcus for it, but it was a question she needed to ask herself. She'd found the power to hurt Amara, but not until after Marcus was dead—when her grief had taken the reins.

But she hadn't saved him. She'd been too weak.

Before Kieran had arrived, she'd wanted to kill Amara. However, he'd stopped her—not because he'd kissed her or made her a better person suddenly. No, she'd stopped because she couldn't bear the thought of losing him too. If it had been Kieran lying on the ground, bleeding out in front of her—an incandescent rage threatened to consume her even at the thought—no one would have stopped her from taking her revenge.

Thea knew without question that if Kieran lay dead in front of her, she would have already been dead.

"I don't know," he finally replied. Thea painted her heart on her sleeve, but his look of confusion told her he didn't understand at all what she felt.

"Tell me something, Kieran." Thea met his eyes, nervous about the words she would say next, because they could shatter her if she was wrong. "If I left you here today and went back, would you ever be the same person again?"

"No." She couldn't even hold her breath; his answer came

instantly. "I would go with you," he added, surprising her. She felt the weight of anxiety lift and rested her head against his shoulder.

"I won't lie to you and say I didn't love Marcus. Amara will pay for what she did to him, but don't be angry with me for my past. I choose to remain here with you, with Ethel and Iris, with Mica and Mirielle. Every single day, I choose you all. I left my entire life behind for—"

"I'm sorry," Kieran said, turning her face towards his. "Of course you have a past. I guess I just forget you lived an entire life without me."

Thea's lips pulled up into a small smile. It was true; she'd lived an entire life without him, but it had been a half-life. She'd been unsure what her purpose was for so long, and now it was completely clear. She didn't know what would happen between her and Kieran, but she knew that she was where she belonged. She'd found her home and her family, even if they were unconventional.

"Tell me about Marcus," Kieran said, pulling her against his chest. She let out a quiet sob as he kissed the top of her head. "Tell me about everything. I've been selfishly pretending your world only existed here. You had a life, and I want to know everything about it."

Thea looked at Kieran thoughtfully. His anger was gone, and despite the smell of alcohol on his breath, she knew he wasn't drunk. His eyes were more green than blue today, and his lashes were wet. She wished she'd told him everything earlier, that he'd known about Marcus before reading her letter, but there was no way to remedy that now. So instead, they both sat with their backs against the wall that bordered the bed, feet outstretched in front of them, as she told him her story.

She started with her parents, explaining how she hadn't known she was adopted until after their deaths. There were so many things she wanted to say. She missed her parents desperately, and the guilt of their deaths weighed heavily on her heart. She'd survived the car accident miraculously, but that had left her with an immense amount of survivor's guilt.

Kieran listened without comment, allowing her to speak freely about whatever plagued her mind. He wiped away her tears when they trickled from her eyes and stroked her hair away from her face when it fell. At one point, he pulled her closer so that her legs splayed over the top of his. It was the most comfortable she'd ever felt with him. All worry of saying the wrong thing, or not seeming like a princess, disappeared, and for the first time in weeks she finally opened up to him.

When it came time to talk about Marcus, Thea's throat threatened to close up. She developed cotton mouth in her nervousness, and Kieran, seeming to sense the discomfort, handed her the glass of water from the nightstand. The cold liquid helped as she reminded herself that anything she said now was about the past, but the haunting thought that Marcus was dead because of her remained present at the back of her mind as she spoke.

She told Kieran that she and Marcus had met in high school and then explained to him what high school was. She talked about Marcus' family and how he would often stay at her house to avoid his terrible parents. When she came to the time of her parents' death and the funeral, Thea's eyes filled with tears as she explained how much Marcus had taken care of her, even though they'd broken up.

"I didn't deserve the way he loved me," she said. "I could never reciprocate it in the same way, no matter how hard I tried. We loved each other, but it wasn't the passionate love writers rave about or artists paint."

"Faeries believe in soulmates," Kieran said, stroking his finger over the back of Thea's hand. "Legend says that Ainé's soulmate was a human, which is why our race is not immortal like the Goddesses. We come from the Goddess' intimacy with a mortal, and although we live longer than most humans, eventually we grow old and pass onto the next life."

"Do you believe in soulmates?" Thea asked.

"Yes. My mother and father were soulmates. When my mother was murdered, it was like my father died too."

"It seems selfish that your father would care more about your mother than you."

"Maybe, but I don't think he meant to leave me. He knew Iris would take care of me if anything were to happen, so he sought revenge."

Thea thought about the revenge she wished to mete out for Marcus' death, but it was not enough to make her irrational now that the initial shock had worn off. Mostly, she felt guilt. She remembered what Amara had said about it being Morrigan who'd killed Marcus. She wanted Morrigan to pay, but she couldn't exactly kill an immortal Goddess, especially the Goddess of Death itself. She blamed Amara for part of what had happened, but the look in her eyes when Thea had begged for Marcus' life had not been malicious or evil; Thea couldn't just ignore that.

"When I saw you standing over Marcus' body surrounded by dark magic, I felt like I was being ripped to pieces. I thought of the person you might have become had you let it consume you, and I would have rather been dead myself."

Thea tilted her head up and pressed her lips to Kieran's. The guilt she felt over Marcus' death overwhelmed her, but so did her need to be closer to the one person who made her world feel sane. He'd saved her from a terrible fate. Despite the pain he felt, he'd stood by her side as he'd promised he would always do.

His current hesitation lasted only a second after her lips met his. She felt his breath catch, but the surprise faded quickly. His lips warmed her own, making her head spin. When he'd kissed her before, it had shocked her. Now, he was the one reacting. His hand slipped underneath her and pulled her into his lap, gently, as if she might break. He shifted his wings into a more comfortable position while she traced her tongue across his bottom lip.

A small sound escaped Kieran's lips; it threatened to make Thea's world explode. The anger and guilt she'd felt since waking up melted away, or perhaps it fueled the passion and eagerness behind the kiss. Her breathing quickened and the only thing in the entire world she could think of was Kieran. All sense of control disappeared as his teeth grazed her lips in a playful bite, and her body's quivering response did not escape his notice. His hands travelled down her back, resting on her hips to press her down against him as his fingertips played with the hem of the sleep shirt she wore. An audible gasp escaped her lips before she could stop herself.

She should have felt shy or embarrassed by the lack of clothing, but she felt none of that with him; everything felt right. At least, until the bedroom door opened.

Thea nearly fell off the side of the bed at the sound, quickly pulling the blanket up to her shoulders. Although she was technically fully clothed, she felt disheveled as she stared at Ethel standing mouth agape in the doorway. She held a pile of fresh clothing for Thea, clothing that Thea noticed did not appear to be dresses, but rather some sort of careworn leather. Ethel's cheeks flushed as she looked between Thea and Kieran, but she didn't say a word. Kieran on the other hand had jumped into a standing position as far across the room as possible, looking exactly like a deer staring into headlights.

"Did you need something, Ethel?" Thea finally asked, unable to stand the silence between the three of them any longer. Her voice shook even as she tried to steady her breathing.

"I brought you new clothes," Ethel said a tad too quickly. "For the…" she looked again between Kieran and Thea with disbelief and confusion.

"For the funeral," Kieran finished the sentence Ethel had failed to. His eyes lowered to the ground. Thea looked at the pile of clothes that Ethel was placing on the bed.

"Are those pants?" Thea asked, unfolding the clothing. Sure enough, there was an outfit very similar to the one Kieran wore in front of her. She hugged the clothes to herself with a smile. "Oh, thank the Goddess!"

A small smile played across Kieran's lips, and Ethel just managed to cover up her laugh.

"You acted like a soldier in the village, when you put your own life at risk for the villagers. You were a genuine leader, and therefore, we may have convinced Iris that a queen doesn't have to follow any rules. Is that how you said it before?" Kieran and Ethel grinned at each other and then at Thea. "I'll leave you to get ready. The funeral is at sunset."

Kieran's look of longing had not disappeared, even with the tension growing in the room, but with a bow, he left Ethel and Thea to get dressed for the funeral. Thea wished he hadn't gone, but seeing Ethel's accusing look, she had a feeling she was about to be scolded.

"You will break his heart," Ethel said, her voice uncharacteristically cold.

Thea just stared at her in confusion.

She would break *his* heart? Was it not clear to everyone that Kieran was completely out of her league and quite literally had done nothing but tell her they can't be together since the moment she arrived?

She realized this may have been confusing to Ethel, who had probably never been in love, but she didn't see herself as being the heartbreaker in this situation.

"When you become queen, no one will allow you to be

together. Don't you understand?" Ethel's voice shook as she tried to explain to Thea what she meant.

"If I'm queen, who will have the authority to tell me who I can or cannot be with?" Thea glared at Ethel, upset that she had just completely ruined her moment with Kieran.

"Thea, this isn't whether or not you're allowed to wear pants to your coronation. These are ancient laws about whom you can and cannot marry!" Ethel suddenly looked much older than thirteen. She was staring at Thea with pleading eyes, but Thea wasn't prepared to give up on Kieran that easily. She crossed her arms over her chest, dropping the clothes she'd been so excited about just moments before.

"But I love—"

"You loved that other boy too and look what happened to him!" Ethel snapped.

Thea was on her feet, standing inches from Ethel within seconds.

"Don't you dare."

Ethel didn't back down. She placed her hands on her hips and stared up at Thea, who was quite a few inches taller than her. Neither one of them said anything else for a long minute. They just stared, unblinking, at one another.

"You are obviously too young to understand how love works," Thea said.

Ethel looked as if Thea had struck her and dropped her arms to her side. She spun to leave the room and then paused.

"If you cared about him at all, you wouldn't lead him on," she said, slamming the door shut behind her.

Thea flopped back onto the bed and stared up at the ceiling, blinking furiously.

She felt ill and tossed her arms over her head, blocking out the candlelight. She hated crying, and yet, it seemed like all she could do lately.

Kieran had talked about soulmates, so Thea figured Ethel

was just as serious about forever loves, but how could someone so young understand what love was? How could she herself understand it? Hadn't she been the one who'd told Marcus that they were too young for marriage when he proposed after her parents' death?

Sitting up, Thea picked the clothes up off the ground, frowning toward the closed door. Ethel's words stung, and with everything else going on, Thea felt overwhelmed. She set the clothes back on the bed, trying to straighten their folds, and then dropped her head into her hands with a hideous sob.

How am I ever supposed to be a queen if I can't even keep my temper with a teenager? she thought miserably. There was a soft knock on the door that made her sniffle and wipe her eyes.

"Ethel, I'm sorry," Thea said, but looked up to meet a different set of eyes.

"I'm sure she means to tell you the same thing when she gets back, but I've sent her out to the stables to cool off," Iris said as she shut the door quietly behind her. "I could hear you two screaming all the way outside."

Thea flushed with embarrassment as Iris came to sit on the bed beside her. She didn't meet Thea's eyes and looked unusually nervous.

"I feel as if I have outstayed my welcome," Thea sighed.

Iris shook her head, placing her hand on top of Thea's.

"Ethel *is* young, but so are you. Neither one of you truly knows much about love yet." She smiled at Thea, but sadness lurked beneath it. "I realize you loved the young man who died, though."

Thea tried desperately not to cry again, but a broken sob escaped her mouth. Iris pulled her close, brushing her hand along the back of Thea's hair as her tears stained the shoulder of Iris' dress. The movement was soft and familiar; it was the same way her mother might have comforted her in a situation like this, and she didn't fight it. She needed to cry. She needed someone else to take care of her, just for a moment.

"It's my fault he's dead," Thea said through her tears, unable to meet Iris' gaze. She closed her eyes, tasting the salt on her lips. "Amara brought him here because of me."

Iris' body was stiff, but her fingers continued to stroke through Thea's hair. Thea felt her warm breath against her skin. She said nothing, but Thea was okay with that. She didn't want someone to argue with her. She didn't want to hear that she couldn't have done anything. She didn't want to hear logic. She only wanted to say what she'd been feeling since the minute the life left Marcus' eyes.

"Losing someone you care about is not something that leaves you, Thea," Iris said. "But those losses are why we fight. We fight so that they aren't forgotten. We fight so that their loss wasn't for nothing."

"Who do you fight for?" Thea asked, looking up at Iris through blurry vision. The older woman wiped the tears away with a handkerchief and tucked Thea's hair behind her ears. "Who did you lose?"

The emptiness in Iris' eyes told Thea she was correct to assume that she'd lost someone. She recognized her own sadness behind those green eyes. She recognized the empty longing for someone who would never return, for just one more moment with them.

"My partner, Cora, was killed in the earlier days of the war," Iris said. "King Malachi said that I ignored my *duty* by loving her, and that I should reproduce our kind..." Iris' eyes grew distant and watery, which surprised Thea. She'd never pictured Iris as someone who would cry, let alone someone who'd allow others to see her cry, but the tears never spilled from her eyelids.

"What happened?"

"The king had Cora executed for treason after I refused to conform. They tossed her into the black lake where the merrow tore her to pieces. I remember she never screamed. She was strong, but her blood turned the water red. I'll never be able to erase the image from my mind, but I also would never wish to. She's who I fight for every single day."

Thea felt like she might be sick. Iris no longer met her eyes, but she understood the anger Iris felt. She also realized that Iris rarely called King Malachi her father. Thea squeezed her hand, which still held her own, and allowed herself to remember the life leaving Marcus' eyes. She allowed herself to feel the pain of that loss and then turned that pain and anger into something else. Marcus hadn't deserved to die. Cora hadn't deserved to die. Her mother hadn't deserved to die. Kieran's parents hadn't deserved to die. The list felt endless.

"How did you escape him?" Thea asked. She'd heard enough about her father to know that he would never have let Iris leave without punishing her as well. It was a miracle he hadn't executed her too. Maybe her bloodline was too important to him to waste. Iris' face paled, and she swallowed.

"I didn't escape him, Thea, but death would have been better than the punishment I received."

Thea stared at the woman she'd grown to admire so much, the woman who had shown so much strength and raised both Kieran and Ethel as her own, regardless of what it cost her. How could that powerful of a woman really believe death would have been better?

"It's about Amara."

"Amara?" Thea choked on the name like it brought a foul taste to her mouth. She looked at Iris with furrowed eyebrows. "What about Amara?"

It had not been intentional, but Thea's voice had grown icy. She couldn't help the anger that boiled inside her when she heard her half-sister's name. She wanted to spit it out of her mouth, to remove the bile from her throat. That same darkness she'd felt last time she'd encountered her bubbled up within her, and she fought it back down. Now that she knew it was there, it flared wildly beneath her skin, searching for an escape route.

She cringed.

"After the execution, they brought me to King Malachi to receive my punishment. As you can imagine, he does not waste Fae blood. Cora was expendable, because she was human. I, on the other hand, could not merely be executed. In the king's eyes, I had committed a far worse crime than Cora by betraying my own kind, as he put it.

"The days after your mother's murder were dark. King Malachi claimed her death was the work of an assassin, but those of us who knew the queen knew exactly who had killed her. I'd gone to Grimwalde to be with Cora during those times. I thought it was the safest place for Kieran, since he would be under the protection of King Aragon. I thank the Goddess every day that Kieran was not with us when Cora and I were captured by the king's men."

"What does this have to do with Amara, though? Is she the one who captured you?" Thea asked, but Iris shook her head.

"This was before Amara was even born."

"Then—"

"Let me finish," Iris said.

Thea shut up, trying not to ask any more questions, and nodded.

"After Cora's execution, They took me to King Malachi's chambers. At that time, I was grief stricken. I tried to attack the king—hopelessly, of course. His men had me on my knees within seconds, and the king laughed at me for my feeble attempt. It was not one of my prouder moments, but I begged him to kill me too. I did not want to exist in a world without Cora. I knew I was responsible for Kieran, but at that time, I couldn't see my responsibility, only my broken soul.

"Of course, the king refused my plea. He said it would be a waste for someone like me to die. He said that my punishment would be that I would perform my duty to the Fae by producing an heir, since someone had stolen you from him."

Thea's mouth fell open as Amara's words to Kieran played over and over in her head. *You wouldn't keep me away from my dearly missed big sister, would you?* Iris didn't notice.

"I told him I would never willingly produce an heir for him, but I was young and foolish then. His guards held my thrashing body down until I had no will left to fight, night after night, until finally it was clear I was pregnant. He never touched me again after that."

Thea felt the warm tears on her cheeks once again. All of her anger had faded, and she threw her arms around Iris without thought.

"Amara is your daughter," she cried, but it was not a question. She understood enough of what had happened without Iris going into any further details. She thought about a younger woman, held down against her will while the king, her father, while he… She couldn't even finish the thought. Disgust, hatred, horror, and a million other feelings devoured her. They threatened to consume her as Iris wrapped her arm back around her.

"You must hate me," Iris said. It was not what Thea expected. She expected Iris to hate her for what her father had done to her, but instead, Iris thought Thea hated her for what Amara had done.

"My father killed your sister, your soulmate, and raped you —but you think *I* hate *you?*" Thea stared in amazement. "Is this why you've been avoiding me?"

Iris looked embarrassed, so Thea wiped her tears away. Although they were quite a few years apart in age, Thea did not feel like a child with Iris. Iris amazed her. She inspired her with her strength and bravery, because even after all that she had been through, she still stood confident and strong.

"I don't blame you for your father's actions," she said.

"And I don't blame you for your daughter's actions," Thea responded.

Both women smiled sadly. Someone lifted a weight from each of their shoulders as they stared at each other in a new light, neither saying anything else.

Thea wondered if she would ever be as strong as Iris; she hoped so. She hoped that one day, she would look back on all the terrible events that had happened and remember that she was strong enough to survive them. That was what a queen would do.

"There's more, though," Thea said, noticing that Iris still looked anxious.

"I know a day will come when you and Amara will meet again," Iris said, lowering her gaze. "I beg you to show her mercy... Your father forced me to abandon her to him. He told me if I tried to fight it, he would kill her and force me to give him another heir until I learned my lesson... I had no choice but to leave. Kieran needed me. Cora's family needed me. I left her with evil, but she was innocent once."

Thea thought about this. She thought about how she might have turned out if her adoptive parents had been like many in the horror stories that other children suffered. She thought even harder about how she might have turned out if her father had raised her. She hated Amara, but she'd grown to love Iris.

"I won't be my father," she finally said. "If there's a way, I'll bring her to you."

They hugged again, but said nothing else. The message was conveyed. Thea could not take a child away from her mother, even one like Amara. She remembered how King Aragon had told her that children were not born evil and wondered if he had known she would need to remember that someday. Thea had a long journey in front of her, and she would meet Amara again. Kieran had told her she needed to fight the darkness. Well, this was one way to exercise that muscle.

A knock sounded on the door and Kieran peeked his head inside. Thea and Iris pulled away, both wiping their faces with a blush. Kieran bit his lip and shifted uncomfortably as he looked at them.

"We need to leave for the funeral," he said, glancing at Thea, who was still not dressed, with a raised eyebrow.

"We'll be out in ten minutes," Iris told him and shooed him out the door.

Dread crept back into Thea's stomach at the mention of the funeral. She glanced at the clothing again and swallowed hard.

"Let's get you ready," Iris said, returning to the bedside and pulling the blanket away from Thea.

"If you could do it all over again, would you be with Cora?" Thea asked.

Iris stopped in surprise, but after a moment, she nodded.

"Cora and I said our goodbyes before her execution. Despite the ending, our love was true. A life without that love would have been a life half-lived."

Thea thought about this as she undressed. It took her a minute to figure out how to put the new clothes on, but with Iris' help, she pulled on the leather pants that clung to her long legs and laced the matching leather waistcoat up over a black tunic. Just like in her dresses, she had to figure out how to breathe and felt extremely uncomfortable with how the waistcoat accented her chest, but she couldn't complain now that she finally had pants to wear. Iris handed her a pair of weather-worn leather boots that stopped halfway up her thighs, and a heavy emerald-green velvet-lined cloak to keep her warm. The boots were the comfiest footwear she'd worn since they had trashed her converse after Ireland; she relaxed as she laced them up.

A comfortable silence fell between them as Thea sat in the

chair in front of the mirror. Iris began pulling her hair into the familiar thick braid she liked to keep down her back.

"He has loved you since you were children," Iris said as she tied off the bottom of the braid. "Your mothers knew it, and that's exactly why he was entrusted with your safety."

Thea glanced at Iris through the mirror, pausing in the middle of tying her boot.

"But Ethel said—"

"It doesn't matter what Ethel says. It doesn't matter what anyone says." Iris finished the braid and set her hands on Thea's shoulders with a sad smile. "Ask yourself if you can live without him. If you can, then let him go. If you can't, then don't lose another moment, because each moment is precious."

Thea didn't respond, but she heard Iris' words loud and clear. She thought of Marcus, dying in front of her, and then the image of Kieran dying flashed completely real behind her eyes. It returned that clenching feeling to the place in her chest where her heart should be, and her stomach twisted into knots. Tears swelled behind her eyelids from the mere thought, and panic took her breath away. She pictured her old life without Kieran and could not imagine returning to it. It felt wrong in every sense of the word.

"See? You don't need anyone to tell you whom you are meant to love." Iris smiled a little, watching her with knowing eyes. "Now, let's go."

Thea nodded, feeling as if she were being pulled from a dream. Today, she would say goodbye to her human life. She would say goodbye to a boy she had once loved, and if she was brave enough, she would allow herself to see what had been standing right in front of her since she'd arrived in the land of Faerie.

As they left the bedroom, she felt him drawing nearer as if an invisible string attached them to one another. She knew, without knowing how, that Kieran stood on the other side of the doorway, waiting for her. She didn't think of Ethel's accusations anymore, or of what it meant for her as the queen. She only thought of Kieran and how complete she felt with him. She would be brave. She would say goodbye to Marcus, and then she would right this upside-down world with Kieran at her side.

CHAPTER 11

KIERAN TOLD THEA THAT THEY WOULD HOLD THE FUNERAL IN THE woods. *I am brave,* she repeated mentally to herself as they followed a path to the pyre that had been arranged. Marcus would be given a proper Faerie-style farewell. Thea thought about his family back home and wondered if they'd even notice he was gone. She knew it was her job to remember Marcus. It was her job to make sure he continued to live on, despite his horrific death. She and Kieran walked a little behind Iris and Ethel into the woods. Mica and Mirielle had also joined them, but they kept their distance from Thea, allowing her room to breathe.

"So, Iris told you?" Kieran asked hesitantly. Thea didn't know why it hadn't occurred to her before that he would have known about Amara, but his words surprised her. She tried not to be upset that he hadn't filled her in on the story himself, because in all honesty, it wasn't his story to tell.

"Yes, she told me," Thea said quietly, but noticed Ethel glance over her shoulder at the sound of her voice. For a moment, the girl looked guilty, but then, seeing the way Kieran held Thea's hand, she glared. Thea just sighed, while Kieran continued to be oblivious.

"What's up with her?"

"You don't want to know," Thea said, frowning as Ethel looked away. She knew they would need to speak at some point. She would need to try to explain what was happening to her, but most importantly, she would need to apologize for what she'd said. Iris leaned down to whisper something to Ethel as they turned another corner, going deeper into the woods, and Thea noticed her shoulders slump.

"I'm sorry I didn't tell you everything," Kieran spoke with hesitation, his eyes watching his feet as they walked.

"I'm not angry with you." Thea squeezed his hand.

No one spoke for the last few minutes of the journey to the pyre, but when they arrived, Thea nearly stopped walking. She didn't know if she could make her feet move any closer as she looked at the enormous structure of logs and branches that had been carefully positioned. It was nearly as tall as herself, and on top of it lay Marcus, or at least, she assumed it was Marcus. They had wrapped his body in white, shielding him from the freshly fallen snow. Kieran's wings fluttered nervously behind him, waking Thea up. She realized she'd stopped mid-step and took a deep breath. Ethel looked at her and her anger disappeared, replaced by sadness.

"When you are ready," Kieran said and handed her the torch he'd been carrying.

"I should say something first." Thea thought her voice sounded like someone else's. They all gathered around the pyre, Thea finally releasing Kieran's hand and clutching the torch as if it were her lifeline. She walked toward the pile of wood that Marcus lay on top of, and although she could not see him, she imagined his blue eyes closed forever beneath the sheet.

She recalled each unspoken word between them with a dreadful understanding that she could never tell him the truth.

He had died thinking that she'd abandoned him—for what reason? She'd never know.

Thea felt her suffocating guilt returning, threatening to tighten her throat until she could no longer take in the breath she needed. Everyone else gathered around the pyre, but kept their distance from her. They observed her, like the darkness she'd shown she was capable of wielding might return at any second, and although the anger in her soul felt untamed, she no longer felt consumed by it. She had compartmentalized that hatred, giving equal parts to Morrigan and her father, while also keeping a portion bottled for Amara.

The memories that those she loved had shared with her about those they'd lost became her driving force. She thought of Cora, whom they'd punished for loving the wrong person. She thought of Kieran, who'd grown up without parents because of a war he wasn't even old enough to be a part of. She thought of her own mother, who had sacrificed everything to protect her.

Thea owed them her life. She owed Marcus her life.

"Marcus... I promise you that this will not have been for nothing," she whispered. Thea knew that Marcus' soul no longer lived within his body, but she hoped that he heard her somewhere. Slowly, her arm lowered the torch, and the flames licked the dried brush at the bottom of the wood hungrily. Within seconds a ring of fire danced along the forest floor, its heat warming Thea's face. She took a step back to find Kieran standing behind her and did not resist sinking against him for comfort.

The fire was beautiful. Blue, red, and orange flames swallowed up the wood of the pyre like a starving wolf devouring its prey. A knot formed in Thea's chest, burning up into her throat, but she refused to cry. She sent a silent prayer to anyone who was listening, begging them to take care of Marcus in the afterlife. She wasn't sure if she'd believed in an afterlife before, but as flames engulfed the white sheet, she hoped with all her heart that there was one. Otherwise, what point was there to Marcus' existence if they could snuff it out in the blink of an eye?

Thea turned and buried her head against Kieran's chest when the sheet burned away from Marcus' body. The smoke stung against her nostrils, and she finally let out a pitiful sob. Her chest felt like something had snapped it in half, bared for everyone to see, and as if reading her mind, Kieran wrapped his wings around her to shield her from their gazes. The fire did not smell like a normal fire. It had a stench to it that made Thea gag. She didn't want to think about the cause of that smell, but how could she not? She knew Marcus' body was melting away. She knew he no longer would laugh at her stupidest jokes, or give her the cute disbelieving smile when she told him interesting facts she'd learned. She would never have the chance to explain to him why she'd disappeared or why she'd broke his heart. She drowned in the unspoken guilt, suffocating in it with her broken sobs.

Kieran rubbed her back gently.

I'm so sorry, Marcus, she thought in desperate repetition, praying it would reach him.

He is at peace now, Thea. Ainé's voice startled Thea enough to make her jump. Kieran looked down at her questioningly, and she frowned, seeing his red-rimmed eyes. He didn't know Marcus, but he mourned him still. He mourned another lost soul in this tragic war. He mourned her loss but differently than she did.

Kieran feels your pain as deeply as you do, Ainé's voice returned, this time softer.

Why didn't you save him? Thea asked, trying to diffuse the anger that she knew lived behind her thoughts. *Why did he have to die?*

Everyone dies someday, Thea.

Thea didn't like this answer and refused to make herself feel any crazier than she already did because of hearing voices in her head. Instead, she convinced herself that the voice was just her subconscious trying to help her understand the traumatic experience she'd suffered. She glanced through the small gap in Kieran's wings and sniffled as she watched the flames once more. It was no longer possible to see Marcus' body, thankfully, and although she knew it would be hours before the flames finally died out, she didn't think she could stay here any longer.

Ethel and Mica were speaking in hushed voices a few feet away. They stared at the fire, and Thea realized they had far more experience with death, despite being so much younger than her. Grief shadowed each of their faces. They'd each lost someone in this war, as Iris had said. Mirielle stood near Iris, wiping her own eyes with a handkerchief. She looked as pale as the snow under the firelight.

"I need to speak with her," Thea mumbled to Kieran, wiggling out of his arms. She was not sure exactly what she wanted to say, but Kieran didn't stop her.

She walked over to Mirielle as Iris, seeming to understand Thea without any words needing to be spoken, dismissed herself to stand beside Kieran.

Tired shadows had formed beneath Mirielle's puffy eyes. She blew her nose loudly into the handkerchief and motioned toward a fallen tree that lay a scant distance from the pyre. Thea followed the older woman to the tree, where they both sat and watched the flames in silence.

Thea figured that Mirielle was waiting for her to speak, but when she was about to say something, Mirielle spoke in a croaking voice.

"You must hate me," she said, catching Thea off guard. She looked at Thea from the corner of her eyes, watching her reaction. Thea opened her mouth to say something, and then closed it again, thinking better of it.

She didn't hate Mirielle, but she couldn't deny her anger. If Mirielle hadn't insisted on her hiding, maybe she could have gotten to him sooner. If Mirielle's vision had been clearer, maybe Thea could have saved Marcus. If Mirielle—

She stopped her thoughts and looked at her companion, her friend.

"People keep telling me that I must hate them today, but I don't hate anyone. I don't even think I hate Amara anymore." This last sentence was hard for Thea to say, but it was the truth. She didn't feel hate toward her sister; she felt pity. She thought about what it might have been like to grow up with her father, and if she were being honest, she couldn't convince herself that she would've been any different from Amara if their roles had been reversed. How could she know, after all? "Morrigan is behind these deaths. She'll use my father and sister until they're unnecessary for whatever she has planned, and the only hate I feel is toward her."

Mirielle exhaled and placed her hands on Thea's.

"You can't blame yourself for your visions, as they come from Ainé herself, don't they?"

Mirielle's nod confirmed what Thea thought. She felt as if she were a pawn in a chess game and wondered if she would be the next sacrifice in Ainé's fight against Morrigan. Her father obviously had fallen prey to the Goddesses' game, but could she actually escape it? Was she not already on the board? She wasn't convinced.

"Don't be angry with Ainé for the death of your friend. It's Morrigan who brings death."

"Couldn't she have helped us avoid it, though?" Thea asked.

"I suppose she could have, but if she helped us there, wouldn't we expect her to help in every death? Would there then be no death at all?"

"Doesn't sound like such an awful prospect."

A sad smile spread across the older woman's face and she patted Thea's hand gently.

"You're very young," she said. "Death is a part of life that we all must accept, and although it pains us, we must realize that it can take us away at any time. That is what makes life so precious."

Thea knew Mirielle was right, but the idea that Marcus' death was unavoidable or written in the stars made her want to cry all over again. Her parents' death had been difficult for her to understand, but in a way, it had been easier because they'd lived longer lives. Marcus was the same age as Thea, and it was possible that what scared her more than him being gone was the fact that she too could so easily disappear.

If she did, who would remember her? What had she done to deserve remembrance?

The fire crackled, sounding like thunder without the echoes of their voices in the forest. No bird's songs could be heard, as if they too acknowledged Marcus' death with their silence. When a fresh flurry of snow fell, Mirielle released Thea's hand, allowing her to pull her cloak more tightly around her shoulders. Snowflakes landed on Thea's cheeks, melting away immediately from their warmth, and she raised her head to the darkening sky where a storm brewed.

"It's time to go," Kieran said, approaching them with an apologetic bow. "There is a blizzard coming."

Thea bit her lip and looked toward the pyre one last time. The flames were no longer as large as they had been. They had dulled from the new wetness in the air, and the shape of Marcus' body was no longer discernible on top of the wood. She stood straightening her cloak and pulled its hood over her head to protect herself from the cold snow.

They'd been here long enough already and Thea knew Marcus' soul had moved on, but she still found it difficult to walk away, regardless of how much she knew she needed to. She needed to do something, anything, to make sense of his death at this point—but that something couldn't just be watching the fire become extinguished by snow.

"Goodbye, Marcus." Thea looked away from the pyre to Kieran. He came to her immediately, and Thea recognized that she no longer needed to wonder if or when he would be there. Kieran always seemed to know exactly what she needed, when she needed it.

He offered his arm, which she accepted gratefully.

Exhaustion threatened her sanity as they walked back down the path toward the cottage. The sun had long since set beneath the tree line, leaving them to walk through the forest in the dark.

Mica asked Ethel if something was going on between Kieran and Thea, and although he whispered the question, Ethel shushed him loudly. The boy's steps faltered slightly, and then he seemed to speed up to catch up with Ethel once more. Mirielle tsk'd her son, advising him to mind his own business, and Thea could almost feel Iris rolling her eyes, even though she never saw it.

These people who had been strangers to her only two weeks ago now felt like a family. Even Mica and Mirielle held a special place in Thea's heart now, and despite the fact that they were all whispering about her, she smiled knowing that they would have her back no matter what she did. Marcus had been her family once, but she still had never quite felt as at home with him as she did among this group of individuals. She wanted to do nothing more than to protect them and make them proud, but she hadn't quite figured out how to do that yet.

"I like this look better on you," Kieran said. Thea jumped at the sound of his voice. She'd fallen into a natural step with Kieran, almost like he was an extension of her own body, so his sudden change in that momentum caught her by surprise. She glanced to her left, looking up at him.

He watched her with a shy smile, crooked as it always was. The gold specks in his eyes sparkled slightly, and the red rim she'd seen earlier was nearly non-existent now. Guilt ate at parts of Thea, reminding her that she'd literally left Marcus' funeral only minutes earlier, but she didn't let that guilt consume her. Part of her had died with Marcus, but it was the human part. She realized that she'd been holding onto that sliver of her old life, trying to capture and keep whatever was left locked in a secure box. She knew now that holding onto her humanity was a mistake.

"I guess I wasn't made for dresses," Thea said quietly to Kieran, but her lips also pulled up into a smile. He chuckled, his wings ruffling with the movement, and the voices behind them faded slightly. Everyone watched their interaction closely.

"You look exquisite in anything you wear," Kieran said. Thea swore she heard someone make a gagging noise behind them and assumed it was Ethel. "But you look happier in this outfit."

Thea lifted an eyebrow at him. He thought she looked happy on her way back from a funeral? The guilt returned.

"Happy is the wrong word," he blurted. "The new clothes just fit your personality better."

Thea nodded, as if to tell him that she wasn't about to break down crying again, and then glanced down at her outfit. The cloak hid a lot, but she could still see the lace-up leather boots as she walked and feel the corset-style waistcoat pressing against her abdomen. She even admitted to herself that she *felt* better in this clothing. The dresses she'd been wearing made her feel as if she was trying to be someone she was not, whereas the black leather told the world she wouldn't fit the mold created by other queens.

"So, this new outfit is because I will be training? Like actual magical training?" She couldn't stand the thought of being left defenseless again. People had died because she hadn't been prepared—both strangers and friends—how could she just sit back idly to watch something like that happen again?

Kieran nodded, looking ahead again as they neared the opening that would lead to Iris' cottage.

"Do you smell that?" Mica sprinted to stand beside Thea, his shoulder blades pulled close together beneath his shirt. Mica was young, and nowhere near as fit as Kieran, but he obviously trained to be one day. Thea sniffed the air and frowned—all she smelled was smoke.

"It's just the pyre..." she started to say, but the looks on Kieran and Mica's faces made her stop uneasily. Iris had run to catch up with them, and Ethel had fallen back to stand beside Mirielle, looking slightly frightened.

"The pyre is too far away to give that strong a smell," Iris said. She ran past them and into the clearing. Thea, Kieran, and Mica ran after her, quickly followed by Ethel and Mirielle. As they exited the tree line, the smell of smoke materialized into a pillar of darkness rising into the sky. The freshly falling snow mixed with thick ash and embers, and Iris stood with her hand plastered across her mouth.

Flames far larger and far less controlled than the pyre's engulfed the stable in front of them.

CHAPTER 12

THEA AND IRIS SCREAMED FOR THEIR FAMILIARS AT THE SAME time, both of their faces stricken with horror. The animals could be heard inside the burning building even from their current distance. Ethel stood horror-struck and speechless in Mirielle's arms, while the older woman stared at the burning building, the flames dancing in her gaze. Kieran felt Thea rip herself from his side and tried to grab her before she could run toward the stables. She glared at him, causing him to drop his hands just as quickly.

"This had to have been my father," Thea said. "He knows where I am." Her eyes darted around, as if searching for any lurking danger. Kieran did the same, immediately shifting into soldier mode. He looked back at Ethel and Mirielle. Iris was already running toward the stables.

"Get them out of here," Kieran told Mica, who didn't question the order. Kieran then turned to Thea, who looked at him squarely. He knew what she would do without a word. He merely nodded at her, fighting the urge to stop her as she ran after Iris toward the stables. Meanwhile, he needed to make sure the arsonist who had created this catastrophe was no longer here. His wings stretched behind him, and he launched himself into the sky, circling just high enough to make sure no unwanted guests were waiting for them.

Iris had used earth magic, her specialty, to break through the wooden stable doors, and to his horror, she and Thea ran head-first into the flame-engulfed structure. He fought the urge to go after her, reminding himself that he needed to trust her judgment and her decisions, no matter how reckless they felt to him. One by one, Kieran watched as horses ran from the stables, obviously having been set free inside, but he did not see Gwendolyn or Faylon.

Faylon's stall is at the farthest end of the stable, he reminded himself.

He circled the perimeter once more from the sky, determining no threat remained, and then landed near the crumbled entrance. Kieran knew there was no world in which he could go inside that building. His wings were far too large and would easily catch fire. He could do nothing but pace, waiting for them to come out.

Kieran reminded himself that hardly any time had actually passed since they'd entered—it just felt like an eternity. Mica had returned, informing him that Mirielle and Ethel were safe inside the cottage. Kieran was questioning him about whether he'd checked the cottage for intruders before leaving them there when a loud crack sounded from the stable.

They both spun toward the thunderous noise and Kieran groaned as he saw the cause. A piece of the roof had caved in. Kieran's concern reflected on Mica's horror-stricken face.

"What do we do?" Mica gasped, looking ready to rush into the flames himself.

Just before Kieran could answer, an ashen shape rose into the sky. Gwendolyn was covered in soot and debris, but appeared uninjured. She soared high into the pillar of smoke with Iris upon her back. Kieran watched her only for a moment before his eyes returned to the door of the stable. He'd counted the horses that had been set free; the only one missing was Faylon.

"Come on, Thea." Kieran's feet shifted toward the burning structure, but Mica reached out to hold him back, pointing.

At first, Kieran didn't understand what was happening. The flames appeared to have parted around the stable's doorway and a dark shape was coming through. Thea's focused eyes and raised hands told Kieran that the flames moved under her control. Her hands shook, but only slightly, and Faylon walked behind her with a cloak draped over him. It appeared Thea had soaked her cloak in the snow before entering the building. The wet material now protected the unicorn from any flames that dared to reach for him.

"She's a fire user," Mica said.

"Possibly," Kieran replied, voice thick with concern. He didn't wait long, though. As soon as Thea was out of the doorway of the stable, he ran to her. Black smudges coated her skin, but she appeared uninjured. As soon as her hands dropped to her side, the rest of the roof of the stable caved in. She fell directly into Kieran's arms, her eyes closing. "Thea!"

He caught her easily, and Gwendolyn landed beside them. Iris quickly dismounted, running to where Kieran held a weakened Thea in his arms.

"She saved us," Iris muttered, astonishment all over her blackened face. "I don't know how she did it, but she made it so Gwen and I could fly out of the stable..."

"She used air magic?" Kieran asked.

"No, she used earth! The ground shook so much that the burning pieces blocking us fell out of our way!" Iris breathed heavily, coughing up a black muck from her lungs. Mica quickly went to her side.

"Help my aunt into the cottage," Kieran told him.

"She can control all the elements," Iris said, continuing to stare at Thea as Mica tried to lead her away. "Only Ainé..."

Mica urged Iris toward the cottage and Gwendolyn joined the rest of the herd of horses, far away from the flames. Faylon nudged the now-unconscious Thea with his muzzle before looking up at Kieran.

"I'll take care of her," he told him and reached to take the soaked cloak from his back. The unicorn gave a thankful whinny, touched his warm nose to Thea's cheek, and then followed Gwendolyn.

Kieran lifted Thea into a familiar cradle and headed toward the cottage. Her body felt lighter than usual, but he figured that was due to the lack of a heavy dress. Soldiers' uniforms were made lighter than most clothes so that they could move more easily. *She controls all the elements,* he repeated. He hadn't seen her use water, but feeling the weight of the dripping cloak, he wondered if she'd also used magic for that. Whatever she'd done, it had exhausted her. He'd never met anyone who could control more than one element, let alone all four. He looked at her closed eyes and sighed. Her lips pulled down at the corners into a frown, and she stirred against him, as if frightened by something behind her own eyelids. He kissed her forehead gently when they reached the cottage door. Mica left it slightly open for him, so he pushed it with his shoulder and walked inside.

Ethel immediately met him in the entryway. Large teardrops spilled from her eyes and dripped from her chin as she stared at Thea in his arms.

"Oh no, oh Goddess above, she's dead!" she cried. "I said such awful things to her, and now... now she—"

"Ethel, she's not dead!" Mica said, running into the room. Kieran looked down at Ethel with a caring smile.

"She's just sleeping," he said.

"AGAIN?"

Everyone laughed, but it didn't touch any of their eyes. Someone had sent them a message. Someone wanted them to know that they were coming for them.

"We aren't safe here," Kieran told Iris as he laid Thea down on the couch in the den. Ethel followed behind him, still sniffling, and placed a blanket over Thea. She then sank to her knees on the floor, gripping Thea's hand.

"This is my home. I can't just leave." Iris said. "Cora's father is still here. I can't just abandon him."

Her eyes, red from the smoke, took in the cottage and its inhabitants slowly. "I can't abandon any of you."

"No one is asking you to abandon anything." Kieran said quietly. "If I take Thea away, they'll follow us and—"

"No." Iris stood and placed her hand on the arm of her chair to steady herself. Her other hand rested on her hip. Kieran recognized the this-isn't-up-for-discussion look she gave him from the many times he'd seen it in his childhood. He thought about his next words carefully before speaking.

"You said it yourself—she is controlling all four elements." Kieran heard Ethel gasp from her place on the floor. He motioned for her to wait before she started asking questions. Mirielle sat near Thea's resting head, showing no sign of surprise at Kieran's words. He watched her as she swept the hair away from Thea's face. It had come loose from her braid at some point, as it usually did. He admired the way it curled around her chin and thought she looked delicate while she slept, vulnerable to whatever evil threatened her. "If her father discovers what she is capable of, he'll stop at nothing to take her. We'll have a lot more to worry about than a simple stable fire or Amara."

He never let his eyes leave Thea. He refused to bow to his aunt's will on security issues, because this was his field of expertise and he knew what needed to be done. All the while, Thea slept, recovering from her magic-brought exhaustion. He tried to imagine the type of power it must have taken her to endure all four elements. Even wielding one could deplete the most well-trained soldiers' energy if used at that intensity. That was why all soldiers trained in both physical and magical combat, so that they never completely exhausted themselves. Kieran moved toward her, and Ethel scooted aside so that he could take her place. His wings shifted into uncomfortable angles as he kneeled beside Thea, but he did not mind; the room was too small to hold them all comfortably.

"What do you say, seer?" he asked Mirielle without looking at her. Instead, he rested his hand on top of Thea's and squeezed it gently. Thea stirred slightly but did not awaken. He knew it might be some time before she did, so he did the best that he could do and transferred some of his own energy into her by magic. He'd done it once before, after her first fight with Amara, but this time he needed to be ready for another assault, so he used the magic sparingly.

Mirielle looked at both Kieran and Thea before closing her eyes. Silence engulfed the room as they all waited to see if Ainé would allow Mirielle to see any sort of guidance, but when she opened her eyes a moment later, she shook her head.

"The future is clouded," she said. "I see many outcomes, but even so, I believe Kieran is right." She looked up at Iris, knowing that was where her opposition would come from. "If she wields all four elements, she is a greater hope for our people than we ever thought to have. The Goddess has chosen her."

Ethel looked at Thea with awe and worry.

"She's still a child," Iris said, but her words did not carry their usual power.

"No, she's not," both Ethel and Mica argued immediately. They glanced at each other with slight grins, and even Kieran smiled a little. Iris just scoffed at them.

"Go watch the front in case of intruders," Iris said to them, and with grumbling frowns, they both left the room.

"They're right, you know." Kieran shrugged his shoulders and finally looked up at his aunt. "It doesn't matter, though. I'm the head of her guard—"

"She is not the queen yet! You'll both get yourselves killed by leaving."

Kieran stood, facing his aunt, and squared his shoulders, his wings raised just enough for effect. However, his aunt was terrifying without wings.

"I'm still charged with protecting her, and that's what I'll do. We planned on continuing her training anyway. The only difference is we'll do it away from Grimwalde."

"And where exactly do you plan to go that you'll be able to train safely?" She now had both hands on her hips, which when Kieran was younger would have immediately caused him to back down.

"You know that I can't tell you that."

"My nephew has lost his mind!" Iris directed this last statement at Mirielle, as if she were looking for backup. Mirielle hesitated a moment and then spoke in a quiet voice.

"We need to protect our children, Iris." She looked toward the doorway that Mica and Ethel had disappeared through with a concerned frown. Iris' hands lifted into the air while Kieran fought the urge to smile at Mirielle. He knew in his heart that this was the way it had to be, but he also knew how stubborn his aunt could be. She looked back at him, a cat ready to strike again, but said nothing. Their similar green eyes bore into each other until a sound from behind Kieran broke their silent glares.

"Do I get a say in where I go?" Thea asked in a small voice. Kieran turned to see her half-sitting up and quickly returned to her side to assist her.

"Princess, you should be resting."

"Cut the crap," she replied to him with a tired but playful smile. He cocked his head at her strange saying, but at least now

Iris was looking at her instead. "Kieran is right. My being here is a danger to you all."

She caught sight of Iris beginning to argue and raised her hand to stop her, sitting herself up straight.

"And before you argue with me, I know this might sound a little crazy, but I know where we'll be safe."

"And how could you know where it might be safe?" Iris asked accusingly.

"Ainé told me." Thea lifted her chin, and iris had to steady herself once more, sinking back into the chair. "I know Kieran has told you about the voice I've been hearing in my head."

Kieran looked down, embarrassed, but Thea didn't notice. He had told them about those voices and his concern that if Ainé could speak to Thea, so could Morrigan.

"She came to me in a dream and told me that—"

"Enough." Iris held up her hands. "If Ainé told you where to go, you need to keep it from us."

She glanced at Kieran with a frown, but he was noticing something else as he looked at Thea. Her cheeks had grown hollower since arriving in Grimwalde. He frowned, angry with himself for not noticing sooner. He'd felt how light she was when he lifted her, but had shrugged it off as mere coincidence connected to her new attire. The truth beamed at him clearly in the form of a thinning young woman on his aunt's couch. Her body had been rejecting the magic—that was why she seemed so exhausted all the time. How could he have been so stupid not to realize?

"Why are you looking at me like that?" Thea asked with a raised eyebrow. She stared at him, her beautiful gray eyes full of a steady determination he'd grown to recognize since her arrival, but the way she looked beyond those determined eyes scared him. If her body rejected the magic, she could die. It didn't happen often, but with someone who mastered all four elements, it amazed him suddenly to think she'd lasted this long.

"How are you feeling?" he asked.

"Tired," she said, timidly looking around the room at everyone. "That's normal, though." She didn't mean it as a question, but her voice rose an octave anyway.

"Kieran..." Iris said, seeming to understand where he was going with his questioning.

"We are leaving tonight," he said without any inflection. If her body was rejecting the magic, he refused to argue with anyone anymore. She needed to learn to control it, so that hopefully... He didn't even want to finish the thought in his own head. The idea of her withering away made him want to throw something across the room.

Thea didn't argue, despite the look of confusion on her face. Kieran saw defeat in his aunt's eyes as she fell back into her chair. He heard faint whispers in the hallway where Mica and Ethel clearly stood eavesdropping on their conversation. Iris, still weak from the amount of smoke she'd inhaled, looked toward the hallway and seemed to debate whether or not to scold the two adolescents.

"If you won't do what I said, you can at least go pack up the leftover bread and stew for Kieran and Thea. They'll need food for their journey," she said loud enough for them to hear. Two pairs of feet scuttled down the hall too quickly.

Thea appeared to relax back into the couch. She tucked her feet beneath her and pulled the blanket over her lap, watching the room with careful consideration. Meanwhile, Kieran went to kneel before his aunt's chair, resting his hand on her leg. He didn't need to apologize for making this decision, but he apologized anyway through the silent gesture. She nodded her head in understanding, patting his hand. After losing his parents at such a young age, Kieran looked up to Iris. She hadn't taken his mother's place, but she'd taken care of him as if he were her own child, and he knew from experience that the look she gave Thea now was the same motherly look she'd often given him as a boy. Iris wanted to protect them all, but at some point, he'd grown up right in front of her.

"You'll have to take care of him," Iris told Thea. Her lips pulled up into a smile, accenting her sallow face. Kieran's heart sank.

"Always," Thea replied, but she watched Kieran with a look that told him she knew they were not telling her something. He wondered if she really thought the exhaustion was normal, or if she was only putting a brave face on for them. He hoped she knew better than to hide things from him, but if he was being honest, he couldn't say he wouldn't do the same to protect her. Whatever was developing between them was becoming more and more complicated by the second.

How could he protect her if he was blind to her? How could he be her soldier, her guardian, if she made him weak in the knees when he was around her? These were constant questions for him, but only one question ever really stuck in his mind.

What will they do to her when they realize she wants me? This questioned felt etched into his soul.

He knew the laws, which clearly drew a line between royal Fae and common Fae. He was the son of a handmaiden and blacksmith. Although both of his parents had been Fae, that did not make him good enough for the princess. In fact, even if he were royal, he still didn't imagine he could ever be good enough for her.

CHAPTER 13

"WE'RE LEAVING BEFORE SUNRISE," KIERAN TOLD MIRIELLE AS SHE excused herself from the den. She promised to return before they left.

In the meantime, Iris left to pack Thea a bag of clothing, reassuring her that it would include plenty of pants. Kieran didn't bother to tell his aunt to rest. He knew she was giving him and Thea space to speak freely. However, he wasn't sure what to say once he and Thea were alone in the room. It was unusual that he felt nervous around her, but their change in behavior brought an unfamiliar wave of nerves.

"So, Ainé wants us to go to Lake Wysteria," Thea whispered, eyeing the open door with uncertainty. Kieran was sure no one was listening to them, but Thea's new information surprised him.

"Lake Wysteria is the largest lake in Faerie. My mother used to tell me that if I was ever lost in the forest, all I needed to do was follow the river because every river led back to Lake Wysteria; it's the source of all four kingdoms' water supply."

"Why do you think she wants us to go there?" Thea asked.

"Well, you were unconscious the last time we were there, but that's the location of the Threshold. She came to you in a dream?"

Thea nodded her head and patted the spot next to her.

"You don't have to sit on the floor, you know." Her usual playfulness had returned, but the same nervousness that he felt seemed to reverberate in her tone. "I won't bite."

"Of course not." Kieran moved to sit beside Thea, knowing he was being ridiculous. He'd sat beside her multiple times before without feeling this way, but something had shifted between them. Despite the fact that they'd been at the funeral of an ex-boyfriend only hours earlier, Kieran didn't feel the intense jealousy he'd experienced before their conversation.

How could he be jealous when she was looking at him like that? It made his heart race.

"I seem to be unconscious a lot lately," she said, seeming pleased by his new spot on the couch.

"Yes, about that—"

"Something is wrong with me, isn't it?" She looked at him guiltily, answering his previous questions. She knew the exhaustion wasn't normal, and she'd been hiding it from him. "I wasn't one hundred percent sure, of course. It's just that none of you collapse every time you use magic." Her eyebrows furrowed, frustration lining her face.

"It appears you can control all four elements, which, no, is not normal."

"So, I'm a freak in the human world and a freak in the Faerie world."

Kieran saw through her amusement to the underlying concern.

"You're not a freak in any world," he said seriously, pulling her against his side. She rested her head on his shoulder while his wings blanketed her shoulders. When she reached out to stroke their feathers with her fingertips he shuddered, his eyelids fluttering closed. "You really shouldn't do that."

"Oh?" she questioned, but her fingers didn't stop. The hairs on the back of his neck and arms rose, but not how they did when he was scouting something dangerous. This unfamiliar feeling drove his heart into a freeze against his chest and made him wish he could pull her onto his lap. Those thoughts, of course, he couldn't voice, but she continued to tease him anyway.

A throat cleared in the room and his eyes snapped open. Ethel stood, blushing, in the doorway.

Mica was a few feet behind her, grinning at Kieran, and they both carried linen sacks.

"Got your supplies for the trip," Ethel said too quietly. Kieran straightened up a little, but didn't move Thea away from his side. "Could I talk to Thea for a minute?"

Kieran did not particularly want to get up at the moment, but the look on Ethel's face was enough to convince him. He nodded then kissed Thea's forehead, which only broadened the grin on Mica's face. The boy started to say something but then yelped as Ethel stomped on his foot. Both Kieran and Thea laughed.

"I need to go get some things together anyway. Camping in those woods can be dangerous."

"Camping?" Thea's eyes widened a little as she realized exactly what it meant to be going deep into the forest for training. Kieran just smiled at her.

"Don't worry, Princess, I won't let the werewolves get you."

"Werewolves!?" Her voice was almost a squeak as Kieran left the room with Mica, both of them laughing.

THEA WATCHED Kieran and Mica leave with a glare.

Just before school started each year, Thea's father took her on a three-day camping trip. They roasted marshmallows, slept under the stars, and talked about what her plans were for the future. Each year those plans changed, but she'd loved those trips. Her mother was not much of a camper. She preferred to shower each night, so it became an annual father-daughter tradition that she looked forward to. She wondered what she would tell her father if they sat eating burnt marshmallows around a campfire now. Her life had consisted of change after change these past few months, leaving her so many things she wished she could say to him. She wished she could tell him about Kieran the most, though. Her father had always known Marcus wasn't the one for her, despite his loving support of any and all decisions she made, and although Kieran had a rough exterior and complicated past, she knew her father would have approved.

"You look deep in thought," Ethel said, finally sitting beside Thea.

It was true that Thea had completely forgotten that Ethel wanted to talk, distracted by memories of the past. She'd become lost in it as she often was.

Live in the present because moments don't last forever, her mother had always told her. Thea knew this all too well now. So many moments that she'd felt would last a lifetime were hardly even memories now.

"I suppose I was just thinking about my parents," Thea replied. "My adoptive ones, I mean."

"Do you miss them?"

"Terribly," Thea replied, fiddling with her fingers. "Ethel, I'm sorry for what I said to you. I had no right."

Thea had wanted to say this the minute Ethel had left the room, but under Iris' advice, she'd waited. Now, she no longer wanted to wait. She hated seeing Ethel so angry with her. She'd grown to look at the girl like a younger sister of sorts and didn't wish to jeopardize that over anything.

"Oh..." Ethel's eyes filled with tears and she threw her arms around Thea's neck. "I feel so dreadful for how I've been treating you, Thea. You've been through so much, and if anyone had no right to act so selfishly, it was me. I should have been happy for you and Kieran, even if it is against the rules. Those rules are ancient, and they also say humans are not as important as Faeries! They're the kind of rules that are meant to be broken."

Thea brushed the tears away from Ethel's cheeks, smiling.

"In my world, breaking the rules was the only way for people to free themselves from oppressors who claimed their way was the only way to live. Well, I think we could use a little of that rule-breaking here too. It's time someone changed the way things were done. Although, I'm not sure Kieran agrees with me about that." Thea couldn't help the downturn of her lips.

Sometimes Thea felt that Kieran was open with her, like when she touched his wings or when he kissed her forehead, but she still saw the fight behind his eyes. He knew they weren't *supposed* to be together according to their world, but would he ever be able to let that go? She wasn't sure.

"Just tell him how you feel," Ethel said, looking as if it were the simplest answer in the world. "Tell him you love him."

Thea's eyes widened at the word love.

Did she love Kieran? Did she believe she was his soulmate? The answer was yes, but could she say that out loud without feeling completely ridiculous? Again, she wasn't sure.

"I don't think it's—"

"It *is* that simple," Ethel interrupted.

The two girls looked at each other for a moment, and then Thea pulled Ethel back into a hug. Ethel knew what Thea needed to say. Now Thea just needed the guts to say it. She imagined being camped in the woods alone with Kieran would give her the perfect opportunity, but the entire idea of being alone with him made her feel like her heart might thump right out of her chest.

"You're choking me." Ethel laughed and Thea immediately let go with an apology.

"I've never been in love before," Thea admitted with guilt. Sure, she'd loved Marcus, but she had never thought of herself as *in love* with him. He had definitely been in love with her. He'd wanted them to get married and have children and live happily ever after in a white-picket-fenced house, but that had never been her dream.

Ethel seemed to understand what Thea was saying and smiled.

"I haven't either, but I've heard it's pretty great. Plus, I've seen the way he looks at you. You have nothing to worry about."

A knock on the doorjamb made them both look up. Mirielle stood there, holding something gold in her hand.

"May I interrupt? I have something for the princess." They both nodded as she entered the room, sitting on the other side of Thea. The object concealed within her hand was a gold bracelet with a large red ruby. It sparkled a little when the candlelight flickered across it. "This will help you."

"What is it?" Thea tilted her head at Mirielle as she held out her hand for Thea's. She clicked the bracelet around Thea's small wrist and patted the back of her hand gently. Ethel let out a soft "oh" as she examined it.

"It is an amulet, blessed by King Aragon and myself. We have prayed to the Goddess for your protection, and when in need, this amulet will return your strength." Mirielle smiled at Thea, who looked at the bracelet thoughtfully. She didn't know much about magical objects. Nor did she feel any different wearing it. But she trusted Mirielle and her great-godfather.

"Thank you, Mirielle."

"It won't work forever, but it should help you if you are ever feeling like your magic is controlling you, rather than you controlling your magic. Sometimes our children wear these when they are first learning how to control their gifts."

Thea tried not to think about the fact that she was an adult needing something a child used, and just let herself be grateful. She knew her body was drained from the magic, and she had a lot to learn, so she would take whatever help she could get.

"How is it that I can control all four elements?" Thea asked. "I heard you all saying it wasn't normal."

"I really don't know," Mirielle said and lowered her head. "There is no recorded history of anyone having that type of power besides Ainé herself."

She paused as if trying to understand something else, watching Thea closely. Thea shifted uncomfortably beneath her blanket while she waited for Mirielle to decide what she would say next. Ethel stared, wide-eyed determination not to get kicked out of the room shining in her eyes. They both knew there was more.

The burden of living up to the expectations of everyone crept back beneath Thea's skin as she waited. All of these people expected her to defeat her father and take her place on the throne, but how could she do that if she could not even manage to not pass out every time she used magic?

"You're not a seer," Mirielle finally said. Her hands were now folded into her lap.

Thea ticked her head to the left slightly. The thought of being a seer had crossed her mind, but everything Kieran had told her about seers, plus what she'd seen with Mirielle and Aragon, made her feel like there was more to it than that. There was something different about the way Ainé spoke with her versus how she spoke with them.

"Seers start receiving visions from the Goddess when they are children, but she never speaks directly to us. It's never conversational." She furrowed her eyebrows slightly and Thea thought Mirielle might be a little jealous of what was making Thea feel like an absolute madwoman.

"Maybe I'm just a late bloomer and living without magic for

so long changed the way it affected me." Thea shrugged because she didn't know if that explanation even made sense. When Ainé spoke to her, it was not to give her visions of the future. Most of the time the words were guidance to help her along in her journey, something she was growing weary of trusting the further along she came.

"No," Mirielle said, unaware of Thea's continuing thoughts. "This is something different. She blessed you with these abilities, but the fact that you are speaking with her directly may have something to do with why you can access all four elements. It seems you are existing, in some ways, on the same realm as our Goddess."

"Okay, so she's trapped in the same prison world as her sister and communicating with me—but why? Why me?"

A knock sounded at the door, interrupting the many questions about to explode off Thea's tongue, and Kieran poked his head into the den.

"We need to get going while the coast is clear. My aunt packed you a bag, and I managed to convince Faylon to wear a blanket for your sake."

"I'm surprised he let you anywhere near him," Thea teased but her shoulders instinctively relaxed when Kieran entered the room. Mirielle watched her with a small, knowing smile.

"Remember to let the amulet help you. If you fight it, it won't work." She patted Thea's hand one more time and then stood up. "I feel I will see you both fairly soon, but stay safe and out of sight for as long as possible."

Mirielle hurried out of the den.

"Are you ready, Princess?" Thea mimicked Kieran's voice, winking at him.

"Oh no, I'm becoming predictable!" He chuckled and nodded his head toward the front of the house. "I'll meet you out there. Come on, Ethel. I need your help."

Ethel frowned, obviously having more questions for Thea,

but followed Kieran out of the room to leave Thea with her thoughts. Thea realized how quickly things had changed. Searching for her adoptive parents had led her to a life she'd never known existed, but now that she was here, she felt the weight of it all.

So many people expected her to save the world and then lead it. And now, on top of that, it appeared the Goddess also expected something out of her, since she'd given her these special powers that she had absolutely no idea how to control.

She felt frustrated by the lack of information she was receiving from someone who was supposed to be far more powerful than herself. However, Mirielle had said Ainé was trapped. Thea wondered if that was why she didn't assist her more in this journey.

You can do this on your own, she reminded herself.

She could hear the voices of the friends she'd made along the way drifting through the open cottage door and smiled, knowing she wasn't alone, as she headed out the door of the cabin and on to the next adventure.

CHAPTER 14

KIERAN REALIZED AFTER A COUPLE OF DAYS THAT THEA DIDN'T have any experience camping for an extended period in the woods. She could perform the basic tasks, like putting up a tent or starting a fire—although he wondered if she'd used magic to start the fire. She cooked decently as well, but overall, Kieran did most of the work as they moved deeper into the forest. They travelled only at night, which made the journey longer than usual, but when they arrived and the coast was determined to be clear, Kieran felt more than a little relieved.

He relaxed with the realization that this plan could actually work, and Thea relaxed with the realization that they could finally stop setting up and tearing down their campsite. Tension and exhaustion radiated from both Kieran and Thea, leaving very little opportunity for conversation. As they camped, one person would sleep for a few hours while the other stood guard, which Thea had never once complained about. Kieran wished he could stand guard at all times, but if Thea was serious about learning the discipline and routine of a soldier. This type of training was as necessary as the physical training.

When they finally reached the lakeside, Kieran watched

Thea's amazement grow. The trees and wildflowers had fascinated her since the day she arrived, but the lake was more beautiful than any forest grove. The water glistened as if someone had sprayed thousands of crystals across its surface in both the sunlight and moonlight. As soon as they arrived, Thea went straight to exploring, the same way she'd done at every other place they'd stopped. When she came to the spot between the trees known as the Threshold, he paused to watch her. He saw the way she stared at the space, seeing what no human eye could, as if called by the buzz of her world beyond it. Kieran didn't hear the calling anymore, because everything he wanted was right in front of him, staring at a world she no longer belonged to. It made his heart ache at the idea of her wanting to return.

"This is where you came through," she said quietly. Her hand reached out to touch the soft glow in the empty space, but Kieran quickly snatched it away. He automatically felt selfish.

Who was he to keep her from her heart's desire if that desire was to return to the place where she'd grown up? She jumped, clearly surprised by his sudden touch, and looked at him with wide, wondering eyes. They were beautiful and curious, but they made his heart ache.

"Now that we've discovered how powerful you are, I thought you might open the doorway," he said quietly, dropping her hand with a look of shame. "I shouldn't have stopped you."

Thea took a visible step back from the Threshold and looked at him with a raised eyebrow.

"You think I want to return? To leave you?" she asked and then quickly added, "And Ethel and Iris? Mirielle and Mica? My great-godfather?" Her cheeks blushed.

"I would understand it if you did," Kieran said with conviction. He knew that they had done nothing but ask her for the impossible since she'd arrived. She hadn't had a chance to even enjoy the beauty of this land, let alone learn to call it home. Any sane person would want to return somewhere safer after all of this madness. He'd even secretly wondered if that was why she'd requested to come to this place of all places.

"My mother used to say that home is where the heart is," Thea said quietly, no longer looking at Kieran. "I know it sounds silly, but I have nothing to go back for. The only thing left there for me is memories. Here, I have a family and something to fight for."

She walked back to where Kieran had unloaded the mare who carried their supplies and began unpacking their tent. He watched her as she looked for the perfect tree to tie the shelter up to and then tied it as if she'd been doing it her whole life.

"You're getting better," he mused.

"If only tent-pitching would help me defeat my father," she replied, but her voice had lowered an octave and he knew she was upset. He didn't know if he should ask her what was wrong, or if he should just let her continue to take her frustration out on their supplies.

"I'm sorry that this is your life," he said finally. "You deserve better."

"I'm sorry that I didn't have this life from the start, but I'm not sorry that this is my life," Thea said, glancing over at Kieran where he had lit a fire. The moonlight cast shadows across her face, shielding her expression from him. He focused and sent a breeze of warm air toward her, tickling her cheek as it brushed her hair back. She smiled, but only slightly.

"I'm terrified that one day I'll wake up and find out this was all a dream."

"Me too," he admitted as the fire grew, warming his hands.

Kieran watched as the rolled-up canvas grew into a shelter and fed the fire without fear of anyone seeing them. He knew no one had followed them, but the fire would have to keep them warm while he reserved his magic for Thea's training.

"So," Thea said as she came to sit beside him in front of the fire. "What now?"

The silence that had stretched between them seemed to melt away as she rubbed her hands together, warming them in front of the fire. She'd pulled her fur cloak off, hanging it on a nearby tree branch, and Faylon had gone to graze on the fresh hay Thea had piled up for him and the red mare. Kieran wanted to look into Thea's starlit eyes and tell her that things would all be okay but didn't feel he could say that honestly. He knew she was nervous about her magical training. In fact, he was also nervous about her training. The idea of her even needing to fight the king made him sick to his stomach. He wished he could protect her from it all, but all he could do was prepare her.

"Now I'm going to teach you how to control your magic so that it doesn't kill you," he finally said. His eyes lowered to his own hands, and he remembered the days when he'd trained to be a part of King Aragon's army. It had taken months, but they didn't have months now. In fact, he had no idea how long they had before the king found them or before Morrigan made her next move. Rumors had come from the Northern Kingdom, Gimmerwich, that the creatures of the darkness had been trying to get past their walls. It was the first time King Malachi had moved against their kingdom.

"So, what first, Captain?"

Kieran lifted an eyebrow at Thea.

"Captain?"

She nudged her shoulder against him and pretended to salute. He didn't know why her joking upset him, but it did. He looked at her, his frown deepening.

"This is serious, Thea. You could die."

Her face fell, and he realized that hadn't been the right thing to say as she folded her hands in her lap.

"You think I don't know that?" She laughed, but it was not out of humor. He heard the anger behind her tone. "You and Iris seem too scared to teach me how to use this magic, but I feel like I'm going to explode! It's like it's tearing at my insides, begging to be used. You don't think I know that my father wants me dead? I do. It's a kill-or-be-killed situation. I already lost one person because I wasn't strong enough."

Kieran winced. He hadn't meant to upset Thea, but her words had been sharp. She'd obviously been bottling things up for a while now, and he felt sure he could use that pent-up frustration to help her. He grabbed her hand and pulled her away from the fire, toward a clear spot near the lake. She protested, but followed anyway.

The moonlight lit the clearing beautifully for his trained eyes, but he knew she still hadn't learned how to use her senses.

"You're angry, and we are going to use that emotion," he said, but she rolled her eyes, actually rolled her eyes. "Is that funny?"

"It's just that every single story you read about the ordinary person growing into a hero goes like this."

"Well, every story has to originate from something, doesn't it? Maybe there's truth in using emotion to fuel your power." His wings stretched out behind him, and he watched Thea's eyes widen a little as she realized what he planned to do.

"You want me to fight *you*?" Her voice cracked. "Using magic?"

"You can't exactly fight Faylon." He laughed, and the unicorn snorted in response. Thea's face paled. "But first, I actually just want you to block my attacks. It's dark, so this won't be a test of using the elements, but we will test enhancing your senses with magic."

She seemed confused, so without hesitation he flew at her and, using the darkness as his companion, knocked her off her feet. He didn't hit her hard enough to hurt her, but he imagined it would leave a bruise for the next day. He'd swept his wing under her leg, tripping her before she could even react, and caused her to land right on her tailbone. She cursed, rubbing her arm, which she'd thrown down to catch herself, and glared up at him.

"Use your senses," he repeated as she stood up again. He circled her, watching her eyes as they followed his foot movement, but not his wings. That was her first mistake.

He lunged in again and used his wing to pin her back against a nearby tree. She whimpered and struggled against his iron grip.

"This isn't fair. You're obviously stronger than me!"

"Am I?" He let her go and tilted his head. "Maybe physically, but you need to use your—"

"Senses, I know." She spat out a little bit of blood from where she must have bitten her tongue and glowered at him.

"Let's try again."

The warriors' dance went on for nearly an hour, but Thea didn't seem to be listening or improving. Instead of using her senses, she kept trying to use the elements, which Kieran dodged with ease. He grew frustrated with her as the time ticked by, and finally, after pinning her yet again to the same tree with one of the same moves he'd been repeating, he quit.

"You're not listening to me," he glowered, crossing his arms.

"I don't know how to use my senses, Kieran." Thea sounded as frustrated as he felt. She'd already said this to him multiple times, but he didn't know how to explain it to her. This was why they were trained as children, not adults. Children were far easier to explain things to, because they didn't overthink what they were being told. Thea, on the other hand, was overthinking everything. "I'm never going to get this!"

Kieran walked over to Thea, who immediately tensed up, as if she were expecting him to throw her on the ground or trip her again. She had minor cuts on her arms and face that made Kieran angry with himself. He hated hurting her, even if it was only minor injuries. He wanted to protect her, not cause her pain and anger.

"I think I'm messing this up," he said. "Let's try something else."

Thea let out an audible sigh of frustration, but nodded that she would try whatever he wanted.

"I want you to think about Marcus." This seemed to catch her off guard. She tilted her head at him, as if waiting for the punchline. "Just trust me. I want you to think about Marcus and his death."

She recoiled. He knew she didn't want to think about it, but this was all he had left. He didn't know how to get her to tap into her emotion without completely overloading, but maybe she needed to overload. Maybe she needed to let herself feel the pain of losing Marcus again so that she could move on. He stepped away from her, giving her space to truly examine him.

"Remember how helpless you felt with Amara? You're not helpless. You have power beyond any other Fae, just waiting to be tapped into, but you need to find a reason to do it. You need to remember that Marcus wouldn't have died if you had been more powerful. You need to remember that you could have saved him."

The words were harsh, and Kieran didn't even know if they were true. Amara had put Thea in an impossible position, but he saw the anger burning in Thea's eyes regardless. She believed she wasn't strong enough to save Marcus, and he needed her to believe she could be strong enough to save them all. Her fingers twitched, and her eyes narrowed on him. He wanted to take back what he'd said, but it was too late, so he stuck by it. He squared his shoulders and stepped to the right slowly. Her eyes followed him instinctively. He saw the animal waiting to pounce. She didn't move, though. Instead, her chest rose and fell in a subtle breath, just giving her away enough that Kieran knew she planned something.

"Focus, Thea," he reminded her and then lunged. She dodged

his move with grace, and he fought back the urge to smile at the improvement. "If you can't beat me, you'll never beat Malachi."

This time, she stepped to the side, mirroring his movements. She glanced at his wings, his feet, and then finally his eyes, never allowing her gaze to settle for too long on one place.

"Marcus is dead, and if you don't get control of yourself, you and I will be dead too."

She lunged at him, but he dodged, causing her to stumble a little. Just as she regained her balance, he moved in her direction, ducking low to try catching her feet with his wings the same way he'd done multiple times before. This time, she jumped gracefully out of the way and landed light as a cat on her feet.

"You're not helping." Her breathing was shallow, and he saw the tears that had swelled behind her angry eyes. It broke his heart, but he knew, despite her argument, that he *was* helping. She had dodged several of his attempts to knock her off her feet, and he hadn't been going easy on her.

They circled each other now, stalking slowly. Since she'd managed to dodge his physical attacks, he thought he'd try something else. He focused his mind and sent a gust of wind toward her without warning, causing her to fly back a few steps. She actually fell this time, but was back on her feet within seconds, not allowing him any time to get a hold on her.

"You said no magic!"

"Actually, I said *you* couldn't use elemental magic." This time, Kieran grinned, knowing it would annoy her. Surprisingly, Thea held up her hands and sent a similar gust of air back at him. His wings fluttered to keep him standing, and he soared into the air, roaring with laughter as she panted below. "Okay, I deserved that one."

He circled her from above and then dove quickly, just missing her as she rolled to the side. Her pants were coated in mud and snow now, and her hair had come loose from its braid.

However, she continued to hold her ground, and her eyes focused on him, despite the darkness. Kieran knew she was finally tapping into her senses, because if she hadn't been, there would be no way she could have avoided him. She could see him more clearly now and hear his wings folding behind him as he stood across from her.

He watched as she ran her fingers through her red locks, brushing them off her face. Her chest rose in quick breaths, but she no longer looked ready to give up. Instead, she lowered to the ground and touched the forest floor with a smirk that made his heart skip. The ground trembled, and the roots of the trees shot up from the earth, reaching for him. It caught him by surprise, and he didn't have time to get himself off the ground before they wrapped around his ankles. They tightened uncomfortably, and Kieran knew he was not off the hook for his comments about Marcus as Thea stalked toward him. He saw the power radiating behind her eyes. Golden specks lined her gray irises and her fingers twitched.

She moved with utter grace and silence toward him.

"See?" he said, trying not to sound nervous as she neared him. He knew there was no way he was getting himself out of her grip at the moment. His wings stretched out, trying to gain momentum, but he was a mouse stuck in a trap. "I knew you could do it."

An orange glow settled over the trees as Thea stopped in front of Kieran. She no longer looked angry, but instead examined the way the roots held Kieran with a fascinated gaze.

"I don't feel like I'm going to pass out," she said suddenly.

"That's because you were using all of your senses and balancing the magic instead of just wearing it all out in one swoop of power."

She kneeled down to touch the roots that twisted around his legs, and he swallowed hard, trying not to look at her kneeling in front of him.

"I can't teach you everything in one night, but this was a good start." Kieran's voice shook just slightly, drawing Thea's attention back to his face. She touched the ground again, releasing him from the magical hold, and then stood straight once more.

"Do you really believe Marcus died because I was too weak?" Thea asked in a small voice.

"No, but I think people will continue dying if we don't train you properly." Kieran looked at her sympathetically. He knew his words had hurt her, but she would not say so. She nodded her head at him and then looked toward the rising sun.

"I'm terrified that I won't be able to learn everything in time to stop him," she admitted.

"You aren't going to do this alone," Kieran reminded her and stepped to stand at her side. "We'll face this together."

He watched her watching the sunrise. The weight she'd lost in the weeks leading up to this point would take time to regain, as would her strength, but new found confidence was clear on her face. He would do everything in his power to get her back to full strength before he let her anywhere near King Malachi, but what scared him was her determination to prove herself worthy. If Thea really had been chosen by the Goddess to stop the darkness that Morrigan brought, then they really needed to prepare. A squeaky yawn from Thea told Kieran they couldn't continue their training tonight. He smiled at her as she blushed and reached out to squeeze her hand. After the adrenaline of the training, Kieran wanted to do nothing more than to pull Thea against himself. They'd been exhausted from their constant movement over the last couple of days, not to mention he'd been worried they might've been followed. Now that they'd found a safe place to camp, the nervousness that she usually brought to him returned.

He wanted to be with her, despite the rules against it, and that want was growing more and more difficult to control. He recalled the way her body had felt pressed against him during that stolen moment in his bedroom and wondered what might have happened if Ethel hadn't walked in when she did. That moment had been a loss of control on both of their parts, but he didn't regret it. If anything, it made being alone with her so much more difficult. They'd hardly touched, aside from some hand-holding and training, since they'd left Grimwalde, and Kieran suddenly realized just how much he hated that. It felt like his body was missing a limb when he was not near her. She'd asked him if he believed in soulmates, and how could he deny a soulmate who was standing directly in front of him?

Is my love real enough to risk it all?

He wanted to do more than touch Thea. He wanted to shout his love for her to the heavens and dare them to take her away from him. His mind spun with ideas of running away, of protecting her from the unknown future ahead of them so that he could selfishly keep her to himself forever. He knew it was wrong, but he wanted nothing more than to keep her safe and with him.

"You should get some rest," Kieran finally said. "I'll take the first shift."

Thea looked toward the tent, oblivious to Kieran's inner turmoil, and nodded her head. The dark shadows under her eyes reminded him just how tired she was, and he felt guilty for wanting to do anything but allow her to recover. He needed to get his head out of the clouds and focused back on the mission at hand. It was his job to get Thea prepared to fight the king, because if he failed, they would likely both die.

She reached out and squeezed his hand.

"Thank you for being patient with me," she said. He could do nothing but nod. Her hand felt tiny in his own, and he fought the urge to lace his fingers with hers. The sun was rising above the trees now, reflecting beautifully on the lake's surface, but the light made them vulnerable. He knew the likelihood of the king's soldiers venturing toward the Threshold was low now that Thea was already in Faerie, but that didn't mean he could just lower his guard. Despite wanting to follow her to the tent, Kieran watched as Thea walked away, disappearing into the shelter.

Just as he was turning to scout the border of the lake, he saw Thea drop her muddy and wet clothing outside the tent's opening. He swallowed hard and launched himself into the sky before his imagination could torture him any longer.

CHAPTER 15

Thea's wet clothing left her shivering even after being discarded outside. She pulled on a dry nightshirt Iris had been kind enough to pack and attempted untangling her hair with her fingers. It felt disgusting, not having been washed in days, and she thought it was a wonder she even managed to get it into a braid that morning. She could hear Kieran flying above their campsite in a way that she'd never been able to before. Her newly sharpened Faerie senses, as she had decided to call them, made her feel like a different person. She wondered how she'd done anything without getting herself killed before learning how to use them. Without worry of exhaustion, Thea concentrated on warming the air inside the tent, and sighed happily when her shivering eased. A week ago, that simple magic would have been impossible for her to do. Now, it took only a sliver of her energy and a little focus.

When her hair was finally untangled enough to lie down, Thea pulled a blanket over herself and rested her head on the pillow. She thought about Kieran protecting her from the skies above and smiled. The last couple of days had been difficult for both of them, and Thea knew Kieran worried about being followed. She desperately wished she could do more to help him relax, but the only thing she could really do was train enough to keep them from getting themselves killed when the time came to face danger again.

Thea tucked an arm under her pillow and turned onto her side so she could watch the entrance of the tent. Training had left her sore and exhausted, so she shifted, trying to get comfortable on the hard ground. She'd done her best to clear the snow from beneath their tent before setting it up, but that left only the icy earth to cushion her sleep. It was not the most ideal. It made her miss Kieran's large, pillow-covered bed, but she'd take the hard ground over putting the rest of their friends in danger any day.

She closed her eyes, knowing the exhaustion would overtake her soon, and let her body relax into the blankets. It was difficult to fall asleep when the world continued to move around you, and having her days and nights switched did not help the dilemma. However, exhaustion won the battle against discomfort and within minutes reality faded into dreams.

In this dream, Thea walked along the edge of the lake. She didn't hear the Threshold calling her the way it had when they'd just arrived, but then again, she knew this was a dream. She walked barefoot through the grass, for in this dream it was spring, and then came to a stop at the sound of children's voices.

On the other side of the lake were two girls; neither realized that Thea stood watching. They looked to be only ten or eleven years old, and Thea watched as their bodies trembled with giggles when one tossed a bundle of flowers at the other, decorating her in shades of blue and yellow. One girl had hair the same color as Thea's, while the other had hair as dark as midnight. They wore crowns of flowers atop their heads and sat in the grass picking daisies. The red-haired girl had tossed the flowers at the dark-haired one, before surprisingly making more grow from the ground with just her fingertips. Both girls smiled as the new blossoms sprang to life.

"Children are always so innocent," said a voice that caught Thea by surprise.

A woman stood beside her, wearing a nearly see-through chiffon gown. Thea recognized Ainé immediately. For a moment, Thea only stared at her, stunned by her beauty. She wore a crown of flowers similar to the ones that sat on the girls' heads, and she smiled sadly as she watched them. Thea looked over at the children who continued to play without a care in the world about who might be watching them.

"That's you." Thea didn't need to ask. The girl's red hair was identical to that of the woman standing beside her. Plus, there was something about the way she held herself, even as a child, that was familiar. "And that is…"

Thea watched the dark-haired girl, tilting her head as if to get a better look. The name of the girl stuck to the top of her mouth like peanut butter, but how could she say it? How could that innocent child be the monster she was supposed to stop?

"My sister, Morrigan," Ainé confirmed without Thea even needing to ask the question. "Before she changed."

"What happened?" Thea asked. She knew it was an intrusive question, but if the Goddess was showing her this memory, she assumed it must be for a good reason.

"She became jealous of my love for humanity."

"And that's what made her a monster?" Thea said in disbelief.

It seemed silly to her, but then again, until recently she'd never had a sister.

"Jealousy is a dangerous emotion," Ainé said, finally looking away from the two girls and at Thea. "You know that, though."

Thea thought of Kieran's reaction to finding out about Marcus and blushed, embarrassed. She wondered just how much the Goddess knew about her and Kieran.

"Is Kieran my soulmate?" she asked suddenly. Thea was

pleased to see that she'd caught Ainé by surprise with her question. That meant she was not as all-knowing as everyone talked her up to be.

"You're so different from the rest of your kind," Ainé said, quietly examining Thea. "Most would fear asking me such a direct question, but you ask without fear."

"I didn't mean any offense," Thea said honestly.

"I know."

Ainé seemed to contemplate what she would say next for an agonizing amount of time. Thea thought she already knew the answer to her question, but still, she ached to hear someone say it.

"Yes, Kieran is your soulmate."

The peanut-butter dryness returned to Thea's mouth, and she couldn't make herself speak. She just stared at her feet, repeating the words over and over again in her head, hoping to the heavens she would not forget them.

"You knew that already, though, so why did you ask?"

"He says we can't be together." The words hurt to even speak, but she said them. "So, I guess I thought if…"

"If I said it then they would allow it?" the Goddess asked in an overly kind voice. Thea nodded. "Unfortunately, I don't control the laws of your land. I have very little control over anything anymore."

"Oh…"

"But that doesn't mean you shouldn't be together."

Thea chewed on her bottom lip while she thought about that. If she and Kieran were soulmates, which according to Ainé they were, then they were meant to be together no matter what some archaic law said.

However, no matter how clear that seemed to her, she did not know if Kieran would ever agree.

"Why did you bring me here?" Thea asked.

"To remind you that no one is born evil." Ainé looked back

toward her younger self and her sister. "It may be too late for my sister, but I don't believe it's too late for yours."

"Amara..."

"She needs you to protect her. And you will need her."

"Protect her? From whom?" Thea looked around, wondering if someone might jump out of the bush at her.

"I can't tell you everything, but you'll soon see. I wasn't able to protect my baby sister..." Her words were full of ancient sadness that made even Thea's heart ache. "But you can still protect yours."

They both watched as young Ainé and Morrigan disappeared laughing and smiling into the woods. They were nothing more than a memory now that would haunt the Goddesses for the rest of their lives. Thea didn't want the same fate for Amara and her. She was still angry for what Amara had done, but she hadn't been born evil, as everyone kept reminding her. Their father had sculpted her into a monster, but she was still young, possibly young enough to save.

"You have a hard journey ahead of you," Ainé said, and Thea knew their time was ending.

"That's why you gave me the gift of the elements?"

The Goddess smiled and stepped into the lake, her dress growing wet at the bottom.

"I gave them to you because you have been without magic for too long. Use them with respect, and they will assist you on your mission."

A million more questions sat on the tip of Thea's tongue, but it was too late. As Ainé's feet entered the water, her body sank and Thea awoke from her dream alone in the tent, feeling as if she had not slept at all.

THEA'S VOICE drew Kieran's attention away from the rabbit he'd been hunting. He knew they couldn't survive on the sandwiches Ethel had packed for them forever and figured Thea would not want any part in the actual scavenging for food. So, after making sure no one waited to ambush the princess, he'd set off to hunt. He'd been listening for her, just in case, so when she called for him he immediately abandoned the lucky rabbit and started jogging back. Normally, he would have flown, but just in case anyone was watching the skies, he figured he'd better stick to the ground.

When he arrived, Thea was standing in only her night shirt, shivering in the snow, with no shoes on. He lifted an eyebrow at her strange appearance and then watched as a stranger look came over her face.

"Why aren't you sleeping? I wasn't going to wake you for at least a couple more hours." He walked toward her and reached inside the tent to grab her cloak, draping it over her shoulders. "And why in the world are you out in the cold looking like this?"

He watched as Thea looked down at her own appearance and blushed. Whatever had driven her out of the tent had obviously been important enough to cause her to forget that it was the middle of winter. Kieran looked down at her bare feet once the cloak was wrapped around her shoulders and shook his head, laughing.

"You're going to catch your death. Come on." Before Thea could reply, he picked her up and carried her back into the tent, carefully maneuvering himself and his wings through the small opening and gently setting her back onto her blankets. "Are you asleep still?"

This seemed to remind her that she hadn't said a word since he arrived, and her cheeks grew a shade darker. He didn't know what was going on with her, but all the thoughts he'd banished from his head earlier returned as he looked at her bare legs peeking out from beneath the cloak. His heart sped up, beating loudly in his ears, and he hoped she was actually sleepwalking so that she wouldn't hear it.

"I'm making you nervous," she said suddenly. Her gray eyes sparkled mischievously, and she shrugged out of the cloak, having followed his eyes to her bare legs. He bit his lip. "I had another dream."

This distracted him momentarily. He looked at her for any sign that the Goddess had told her of oncoming danger, but she only shook her head to reassure him that it was not that type of dream. He didn't know how she read him so easily, but apparently she knew what he thought without him saying a word now. This both enthralled and terrified him.

"What did she say?" Kieran knew by the way Thea had said it that she'd definitely spoken to the Goddess again, but something about the way Thea avoided eye contact made him want to know desperately what had happened.

"Well, she wanted to tell me not to give up on Amara," Thea said, but Kieran sensed that there was more. He looked toward the entrance of the tent, thinking about what could lurk in the woods just waiting for them to be vulnerable, and then sat beside her. He couldn't be on alert at all times, and even if he could, he'd walked the perimeter enough that he was sure there was nothing there. They were safe, which meant he actually had a chance to sit down and talk to Thea, something that he both wanted and was terrified of at the same time. She looked surprised that he was sitting with her, but also pleased.

"And?" He elbowed her with a gentle playfulness. "I know you're not telling me everything."

"I asked her a question... about us." She said the last two words just above a whisper, and his heart nearly stopped.

"And?" he repeated, this time at almost as low a tone as she had spoken.

"I wanted to know if we were soulmates."

He stared at her, unable to make himself ask any further

questions. A million thoughts raced through his head, but he didn't know if he wanted to know the answer. On one hand, he thought that he already knew the answer, but on the other, what if Ainé had told Thea that they shouldn't be together? What if she was about to break his heart? He couldn't speak.

"Don't you want to know what she said?" Thea asked, suddenly looking as nervous as he felt. She watched his facial expression, carefully reading his reactions, and he took a deep breath. He wanted to know what the Goddess had said, but more than that, he wanted to kiss her for even asking such a question. If Thea wanted to know if they were soulmates, it was because she felt that they were, and that made his heart soar. If he was being honest, he didn't care what the Goddess had said in that moment, because all he heard was that Thea believed they were soulmates—and so did he.

"Kieran?" He heard her say his name, but never in his entire life had he felt so compelled to kiss someone. It was as if his body's survival depended on her touch, so without another second of hesitation, he pressed his lips against hers and let the world explode around them.

CHAPTER 16

THEA'S NERVES MELTED AWAY WHEN KIERAN'S LIPS TOUCHED HERS. The same electric passion that she'd felt the last time they'd kissed sent shivers down her spine. Her eyelids fluttered closed. She remembered the dream. She remembered Ainé confirming Kieran as her soulmate. That was what she'd wanted to tell Kieran, but this worked too. Her entire body burned hotter than fire as she let him pull her into his lap the same way he'd done before. It felt like the moment in his bedroom had been paused and someone had just slammed the play button in the middle of their conversation.

"Kieran," Thea mumbled against the kiss, but she wasn't sure if he even heard her. He rested one hand on her lower back, while the other twisted into her already tangled hair. Her breathing quickened as his lips left hers to kiss along her jaw, leaving a gentle trail down her neck to her collarbone. Her own hands rested on his chest, clutching at his shirt tighter after each new touch of his lips. Every kiss left her a little more breathless and a lot less in control. She cupped his chin, pulling his lips back to hers, and he rewarded her with a breathless groan of approval as she traced her tongue across his bottom lip, tangling her fingers into the back of his hair.

When his hand moved from her back to rest on her bare legs she thought she might lose it. She wanted to be closer to him, and the entire world was fading away around them. She no longer thought of the journey ahead or behind. She didn't think of where they were going. The only thing that mattered was Kieran and how much she needed this moment here and now. She knew the road they travelled would likely lead to their deaths, and that was why she was done caring what anyone else said about them being together. She needed to be with him as much as she needed oxygen or water to live.

Thea's mind swirled as they kissed, and when he began to lay her onto her back she whimpered in protest at the growing space between their bodies, reaching up for him. He hovered over the top of her, propped up on his hands, and she quickly wrapped her legs up and around his waist, pulling him back down against her with a triumphant grin. She could feel how much he wanted her, even through his clothes. She felt like her heart might beat right out of her chest as he kissed her again, this time more gently, and brushed the hair away from her face so he could look at her. She didn't mind, though; she wanted him to see her.

After a moment of nervous contemplation, she reached down to grab the bottom of her nightshirt. He raised himself up just enough for her to pull it over her head, watching her with a deep-rooted animal hunger. When she lowered herself back beneath him her hair fell away from her shoulders, leaving her completely exposed. She watched as his eyes travelled over her body slowly and let her legs fall from his waist to settle on each side of him. His wings unfurled above them, stretching to the edges of the tent.

"You are perfection," he said. His voice was rough, lower than Thea had ever heard it. It raised the hairs on the backs of her arms and made her lick her lips. She reached up to trace the bottom of his black tunic and saw him smile. "It's a little more difficult with the wings."

She watched as he expertly unbelted his baldric, setting his sword to the side, and then pulled the tunic off with perfect ease. She wondered if she would ever be able to do that for him as quickly and gracefully. As soon as it was gone, her hands dropped to rest on the hard muscles of his chest and examined the lines of abs he'd been hiding beneath it with appreciation. She saw the scars along his skin, as well as a tattoo just above his heart, and traced them with a light finger, looking up at him with questioning eyes.

"It's Ivandor's crest," he said looking slightly embarrassed. "I got it when I joined the king's guard to remind me what and who I am fighting for. I will always be a soldier of Ivandor at heart."

Thea traced the crest delicately. She could make out a dragon, a bushel of thistles, and a set of swords, all held together by the dragon's tail.

"You're amazing," Thea said quietly, and then pulled Kieran's lips back to hers.

At some point during the kiss, Thea's hands found Kieran's wings, her fingers tracing the velvet feathers with gentle fluidity. She felt his body tremble beneath the touch and moved her kisses from his mouth down his neck and chest. He groaned in response, his fingers digging into the blankets beneath them, and Thea smirked. She was beginning to understand just how sensitive his wings were.

As she pulled his body down closer to hers, she kissed his earlobe gently.

"We are soulmates," she said quietly. "I am yours, and you are mine, forever."

Before meeting Kieran, Thea would have run for the hills if someone had said that to her, but everything about them felt right. She knew Kieran would not run. In fact, she wasn't even scared to be the first one to say it out loud. She needed him to know that this was what she wanted, that she wanted to be with him.

"I love you," Kieran said in return. The smile on his face was unlike anything Thea had ever seen, and the passion in his eyes was unmistakable. With every second that passed by, Thea felt the need to be closer to him growing more unbearable. She traced the tops of his pants with her fingertips, letting her nails graze his skin gently, and smiled back at him.

"Show me," she whispered, and his wings came down around them, cocooning them in warmth until his body met hers.

KIERAN WATCHED Thea sleep against his side for a long time after their energy had depleted. She'd collapsed against him and exclaimed through her ragged breathing that if they didn't take a break she would be asleep for days. Despite both of their bodies being coated in sweat, she'd fallen asleep shortly afterward, her chest rising and falling more slowly the closer her dreams came. He noticed she smiled in her sleep and kissed her forehead every so often, as if to confirm she was still there, still his.

He stroked his finger gently across her arm, enjoying the view of her naked body against his. It was difficult for him not to wake her and make love to her all over again, but he knew she needed rest. If he were being honest with himself, he also could probably use the rest, but the memory of their bodies connected as one was enough to raise his spirits, among other things.

Watching her sleep this time felt completely different to when she'd been recovering. He didn't worry about her fragility or that she might not wake up. Instead, he enjoyed the fact that she slept safely in his arms. He rested his head against hers, playing with her hair between his fingers, and listening to her steady breath. He believed he could do that forever.

A rustling in the trees outside drew his attention away from Thea, though, alerting him to another presence. He used his foot to nudge the flap of the tent open, just enough that he could look out. It was late in the afternoon now; they'd spent plenty of their day in the tent, much to his liking. The high sun made it easy for Kieran to recognize a smiling face staring directly at him from the opening in the trees: Mirielle.

He quickly let the tent shut, knowing full well she'd just seen more of him than he wanted her to, and slipped a pillow under Thea's head in place of himself. She stirred slightly in her sleep, mumbling something unintelligible.

"Get your rest, Princess. I won't be far away." He kissed her cheek and watched her fall back asleep while he pulled his clothes on as quietly as possible. By the time he slipped out of the tent, Thea's breathing had dropped low and steady once more. Mirielle was sitting on a log near the lake's edge, watching the water and waiting for him.

"I didn't mean to disturb you," she said without looking at him as he approached. He was glad, because his cheeks felt warmer than normal.

"How did you find us?" Kieran looked around anxiously. The whole point of telling no one that they were here had been to keep Thea safe. If Mirielle could find them, then what if someone had followed her? What if the Princess was in danger again?

"Ainé told me," she said, meeting his eyes.

"You came alone?" Kieran asked with an edge of panic. He didn't know why Ainé would have told Mirielle where they were, but he feared the worst. "Did something happen? Did Malachi come?"

"No, no." She set her hand on his shaking knee, meeting his

eyes. "I took the children to a safehouse, and Iris has been patrolling the village with Gwendolyn since you left. There has been no news from Malachi or Amara."

"I don't get it," Kieran frowned. "Why would they attack like that and then just back off? We must be missing something..."

"I don't know, Kieran, but Ainé sent me to speak with Thea."

"About what?" he asked, but she met his question with a silence that made his eyes narrow. "Mirielle, I can't protect her if I don't know what I am protecting her from."

Instead of answering, Mirielle folded her hands into her lap and continued to look out over the water. "I haven't been here since I was a child. They used to say that if you stared at the water's edge long enough, you would see both the Goddesses playing on the bank."

"Both of them?"

"Yes, as children."

Neither of them said much else, but Kieran looked out toward the other side of the lake, wondering what two Goddess children might look like playing there. He couldn't picture it.

"Please tell me why you're here," he pleaded. *"Please."*

He wanted to return to the tent, to be with Thea and pretend Mirielle hadn't shown up to ruin their moment, but he needed more information.

"Kieran, I need you to trust me," she spoke in a level tone as she looked back at him. "The goddess was clear about my instructions."

Then she looked toward the tent with a smile that didn't match her age. "So, I see I was right about you two."

Kieran's mouth fell open. He wanted to respond but the words wouldn't come. The argument died on his tongue at her next words—as did his questioning of her intentions here.

"I knew you were soulmates from the moment I laid eyes on you two."

"You did?"

She laughed again, this time a little louder. Kieran heard a rustle in the tent and knew that they'd woken Thea up.

"Kieran?" Thea called out groggily. He got up, but Thea came out of the tent wrapped only in her cloak and froze as she saw Mirielle. "Oh!" Her cheeks burned as red as her hair as she stumbled back into the tent quickly. Kieran couldn't help but smile at her clumsy attempt to cover up all the skin that had been showing. He also couldn't help wanting to follow her back into the tent.

"Poor girl," Mirielle said, shaking her head. "Always so embarrassed for no reason."

A few moments later, Thea returned fully dressed, with her hair pulled back into a braid. When she reached Kieran, he pulled her close against his side, unable to be so far away from her any longer, and kissed the top of her head. Thea looked surprised for a moment, but then relaxed into his arms. He wanted her to know that he was serious; he was done hiding how they felt from everyone.

"Mirielle was just telling me how she knew we were soulmates," he said as his fingers laced with hers. He knew this wasn't the most important bit of information that Mirielle had mentioned, but it was the freshest in his mind.

"Oh?" Thea tilted her head at Mirielle. Her cheeks were still flushed, but her energy had returned. He didn't want to look away from her and felt a new appreciation for just how beautiful she was.

Mirielle smiled at them both and nodded her head. Then she shivered and looked at Kieran.

"Kieran, dear, would you be so kind as to get a fire going for me? I promise not to stay long, but I'd like to warm up before I start my journey home."

Kieran knew then that Mirielle wished to talk to Thea alone. He didn't particularly like the idea of being left out of the conversation, but she'd made it clear that whatever she had to say could only be said in front of Thea. It infuriated him. He looked at Thea, who nodded that she'd be fine, then back to Mirielle.

"I'll go gather firewood," he replied stiffly and squeezed Thea's hand one last time before heading for the tree line. Whatever Mirielle needed to say, she would not say it in front of him. He felt an unexplainable sense of dread creeping over him, twisting his stomach into knots, as he glanced back one last time to see Thea sit beside Mirielle.

CHAPTER 17

THEA DIDN'T ENJOY BEING AWAY FROM KIERAN, BUT IT WAS obvious Mirielle had something she wanted to tell her. So, reluctantly, Thea had let go of Kieran's hand and watched him disappear into the tree line. She knew he would not go far, for fear that something might happen to her, but any distance between them felt like an infinite space now. Her body ached to be back against his.

Thea didn't know whether or not Kieran had had a lot of sexual experience in his past, but from her own limited experience, that had been the best sex of her life. She felt complete being with him, like she could not describe where her body ended and his began. She'd wanted nothing more than for that feeling to go on forever, but physical exhaustion had become a barrier. Now, after having rested, she'd awoken missing his warmth.

"I'm sorry to have interrupted," Mirielle said, pulling Thea from her thoughts. "I needed to see you, though."

Those words drew Thea's attention away from the tree line where she'd been searching to see if she could see Kieran. She looked at Mirielle's serious face and her back straightened. She recognized the look in Mirielle's eyes. It was the same look that had haunted Marcus' face when he'd come to her hospital room and explained that she was the only survivor of the car accident.

"What happened?" Thea's voice was sharp, but she hadn't meant for it to be harsh.

"I had a vision," Mirielle started to say, and Thea's heart began beating again.

She'd thought Mirielle would say someone was dead, or that her father had razed the village and killed Iris, Ethel, and everyone else she knew, but why would Mirielle not want Kieran here if all she wanted to share was a vision? Should he not know what was coming as well?

"A vision that involves Kieran."

Thea's throat felt as if it'd closed, her mouth growing dry. She would surely suffocate, or puke, or both.

"Breathe, dear." Mirielle reached over and squeezed Thea's hand, causing her to let out a breath. "I came to warn you.

"I had a vision of your fight with King Malachi. I saw the solstice which is in two days' time. If you arrive before Yule begins, you can defeat the king."

Thea's eyes widened. *Two days,* she had *two days* to get to Ivandor and defeat her father. Considering her lack of training, she didn't feel that was anywhere close to the amount of time she needed to be ready.

"Wait," Thea said suddenly. "Why didn't you want Kieran to know this?"

Mirielle's face saddened and she no longer looked at Thea.

"You must face Malachi alone. If you take Kieran with you, he will die."

Thea's blood turned to ice, burning through her veins with the pulse of her beating heart.

"How?"

"He'll use dark magic to protect you, and it will consume him."

"He would never do that!" Thea stood, staring at Mirielle. "He knows the consequences of using dark magic. That's why he stopped me. He'd never use dark magic."

Even as she said the words, Thea wondered if they were true. She'd used dark magic by accident to protect someone she loved. Did she really believe Kieran would not go to any lengths to protect her? And if Ainé had given Mirielle this vision as a warning... Thea sat back down, putting her head in her hands. Mirielle rested a hand on her upper back.

"Kieran knows I am here to tell you something. He won't stop until you tell him what it is. The safest thing you can do to protect him is leave as soon as possible."

Thea let out a strangled sob, the happiness that had filled her moments earlier draining away.

"He will kill me."

"Not if you arrive before Yule. I don't know what he's planning, but I know you need to be there by then."

"The Goddess doesn't like to give specifics, does she?" Thea said, more under her breath. She was angry. She was angry at Ainé for not just telling her this information herself when she'd spoken to her last. She was angry at Mirielle for interrupting the happiness she'd found. Most of all, though, she was angry at herself for the lies she would need to tell Kieran. "I can't lie to him."

"Not even to save his life?"

Thea wiped the frustrated tears from her cheeks, trying to hide the evidence before Kieran returned, and glared at Mirielle for even insinuating she would let anything hurt Kieran.

"I'll do whatever it takes to keep all of you safe, but I don't know how Ainé expects me to defeat my father with such little training!"

"I can't begin to comprehend the Goddess' plan for you, but if I had to make a guess, I would say Morrigan is plotting something that you can stop if you arrive on time. You need to trust in yourself and your abilities. She wouldn't send you to do the impossible."

Thea wasn't convinced that was true, but there was no point in arguing. If Mirielle had seen Kieran's death, that was not something Thea could live with. She would protect him, even if it meant doing this alone. She just wondered if he would ever forgive her for it.

"Faylon is one of the fastest creatures in the lands. If you make haste, you'll arrive before the solstice. The castle is only a day and a half's ride from here."

Thea nodded as Mirielle stood, looking at her with sad eyes. *Don't shoot the messenger* came to mind, but Thea couldn't disguise her anger. Nor could she disguise her fear. She knew she was unprepared for this fight with her father, but if Kieran's life was at risk, she had no choice. She stood, like a queen would, and lowered her voice, just in case Kieran was nearby.

"Go back to Grimwalde and send Mica to stop Kieran. He's going to come after me."

She knew with undeniable certainty that as soon as Kieran realized she was gone he would go after her. There was nothing she could do to stop that, but she hoped Mica could slow him down long enough for her to do whatever it was she needed to do. She didn't have a plan yet, but she'd figure one out. Mirielle nodded her agreement and then reached into her pocket and retrieved a small vial with clear liquid in it.

"This will help delay him. It's a sleeping potion, the same type your mother used to keep you asleep on your journey through the Threshold."

Thea took the vial and examined it with a frown.

"How long will he be asleep for?" Thea asked.

"Until you wake him up."

Thea looked at Mirielle in surprise.

"And what if I don't come back?" She swallowed hard.

"Then we are all lost."

Thea cursed and tucked the vial under her cloak as Kieran reappeared with an armful of firewood at the tree line. Thea did her best to mask the worry on her face, to hide the anger, and to pretend nothing had changed in the time he'd been gone as he walked toward them. Seeing him made her heart throb, and the vial in her pocket felt more like poison.

As Kieran reached them, Mirielle apologized and said she needed to return to Mica. Kieran protested that she needed to rest before journeying home, looking suspicious, but she told him she had her ways of staying awake and alert, revealing another small vial in her hand; this one contained a liquid the color of the sky on a cloudless day. Thea told Kieran to let Mirielle make her own decisions, as kindly as possible, but his eyebrows rose in surprise at her suggestion. He eventually gave up arguing with them, and Mirielle left without looking back at Thea.

The day had officially gone from the best day of her life to the worst.

Thea watched Kieran make a fire for them to sit by. She felt numb as she stared at the flames dancing to life before them. She knew Kieran was watching her with worry, but neither of them said a word. She needed to say something, anything, to calm his worry, but words wouldn't come. Her heart remained broken in her chest, throbbing and threatening to turn tears loose on the world around her. She would not cry, though. She would not show weakness or fear. She would just continue to stare at the fire.

"What did she say to you?" Kieran finally asked after what felt like an eternity of silence. "You're obviously upset," he added when Thea did not reply. She'd been formulating a plan in her head during the entire time they'd sat there, but now that she was being given the opportunity to put that plan into motion, she didn't know if she could go through with it.

Save his life, she reminded herself.

The sunset was already approaching, and Faylon stood nearby as if knowing she was going to need him soon. He looked alert and paced as nervously as she felt.

"I'm just nervous about facing my father. Mirielle said that Morrigan is growing stronger and that my father is getting closer to finding me," Thea said—not a total lie. If she lied to him, he'd see right through it, but hopefully twisting the truth was the next best option. She stood up and grabbed a kettle from their supplies, filling it with fresh water. "Don't worry, I'm just going to make some tea. My mother used to do that to calm my nerves." She attempted a smile at Kieran, but he didn't look convinced. He walked over to take the kettle from her and placed it on the fire, then pulled her down into his lap as they waited for the water to heat. The vial Mirielle had given her burned the inside of her breast pocket like hot iron against her chest.

"I told you, you don't have to go through this alone. We're going to prepare and be ready for this fight together."

Thea had to fight the urge to cry. She blinked furiously down at her hands, and thankfully, Kieran didn't notice. He stroked the back of her head—a comfort she didn't deserve—and kissed her face quietly. She was a traitor, lying to him like this, but she reminded herself that if she didn't lie, she would lose him forever. She'd also lose him forever if she didn't succeed.

No pressure.

When the water in the kettle boiled she reached out with shaky hands to pour it into a cup.

"Would you have some with me?" Thea asked as innocently as possible. Kieran nodded, suspecting nothing. As Thea turned her back on him, she emptied the vial into his tea, handing him a cup before making her own.

They sipped in silence, Thea watching as discreetly as possible for any sign of tiredness on Kieran's face. When he began yawning, she commented about the last time he'd slept and asked him if she could take the guard shift tonight.

"I was hoping you'd come to the tent with me. I'm sure things will be fine out here." Kieran yawned again and put his mug down on the ground, stretching his arms and wings wide.

"Of course," Thea said. She knew she needed to leave soon, but she would savor any last moments with Kieran, for fear that she would never have them again. She didn't know if she would come back from this journey, but having him here waiting for her was enough to motivate her to do her best.

They walked toward the tent hand in hand, and Thea glanced at Faylon, communicating with him without saying a word. *We need to be ready to leave.* The horse gave a low bow of his head, but his eyes looked sad as Thea and Kieran entered the tent.

Kieran immediately settled himself down onto the blankets, pulling Thea with him so that she fell into the protection of his wings. His eyes had grown far more tired, and she knew it would not be long before he was asleep. He pressed his lips to hers, catching her by surprise, and she melted into the kiss, allowing herself to forget her fear for just one moment.

"I love you," he mumbled against her lips with a smile. She fought back the sob that threatened to escape her throat.

"No matter what?" she asked, unable to help herself. He pulled back to look at her face.

"No matter what. I am yours, and you are mine, forever." He repeated her words, but on his lips they sounded like poetry.

"Then hold me until the morning comes," she whispered, her head resting on his chest. She felt his breathing slowly relaxing and knew he was falling asleep. Tears streamed down her cheeks as she listened to his steady heartbeat and felt his warm arms holding her safely against him. She would have given anything in the world to stay in his arms. She would have given her entire kingdom to continue to feel safe like this, but that was not what a queen would do.

A queen would do whatever it took to protect her kingdom and those she loved.

A queen would sacrifice herself if it meant there would be a chance for her people.

A queen would be brave. So Thea would also be brave.

"Kieran?" she said quietly. No response.

She shifted her weight in his arms, wiping the tears away from her face, and sniffled quietly as she sat up to look at his sleeping face. He looked at peace for the time being, although Thea knew it would not last forever. She hated herself for what she was about to put him through, but even if he never forgave her, that would be better than the alternative.

She thought of kissing him one last time, but something about the way Mirielle had told her he would not wake until she woke him stopped her. Instead, she squeezed his hand and adjusted his baldric to hang across her body. She sheathed his sword and slipped one dagger into the strap of her boot and the other into her belt, before sneaking quietly out of the tent. The potion had worked.

Outside the tent, Faylon waited for her with a blanket over his back. He'd somehow placed it there himself. She walked over to him and stroked his warm nose with her palm. He pressed it against her wet cheeks and let out a heavy breath.

You're sure about this? he asked her, and she nodded her head, unable to speak. He lowered himself to the ground and Thea climbed onto his back easily. Her body felt like a stranger's as they walked away from the tent. Her heart remained with Kieran, but today, she could not be his lover. She needed to be his queen. She looked back once more at the tent, seeing no sign of movement from within.

"I am yours, and you are mine, forever," she said to no one

but the wind, then pulled her cloak's hood over her head and tangled her fingers into Faylon's mane.

"Take me to Ivandor as quickly as possible." Her voice was no longer that of a human girl, and tears no longer fell from her eyes. She wouldn't show fear entering the lands that rightfully belonged to her. She wouldn't allow her father to break her, and she would save those she loved.

There was no longer time to be a princess. She was a queen of Faerie, and it was about time she started acting like one.

CHAPTER 18

KIERAN KNEW HE WAS ASLEEP BY THE FACT THAT THERE WAS NO snow on the ground, but he still found it hard to distinguish the dream lake in front of him from the real lake he knew he and Thea were camped beside. He walked along the shore of the lake, his wings dragging along the ground slightly, and found himself beside a red mare much like the one they'd brought with them. She grazed in the fresh green grass, her tail swishing behind her, but she looked up with startlingly human eyes as he approached . He stepped back, but the mare stared at him, her golden eyes sparkling the same way that a Fae's would when using magic. He tilted his head and reminded himself that this was just a dream.

"You're a pretty one," he said quietly, not sure why he was saying it at all. The horse only continued to stare at him. He walked toward her slowly, reaching out his hand, but he did not really feel like he was controlling his movements. It seemed the dream was taking control of him now.

When he reached the mare, she pressed her nose against his palm and he gasped at its icy temperature. His eyes widened as the mare transformed in a swirl of green and yellow light into a woman in a green dress with hair the same color as Thea's.

"Ainé," he breathed, unsure of how he knew this was the goddess but having knowing that it was. "You're Ainé."

He dropped to his knees, bowing his head before her.

"Rise, young Kieran. That is unnecessary," she spoke kindly, and her voice was like a melody sung by the birds.

He looked up at her and did as he was told, rising to his feet. She had a soft glow to her skin that made him feel like he should avert his eyes, but when he did, she rested her hand beneath his chin, pulling his gaze back to her. He noticed then the seriousness upon her face.

"I need to tell you something, and you need to accept it calmly," she said, and Kieran knew a look of pure confusion must have crossed his face. She brushed her thumb along his cheek. Her hands were as cold as the horse's muzzle had been. "Thea is in trouble."

"What?" This brought his attention away from the feel of her skin. His body straightened into the familiar stance of a soldier on alert and he looked around for the danger, as if it would approach him in his dream.

"My sister has tricked her," Ainé said, her voice distant and sad. "It's difficult for me to speak with you. I'm not sure how much time we have, but I reached you because of your bond with Thea." Now, she smiled at him as if approvingly. His mind was swirling, though. Thea was in trouble and he needed to wake up, so why wasn't he waking up?

"Remember, I need you to be calm. Thea gave you a sleeping potion." Kieran felt a pang of hurt, remembering the tea Thea had given him and the exhaustion that instantly followed.

"But, why would she…"

"Morrigan showed the seer a vision of your death, Kieran. You mustn't be angry with Thea."

Kieran wasn't in the mood to be told who he mustn't be

angry with. He was in the mood to wake himself up from the endless nightmare he'd just stumbled into.

Ainé watched him with a sadness he wanted to slap off her face.

"You can't wake yourself up, Kieran. Do you remember the night you took Thea through the Threshold?"

"Of course."

"Then you remember how soundly she slept. That was until you kissed her."

Kieran recalled the very moment. He'd kissed the top of her head and watched her wake up immediately. It had surprised him at the time because she had not stirred for a second when he'd taken her through the clashing of swords or as they'd rushed through the forest.

"It's a love potion?"

"Of sorts," Ainé said with a small smile. "Thea's mother knew you loved Thea, although I don't think she knew exactly how that love would grow. She knew that you'd be able to wake her before you left her in that other realm."

"So how am I supposed to help Thea then, if she is the only one who can wake me up?" Kieran's anger was growing. He understood now why Thea always seemed so frustrated after talking to Ainé. He felt as if she were speaking in riddles.

"You're going to help her by being prepared when you're captured," Ainé said, only increasing his confusion tenfold. "After speaking to Mirielle, my sister figured out where you'd taken Thea. The king's men expect Thea to come to them, but he has sent others for you."

"But why? He needs Thea, not me."

"Because to get to Thea, he needs you, and right now, you are completely vulnerable."

"I still don't understand how I'm supposed to help if I'm unconscious." He glared at the lake, feeling it might be rude to show the Goddess how he felt towards her right now.

"It won't surprise you when Thea wakes you up, and trust me, she will wake you up, Kieran. I came here to warn you so that you would be ready, but now I fear I'm growing weaker and cannot hold this connection much longer."

Kieran noticed the environment around them fading, and even Ainé looked duller.

"My sister plans to use Thea's blood for a ritual on the solstice," she said, her voice sounding distant.

"A ritual? A ritual for what?" He tried to grab Ainé's hand, to stop her from fading away, but he could not touch her.

"There's no time, Kieran. Thea needs you to be ready. We all need you to be ready."

Kieran could hardly see Ainé anymore. He felt exhaustion pulling him back into the darkness, but before it completely engulfed him, he heard her whisper three more words.

"Trust your bond."

And then he saw nothing.

THEA FELT grateful for the extra sleep she'd gotten the day before as she rode long into the night. Her legs and back ached, but she didn't dare stop. Faylon had left her to her thoughts almost as soon as they'd left camp, but Thea wondered what he thought of this mission. Having a familiar was still a new concept to her, but she hoped he didn't *have* to go with her on a suicide mission.

It's not a suicide mission, she told herself, yet again. The thought of facing her father made her sick to her stomach, but as they rushed through the forests of Ivandor in the general direction that Thea believed she needed to go, she reminded herself that the Goddess would not give her something she couldn't handle. She replayed each and every piece of advice Kieran had given her in their short amount of training. She'd been riding for nearly ten hours, but not long enough for her to stop looking over her shoulder for enemies. She hated riding in the broad daylight; it left her open to too many dangers.

On any other occasion, she would have enjoyed the beautiful landscape. It was her first time traveling outside of the Grimwalde territories, and the snowy forests soon turned into stunning rolling green hills as if the seasons could change overnight. She wanted to stop and sketch the massive mountains in the distance or the way the sun rose over the hilltops. Sketching would have been a much-welcomed distraction at this point, but it was a luxury that would have to wait until after she survived this encounter.

Thea's feet tightened around Faylon's sides as a sudden gust of wind swept around them. She'd sensed it seconds before it touched her skin and known it was not an ordinary breeze. It caressed her cheek and tickled the back of her neck; she shivered. Faylon made a noise of protest when it blew the hair of his mane into the air, his nostrils flaring at the intrusion. Thea shushed him, certain to have heard something, but saw nothing as she looked around. The gust picked up once more, this time spinning around her body like a small tornado. It made her catch her breath as it whistled against her ear. She felt the magic pulsing in the air and imagined for a moment that Kieran had escaped the sleeping potion.

Could he be trying to get my attention, she wondered.

The wind pressed down upon her, forcing her to listen, and so she did. She listened, trying to understand exactly what message the magic was trying to convey.

"What is it?" she asked, frustrated. If Thea was right, she only had a couple of hours' ride left until she reached the castle gates. Faylon had slowed his pace, concerned about the gust of wind around them, but Thea gave him a quick nudge. They couldn't afford to slow down.

She lowered herself against Faylon's back, her eyes stinging from the wind. He lurched forward, and as they tried to outrun the magic, Thea swore she heard the word *Trap* howling around her. A fresh flutter of nerves twisted inside of her, but she tried to focus straight ahead.

"How much farther?" She spoke loudly because the wind had not yet died down. Instead of whispering messages of traps, it tried to throw her off Faylon's back. She clung to him as tightly as she could without tearing his mane out.

We're nearly to the outskirts of Ivandor now. It is only a couple of hours from there to the castle.

Thea nodded her head but said nothing more. She looked behind her again, imagining an onslaught of enemies at her tail, and ignoring the nagging feeling inside of her chest.

She'd done the right thing by leaving alone. After all, it had been Mirielle's idea, and she'd gotten the vision directly from Ainé.

But as she thought the words to convince herself, they made less and less sense to her.

As they neared the place where Faylon said the borderlands of Ivandor were, Thea's emotions took center stage. This was her home, or should have been, if her father had not been such a terrible man. She should have grown up on these lands, learning how to control her magic, but instead, she'd grown up knowing nothing about who or what she was. She knew her adoptive parents had loved her, and she hated the thought of never knowing them. However, she also had never known her biological mother. This land was full of things that should have been, but never could be.

That would change.

She thought of the life Kieran had given up here for her. She thought of all the people who had fled because of her tyrannical father.

That would change.

She thought of Morrigan seducing her people with darkness, corrupting them and corrupting the beauty of these lands.

That would change.

She saw the destruction that the darkness had brought upon her lands as they entered it. The grass grew less green the farther in they came. The trees died, and the birds ceased singing. The still, icy air cut her to the bone, and she clutched her cloak tighter around her as Faylon slowed to a walk, his breathing steadying. She knew she had asked a lot of him by the telltale signs of his exhaustion. She felt an immense amount of gratitude for her familiar's strength and determination but noticed the way his ears flattened against his head the closer they came to Ivandor. The tension in both of their bodies electrified the air.

"Tell me it wasn't always this way..." Thea said quietly to Faylon.

Ivandor used to be the most beautiful of the four kingdoms, he told her, his voice thick with grief. Thea continued to stare at the death and destruction that surrounded them, but stopped when her eyes focused on a single image just barely visible ahead of them: a woman.

Faylon tensed, having spotted her at the same time as Thea. She walked toward them swiftly, an army of creatures Thea had never seen before following behind her. Some, who appeared as men, held swords and wore soldiers' armor. Others had wings like Kieran and soared into the sky above Thea and Faylon. Most, however, were hideous creatures that skulked and crawled behind their leader. Thea and Faylon stood frozen, watching as the mass approached, led by a single female Fae, Amara. The word *Trap* whipped around Thea like a slap in the face.

CHAPTER 19

"WELL, WELL, WELL," SAID AMARA IN HER CASUAL, SING-SONG voice when she got close enough. "My big sister has finally come home!"

Thea's fingers twitched in Faylon's mane as she contemplated turning tail and running, but seeing the Fae flying above kept her in her place. She knew when she was outnumbered, and Faylon had exhausted himself getting here. There was no way they could outrun anyone. Her heartbeat quickened as Amara stopped about a hundred yards away from them, taunting her with a knowing smile.

"Morrigan knew you'd be here," Amara continued, not waiting for a response from Thea. "Daddy sent me to bring you back to the castle. Afraid your pony won't be welcome, though." Faylon made a vicious-sounding noise, and for a moment Thea pictured him impaling Amara with his horn. She stroked the side of his mane carefully and leaned down to press her lips to his ear.

"Go to Iris. She needs to hide Kieran," she whispered, before slipping off of his back. The only response he gave was to press his nose to her cheek momentarily and then he was gone, quicker than Thea had ever seen him move, despite his exhaustion. She knew he would do what he was supposed to but feared she would be the death of him at this rate. If this was a trap, then Thea needed her family to know she'd been captured. She definitely couldn't fight them all by herself, and she had officially lost the element of surprise. She would have to figure out another way to not get herself killed, all while hoping Iris could save Kieran.

"Leave it," Amara told her soldiers, who looked like they were about to go after Faylon. Thea let out a breath of relief and then held her hands up as if to show she did not mean to attack.

Time for plan B, she thought and pulled her hood off. She looked directly at Amara, meeting her sister's eyes with a look of pleading.

"It doesn't have to be this way, Amara. You don't have to do what he says." Thea didn't know if this type of negotiation would work, but she imagined she'd survive longer with Amara on her side, especially since Amara probably knew how to control the others. She thought of all the things Amara had done since her arrival here and tried to push back her hatred by thinking of Iris. This was Iris' daughter, and she was only a child. Thea needed to protect her.

Amara didn't seem to see it this way, though. Instead, she laughed along with rest of group closest to her. As the group of about two-dozen began circling her, Thea felt like a rabbit in a trap.

"Father only needs you for the ritual. After that, he'll realize that I've been the loyal one." She spat on the ground beside her and then raised her arm.

So this was about gaining a father's love and approval; that was predictable teenage girl behavior if Thea had ever seen it before.

Amara stretched her fingers toward Thea and then curled them inward, pulling her body forward by force of magic. Thea fought against it, but it was no use. She could only pray that Faylon would get to Iris in time to get Kieran to safety. She realized now that she'd left him completely defenseless and kicked herself mentally. If anything happened to him because of her, she'd never forgive herself.

"What ritual?" Thea asked, trying to stall. She was curious what ritual Amara spoke of, but that didn't change the extremely dangerous situation she was in.

"You'll see." A smirk pulled at the corners of her lips and her red-rimmed eyes sparkled.

"Amara, your mother—"

CRACK.

Thea's head jerked to the side as Amara's palm met her cheek. Her smile had disappeared and Thea's eyes stung as much as her cheek did. She turned to look at Amara with a glare and found her anger mirrored back at her.

"Don't talk to me about that whore," she growled. "She *left* me."

The crowd had gone quiet, and everyone watched Amara with curiosity. Thea momentarily felt bad. Amara had never known her mother. She only knew what her father had told her, and Thea thought she'd probably look for someone to blame too if Malachi had raised her. Her own mother had made sure that would never happen.

"She loves you, Amara. She had no choice but to leave." Thea reached for her sister's hand, her voice thick with sympathy. Amara snatched her hands away, but for a second, Thea swore she saw a glimmer of wondering in the younger girl's eyes. It quickly changed back into anger, though.

"Get her out of my sight," she snapped to two creatures standing closest to them. Thea was not sure, but she imagined they might be ogres. She swallowed hard and then tried not to gag from the stench as two sets of meaty hands closed around her arms and pulled her away from her sister and into the mass of other soldiers. Thea looked around at the creatures she'd read about in books as a child, but they didn't look friendly in the slightest. Centaurs stood around her, shirtless, with pointed ears—they were all men. Their manes flicked from side to side just as Faylon's did, and their human hands gripped swords and shields. One smiled at her as the ogres pulled her past, showing a shiny row of pointed teeth that made Thea's breath catch.

"Don't get too close; they bite," one ogre growled while the other laughed a thick, liquid laugh. Snot shot from its nose as he looked at Thea, landing on her cloak in a green mess. He grinned.

"You're a little thing. Not even enough for a snack." He pushed her, and it took all her might not to fall over. Her arm ached from the contact, and she could tell a bruise was already forming on her skin. The ogres were twice her size, but she had one thing over them: magic. She focused her energy on the earth beneath her feet, and as it began to shake they let go of her, stumbling backwards. Everyone around her looked over in surprise, and Amara rushed over.

"I suppose we are related," she said as vines shot out of the ground to bind Thea's arms behind her back. "I'm an earth user as well."

Thea stared at her sister. She was sure that her father must be aware she could control all the elements by now, but it appeared that she still had a little surprise left in her. He hadn't shared all his knowledge with the captain of his army. She wondered if it would be enough to save her life.

Thea said nothing in response to her sister and did not bother fighting the hold on her wrists. She knew she could have burned the vines off, but she didn't need to waste her energy or give away the element of surprise. Instead, she allowed herself to remain bound and stared ahead as they continued to walk. Amara whistled and two wolf-sized dogs appeared at her side. They each had glowing red eyes and snapped viciously at Thea's ankles as they walked. Their paws were no ordinary paws. They were monstrous, with razor-sharp claws that tore the earth they walked on. The part of these canine creatures that Thea found most interesting, though, was their hackles, which appeared to be made of actual fire that danced wildly down the center of their backs.

Above her, the winged Fae flew ahead to scout for trouble, while to each of her sides the ogres and centaurs chanted about returning the Lost Princess to her tower. Thea had never felt more alone than now. She wished desperately for Kieran's strength beside her, all while being thankful he was nowhere near the catastrophic mess she'd gotten herself into.

Amara chatted loudly ahead of Thea with a centaur about how proud her father would be of her. The centaur didn't look interested, but Thea imagined Amara forced him to listen to her talk often. She was nearly skipping, and kept looking back with a wicked grin, to make sure Thea was still there. She'd sometimes tighten the hold on Thea's hands uncomfortably, letting the vines dig deep into Thea's wrists, but Thea never let her pain show. After her one failed attempt at reasoning with her sister, she'd decided to save her energy for the meeting with her father.

When they reached the gates of the castle, Thea held her breath. Large vines of thorns climbed the high castle walls, making it impossible to climb. Amara walked Thea directly through the village on the way there, so that she could see the terrible life and suffering of the humans who lived there. They wore simple rags as clothing, and the children were filthy and thin. The laughter and pleasantry of Grimwalde was the polar opposite of Ivandor. They stared at her with wide eyes as Amara taunted them, saying that their savior had been captured and posed no threat to Malachi. She threatened violence against anyone who dared to disobey the king or her, and Thea regretted the promise she'd made to Iris. There were no Fae in the village, only malnourished humans. One man threw a stale loaf of bread at Amara. Thea only knew it was stale because of the loud sound it made when it hit Amara upside the head.

Two centaurs beat him unconscious while Thea screamed herself nearly hoarse trying to get them to stop. The man shielded his face from their hooves and cried out curses at the king and Amara while his blood pooled into the cobblestone street. He met Thea's eyes with a look that told her he believed in her, but how could he while she just stood there, tears streaming down her cheeks? Unable to control her need to save the poor man, Thea set the vines around her wrists on fire and ran toward him, but the centaurs pushed her out of the way so that she could not get close. Thankfully, Amara was too distracted to see what Thea had done to get loose. She didn't like being showed up at her own game, though; that much was clear. She turned her wrath on Thea, who received a hoof to her ribcage and was knocked over, gasping for breath into the dirt. Thea heard a distinct crack and knew at least one of her ribs had broken from the impact. It made it difficult to breathe as she clutched at her side. The centaurs laughed, and those who'd remained to watch her take a beating fled the streets for fear of being the next victims of Amara's rage.

Thea was re-bound and taken directly to the castle after that. She knew she'd weakened herself by trying to help the man, but there was no way she could have just let them kill him in front of her, which she was sure they would have done if she hadn't diverted their anger to herself.

"Don't be stupid," Amara had told her with a roll of her eyes, but Thea felt anything but stupid. She felt angry, and that anger would be her driving force.

As they crossed through the gates, she heard the whispers around her begin. Servants, clearly human, were standing against the walls, awaiting orders. There were also a few more centaurs, and to Thea's horror, she saw a slimy green creature swimming in the river around the castle walls, staring up at her with glowing silver eyes that had black slits for pupils.

"The merrow are nasty creatures that feed on disobedient humans," Amara teased, glancing at Thea's paling face. Thea noticed then the white pieces of bone scattered along the banks. Bile rose in her throat, and she could not control it. She threw up all over the ogre next to her. He jumped back with an angry roar, grabbing her by the neck and lifting her into the air. She kicked hard, trying to strike him, but he'd caught her by surprise and her vision blurred.

She thought of the human bones that lined the river and the creatures that existed within. It made her want to kill Amara. It made her want to succumb to the darkness that boiled beneath her skin, but she tried to think of Kieran bringing her away from that darkness. If she used it, she could never save the rest of those villagers.

"Put. Her. Down. You, big, stupid beast!" Amara grabbed a sword from the centaur that always stood by her side, and held it against the ogre who dangled a choking Thea five feet in the air by her throat. He dropped Thea immediately, but she didn't have time to fall correctly and ended up rolling her ankle on the stone ground. Everyone but the surrounding humans began laughing as she limped into a standing position, rubbing her aching neck. If she'd had any chance before, it was becoming less and less possible with each new injury.

A throat cleared loudly and silence fell across the bridge. Amara stood a little taller, and even the ogre who had just been holding Thea into the air shrunk down, trying to fade back into the crowd. Thea couldn't see where the noise had come from, but she dreaded she already knew the answer. A pathway parted, and Amara stood just slightly in front of Thea, as if wanting to make sure whoever was coming knew that Thea was her property.

"You've done well, daughter," said a gruff voice as a tall man walked toward them. He wore a black velvet cloak over his leather warrior garb. Thea was sure he was over six feet tall, and even at a distance, she could see the sword secured to his hip. His eyes were a darker red than Amara's, and gray hair tinted his black beard. Most importantly, though, he wore a jeweled crown upon his head and had a wicked smile that never touched his eyes. He strode toward them as only a king would, with a confidence that did not falter. Amara bowed low when he drew close and looked at Thea with eyes that told her she should do the same.

Thea only stood taller, and the king let out a booming laugh.

"You look like your mother, and you are right not to bow to me. You are royalty and will bow to no one." He walked right past Amara and cupped Thea's face in his hands, turning it side to side for examination. "So much like your mother."

Thea wanted to cry out for him not to touch her, but she did not. She wanted to spit in his face and tell him he was a murderous bastard who killed her mother, but she did not. She wanted a lot of different things in that moment, but reminded herself that she was a queen and would show all of these creatures and people exactly what that meant.

"What happened to her?" the king asked Amara, noticing the bruising on Thea's neck.

"She put up a bit of a fight and—"

"I told you to bring her to me unharmed." A similar sound to the one Thea had heard when Amara slapped her echoed through the hall, but this time no one laughed. Everyone looked around uneasily and Amara lifted a hand to her cheek where blood spilled from a gash left from the contact with one of the king's rings. Thea saw the anger behind her sister's eyes for only a split second before she lowered her head, apologizing to their father. Thea could tell this was not the first time the king had hurt Amara, but she said nothing as he focused his attention back on her.

"The servants will draw you a bath, and then we will speak."

"No." It was the first word Thea had said, but she kept her voice steady. Looking at her father, she saw the similarities between his face and her own. She saw his lips move in the same way that her own did when she spoke. She noticed the slight crookedness of his nose that she often saw in her own reflection, and she even saw her own jawline mirrored on his face. It made her feel sick. She wanted to see nothing of herself in him, but there it was. He seemed surprised by her refusal, and for a moment, she thought he might hit her too. In fact, she noticed Amara's surprise when he didn't, but she said nothing else.

"You don't wish to have a bath?" he asked, looking at Thea's grimy attire.

"Tell me about the ritual," Thea said, happy her voice was not quivering. Amara shrunk down a little smaller as the king glared at her.

"I see someone couldn't keep her mouth shut."

"Father, I—"

"Silence."

Silence followed, and Thea did not move as she waited for King Malachi to decide. He seemed contemplate, but finally, he spoke again.

"If you don't wish to bathe, that is your choice. However, the servants will take you to your bedroom until I am ready for you."

Your bedroom, Thea thought with a jolt of surprise. After all these years, her father had kept her a bedroom in their home? She knew the surprise showed on her face by the smile that touched his lips.

"I'm not the monster they make me out to be," he said in what was almost a soft tone. "You will see that."

Thea doubted it.

She wanted to say more, but he turned, grabbing Amara by

the arm, and headed out of sight. Immediately two humans appeared to usher Thea into the castle. As the castle gate locked shut behind them, Thea tried to make a note of how she could get out of there if she managed to escape her bedroom. She made a mental note of each corridor they turned down and each staircase they climbed up, but it felt like she was being led in circles through the endless halls. Unlike Grimwalde, Ivandor's castle was dim and dreary. Spiders scurried up the walls as their footsteps echoed endlessly, and Thea actually screamed at one point when they turned a corner to find an ogre beating a bloodied human body that was already crumpled and lifeless on the floor. The ogre's malicious laugh boomed against the stone walls as he saw them and Thea felt her two human escorts stiffen. They did not meet the ogre's eyes as they pulled Thea past and toward another staircase.

Thea had known that her father hated humans, but somehow, actually seeing that hatred manifested was far worse than anything she'd imagined. The ogre's smile haunted her as her escorts dragged her toward a final door—one Thea prayed was her bedroom. She had absolutely no hope of finding her way out of this castle, but she could at least take a moment to recover there. Her father needed her for something, something that, according to Mirielle, was supposed to happen during the solstice. Maybe she could stop whatever his plan was and then regroup with Kieran and the others if she could just come up with a solid, non-suicidal plan.

Her escorts were an older lady, probably in her sixties, and an adolescent girl no older than Ethel. Neither of them said a word until they reached the door to what she assumed was her bedroom. Then it was the older woman who spoke while the younger one stared at her own feet.

"Don't go doing anything stupid, girl," she said, causing Thea to look up at her in surprise. "If you disappear, who do you think they will punish?" She looked at the other servant.

Although the older woman's hair was graying, Thea saw the resemblance clearly between their faces.

"I'm here to help, not hurt you." Thea looked between the women and frowned. "What are your names?"

They ushered Thea into the bedroom so quickly that she almost tripped over her own feet. She ached from the beatings she'd taken outside, and despite what she'd told her father, she actually did desperately need to bathe. The room they entered had light blue walls and a large four-poster bed with a dark blue comforter. A black velvet curtain hung around all four sides of it. Unlike what she'd seen of the kingdom so far, this room was warm and welcoming. A few stuffed animals sat on the bed. One was a lion, another was a rabbit. There was also an enormous wardrobe and an empty porcelain tub. The windows, to Thea's dismay, had been barred over.

"My name is Elizabeth, and this is my granddaughter, Millie." The younger girl drew a bath but said nothing. Thea frowned and told her that she didn't need her to do that, but Elizabeth shook her head. "She doesn't know what else to do. She grew up in this castle as a servant."

"That doesn't mean she has to be one. She's a human being." Thea heard the anger in her voice and saw Elizabeth smile slightly.

"Yes, she is a human being, and therefore, a servant."

Thea walked to the window and stared out at the decaying kingdom. She wanted to bring life back to these lands, but how could she if she was locked away?

She asked herself what Kieran or Iris might do in this situation, but they probably would have never allowed themselves to be captured to begin with. She'd left their protection and decided to do this on her own, so now she would have to.

"I knew your mother," Elizabeth said, drawing Thea's attention back into the room. "You are brave, like her, to want to free us. Just know that when the time comes, we'll be at your side.

Even those of us who don't remember what freedom tastes like."
She looked toward her granddaughter and the steaming tub.

Thea walked to stand by Elizabeth and took her hand. She
wanted nothing more than to live up to the expectations that
others had of her, but she needed to figure out how she would
survive this. She watched as Millie motioned for her to come to
the bath and allowed Elizabeth to help her undress by unlacing
her black waistcoat. The last thing she wanted was for them to
see weakness, but she winced as they stripped the clothing from
her bruised body. She had been sore from her training with
Kieran, but the beatings the ogres had given her on her way in
had left her sides black and blue. She heard Millie gasp, seeing
her injuries. Her hand flew up to her mouth and tears welled in
her eyes.

"No, no, don't cry," Thea blurted, feeling embarrassed as she
stood naked in front of them. "I'm fine, really."

Millie seemed to take her words as a command and quickly
turned away to hide her tears. Thea sighed in response and
winced as her broken rib shifted.

Elizabeth tossed Thea's filthy clothes into a sack and left
them by the door. She said she would wash them for her, and
Thea gave a grateful nod. Dried blood coated her lip and legs
where scrapes and cuts had semi-healed. She walked toward the
tub and rested her hand on Millie's shoulder.

"Thank you for the bath, Millie. I think it will help me heal."

Elizabeth had disappeared out of the room for a moment as
Thea lowered herself painfully into the tub, but she returned
quickly with a small drawstring bag of salts that she poured into
the steaming water.

"This will help with your injuries. It will not heal them, but it
will strengthen you." Elizabeth looked at Thea's bracelet and
frowned. "Don't you want to take that off?"

Thea shook her head and lowered her arm into the water, as
if hiding the bracelet from her. She hadn't used its magic yet,

but she didn't want to be separated from it. She imagined she would need the extra strength soon and didn't want to be left without it. Sinking deeper into the water, Thea let herself relax for a moment. She didn't feel frightened of these servants. After all, they were some of the people she was here to help. She worried that Amara or the king might return to take her away, though.

"He'll give you time to think," said Millie. Thea's eyes had closed, but she immediately opened them to look at the young girl. "I overheard him talking about the ritual—"

"Hush!" Elizabeth scolded, smacking Millie's hand. "You know better than to be snooping in the king's business."

"But, Grandmother—"

"No."

"I need to know," Thea interrupted, reminding them that she was there. They both turned to her, Elizabeth looking angry. "I can't help you if I don't know what I'm getting myself into."

"As stubborn as your mother, I swear!" Elizabeth crossed her arms, staring at both of them as if they were disobedient children. Thea lifted her chin a little higher, wishing she looked more like a queen and less like a beat-up child.

"I can't help if I don't know what I'm trying to stop."

"He's figured out a way to free her," Millie said quickly, ignoring the glare from her grandmother.

"Whom?" Thea asked. She gripped the sides of the tub and pulled herself into a sitting position. Whatever Elizabeth had put into the tub, it was helping. She already felt less achy.

"Morrigan."

The name was a whisper on Millie's lips, but Thea heard it loud and clear. She knew that, according to legend, her sister, Ainé, had imprisoned Morrigan to protect the land of Faerie from her wrath. Ainé loved the humans and wanted to protect them from her sister's jealousy. However, this meant that both Goddesses had been imprisoned in another realm. If Ainé had been the one who had sealed the doorway to that realm, then how did Thea's father plan to open it?

"He can't free her... Ainé is the only one who can open the door." Thea said the words as if they were the truth, but was there not always a loophole in stories like this? Hadn't Kieran called her that loophole?

"Through you," Elizabeth said as she rubbed her arms.

"What do I have to do with some ancient prison, though?"

"He believes you are a direct descendent of Ainé." Millie finally met Thea's eyes as she spoke. Her own gaze was full of hope, a deep longing for whatever Thea could offer them. Thea, on the other hand, felt bewildered.

How could she be a direct descendent of a Goddess? That made no sense at all.

And yet, had they not all been wondering why the Goddess could speak to her directly without her being a seer? And had she not asked herself a million times why Ainé gifted her with control over all four elements? She frowned as it began to make more sense, but she didn't know how that helped anything the king wanted to do.

"If the rumors are true, then it seems he has a plan to use your blood in a ritual during Yule, the winter solstice."

"My blood? Why not just kill me now then?"

"I don't know." Elizabeth frowned and then grabbed a towel for Thea, holding it up. Thea climbed out of the tub carefully and wrapped herself in the fabric's warmth, trying to take in all the recent information they had given her. Kieran's mother had known Malachi wanted to free Morrigan using her, and that information had caused Thea's mother to send her away. Was this the reason they had not allowed her stay in Ivandor? Because somehow she was a direct descendent of a goddess?

Thea panicked, realizing Kieran and Iris knew nothing of the king's plan to free Morrigan. If Thea hadn't come here, they would have been in the dark. However, if Thea hadn't come here, they also wouldn't be at risk of the Goddess of all Evil being released in the first place. She tried to steady her shallow breathing. Her lungs felt as if they were on fire, but if she was going to survive this, she needed to fight through the pain.

"He must need something from me that he can't take by force," she said quietly, looking around the room. For a moment, she had allowed herself to think that some part of her father still cared about her. However, now she saw the truth. This bedroom was a ruse. He wanted her to believe this was her home because he needed something from her. He wanted her comfortable and unguarded so that he could take what was necessary. She didn't know why it hurt her to realize this, but it did. She supposed the thought of a biological father caring about her was too good to be true. Thea thought of Kieran and Iris; Ethel, Mirielle and Mica; and she thought of the challenge she faced. She couldn't allow Morrigan to be released, but first she needed to determine exactly what her father needed from her and how far he was willing to go to get it.

"There's clothing in the wardrobe for you. It should be about your size, I hope," Elizabeth said. She motioned for Millie to leave the room, but she met Thea's eyes before she left. "Remember what I said. We'll be at your side when the time comes, my queen."

Elizabeth bowed her head low and then disappeared from the room, leaving Thea stunned. She appreciated the fact that the humans would fight with her, but she didn't know if that would be enough. Did a few humans and one untrained Faerie stand any chance against a powerful king and his evil army of followers? Her logic told her the probabilities that she did not wish to hear, so she focused her attention on the wardrobe instead. However, as she opened it up, a new sense of dread settled over her on seeing what was inside.

"Goddess above—how in hell am I supposed to fight in a damn dress?"

CHAPTER 20

When a centaur knocked on her bedroom door to inform her that King Malachi invited her to dine with him, Thea was wearing her muddy leather clothing once more. The centaur seemed surprised by her appearance, but said nothing as he stepped aside for her to pass. She'd stared at the dresses in the wardrobe for nearly an hour trying to picture herself defending anyone while wearing one of them. This led to the decision to put her dirty clothes back on. She'd done her best to scrape off the dried blood and mud from them, then tamed her unruly hair into a neat bun on top of her head. The rest of her time had been spent in meditation, trying to reach Ainé, but by the time the knock sounded on her door she'd all but given up on the Goddess' help.

The centaur led her to a set of double doors, where Thea thanked him and received a stomp of a hoof in response. He stormed off, seeming insulted by her gratitude, and Thea entered the dining hall with a look of bewilderment on her face. Several human servants set the table inside with a luxurious amount of food. The last time Thea had seen anything close to that amount of food had been her Thanksgiving with her adoptive parents. Her mother had cooked two turkeys, because she couldn't decide which recipe to use, and they'd had enough food for the entire neighborhood. Her heart ached at the thought of her mother and what she would have given to speak with her just one more time before her plan to come to Ireland would possibly get her killed. Instead, she faced her biological father, who sat at the end of the table looking at her with disappointment.

"The dresses didn't fit you?" he asked. Amara sat on his left with her hands folded neatly in her lap. She wore a purple gown that matched the newly forming bruises on her face; it made her look far younger.

"I'm more comfortable in my own clothing, thank you." Thea knew the king felt the forcefulness of her speech, but she didn't care. She stood in the doorway, examining each exit carefully while she waited for him to tell her what he wanted. She figured this was not just a family dinner to make up for all the family dinners she'd missed.

There were only two doors in this hall. One being the set of double doors she'd come in through, and the other, she assumed led to the kitchens, because that was where the servants were bringing food from.

"Come, sit at my right," King Malachi finally said, motioning to the seat on the other side of him. "We have much to discuss. But first, you must be starving."

Thea walked to the seat he'd indicated and sat, placing a napkin across her lap as the servants piled food onto all three of their plates. Each of the humans was malnourished, but they didn't look at the table with envy or hunger. They merely placed the food down as quickly as possible before returning to the kitchens. King Malachi never thanked them or even acknowledged their presence, but Thea continuously did, which seemed to make them all even more nervous.

"So, it's true that humans raised you?" Thea had wondered

what the first topic of their dinner conversation would be, but this was not what she'd expected. She looked up at King Malachi—her father, she reminded herself. His nose had scrunched up a little as he spoke.

"Yes, I had two wonderful, loving, *human* parents."

Thea watched as the king's hand, which had been about to cut through a piece of beef, tightened around his knife. He made a noise that was most like a grunt, and Amara said nothing.

"Tell me why I'm here." Thea hadn't touched her food, nor did she plan on eating. For all she knew, he could have put some type of potion or poison into it. Amara glanced up in surprise at Thea's sudden change in tone, then looked at her father, who had stopped mid-bite.

"This is your home," the king said through tight lips.

"No, it's not."

"I told you, Father—" Amara stood, looking angry, but was cut off sharply.

"Silence, Amara."

The entire room fell silent and Thea folded her hands in her lap. She had no intention of making this easy on them. Thankfully, she was one step ahead in knowledge, now that she knew about the ritual, but she needed more information before she could figure out the next step in her plan. The staring contest between herself and her father was enough to make anyone want to scream. It stretched on for what seemed like ages, and while Amara half-stood at the table, Thea remained calm and seated.

The king set his fork and knife down, not daring to back down from the visible power struggle between them. He looked as if he were contemplating his next words very carefully, rolling them over on this tongue, but at that same moment, a raven soared in through an open window near the ceiling. It must have once been a skylight, for otherwise Thea could not think of any logical reason to have a window so far out of reach.

The large bird landed on the king's shoulder, the same way it had done to Amara in the village, when she was torturing Marcus. The difference was that the bird did not dig her talons into the king's shoulder. Apparently, pain was not needed to make the king obey. The raven's yellow eyes stared Thea down, raising the hairs on the back of her arms and neck. For a moment, she just stared, her mouth slightly open as a vision flooded her memory, a vision of two girls playing by a lakeside.

"Morrigan," Thea said, her tone cool and collected. She didn't doubt her deduction, and the bird cawed in approval; it sounded amused. Amara lowered herself back into her chair, appearing to shrink away at the sight of the Goddess of Death in her imprisoned form. Thea's entire body reacted to this new danger. She examined her exits once more, now adding the high above window to the mix, as impossible as it would be to reach.

The bird's eyes twinkled, a smirk hidden behind their golden glow. Thea glared, gripping the arms of her chair a little harder. The darkness Amara had commanded was nothing compared to the shadows that now stretched out from behind the king's chair. He glowered as they crept along the floor beneath the table, tangling themselves around Thea's ankles. It took every bit of control she had not to scream at the curdling feeling their touch brought to her skin.

"I have tried to be kind to you, dear daughter," the king said with a newfound confidence. "But you are only a child; I owe you no explanation for my actions."

For some reason, this angered Thea more than anything else he'd said. She'd been called a lot of things over the past few weeks, even over her life, but a child was something she was not. She'd travelled across realms to come to this point, and he underestimated everything about her, including her age. She rose from her chair, summoning as much of that raw confidence that she saw in her father's eyes as she could. She thought of her mother's sacrifice and of Kieran. She thought of all the reasons she needed to stop her father from what he planned to do. As she stood, his eyes widened and Morrigan flapped her wings, as if ready to soar toward Thea.

"You don't frighten me, *Father*. You may bully your youngest daughter into doing your bidding," she glanced at Amara, whose eyes looked like they might bulge out of her head, "but I am not a child; I am the Queen of Ivandor."

A redness burned across the king's face, and it reminded Thea once more of their relationship, recognizing that same scarlet shadow that often plagued her own facade. He stood then, staring down at her, and Morrigan soared into the air with what sounded as close to a laugh as a crow's caw could come. The king's fist slammed down, sending his plate to the floor, and the few humans disappeared quicker than light from the room. Amara had lost all confidence that she'd shown with Thea alone, now quivering in the face of her father's anger, fearful that it would turn on her.

"How dare you—"

"No. How dare you! How dare you stand where she stood and pretend you are worthy of that crown?" Thea spat the bile that had risen to her throat from her mouth. Her anger surprised even her, but the more she imagined what her mother had gone through to keep her safe, the more she hated her father. The darkness danced beneath the surface of her skin, but she refused to let it out. Instead, her anger boiled her blood. Her fingers twitched, and when Morrigan dove at her, she held up a hand to set an invisible wall of air between herself and the bird. The raven gave an angry squawk as it tried to recuperate its flight pattern, and the king's eyes turned on Amara.

"You told me she was an earth user." Thea had never heard a voice sound so animalistic. Amara just stared with wide eyes at them both, stumbling over her words.

"Oh, I am." Thea smiled, finally feeling like she had the upper hand. So she'd been wrong. Her father really did not understand what she was capable of. She steadied her stance the way Kieran had taught her to when preparing to face an enemy and planted her feet into the ground. She wasn't about to stick around here any longer than she needed to, nor give them a chance to react. The king's reaction was slow and confused, giving Thea only moments before the castle guards realized what was happening.

I only have one shot at this, so don't let me screw it up.

The prayer floated into the abyss as she crouched, placing the palms of her hands against the wooden castle floors and reached for the earth beneath the surface. She knew it was there, even if long forgotten, and soon the roots of plants as old as the land itself sprang from the cracking tiles. They shot upward beneath the table, lifting it into the air as plates of food and goblets of drinks clattered and splashed around them. Thea watched the king stumble backwards as the ground quaked beneath them and smirked as a vine wrapped around the base of Amara's chair, dragging her toward the kitchen doors.

"That's impossible," King Malachi said, regaining his composure. Morrigan screeched in the air above, diving at Thea, who quickly rolled her body across the floor to dodge her razor-sharp beak. She didn't want to know what that would feel like piercing her skin. She had enough scrapes and bruises right now. The shadows, which had scattered in the chaos and loss of focus from the king, returned to him, rising nearly to the ceiling, and Thea knew she needed to decide before the king did. She could not fight them all, but what was it Kieran had said when they'd first started training?

There is no shame in running. Sometimes that is all that will save your life. She'd rolled her eyes at him for that, thinking that running was an absolute waste of time when she could learn to control her magic. Well, maybe running was exactly what she needed to do.

She glanced back toward the doorway, aware that the king was calling for his guards and screaming at Amara to get up and stop Thea. It was just like her father to want a sixteen-year-old girl to fight a battle he was too scared to fight himself.

Thea glimpsed the guards coming in through the double doors, but it was either take them on, or the king and Amara, who stood between her and the kitchen. She stopped debating and pushed her feet as quickly as they would carry her toward the only plausible exit. The king screamed and scrambled as roots tangled around his ankles, and Amara dove out of the way just in time to escape a large branch's grip on her arm.

The guards in the doorway looked baffled by the scene inside the dining room, but they quickly discovered Thea was the new threat the king had summoned them to face. Both guards were Faerie, and Thea figured the king only trusted his own kind to protect him. They each had wings that made Thea's heart ache for Kieran, but she had no time for emotions right now. It was fight or flight, and flight was the only option she had. She breathed hard as she barreled towards the two Faeries, watching their eyes widen in surprise at her lack of hesitation. Air and earth were really the only elements Thea knew how to use in combat, although she wished desperately that she could just make fire shoot out of her hands, knowing full well that was not how it worked. The magic it had taken to control the earth below her had been enough to bring a strain to Thea's energy. She focused on the bracelet on her arm, not quite sure how to use it, but saw the red gem begin to glow in response to just her thoughts. She immediately felt her strength returning to her and sent a tornado of air toward the Faeries. They had their swords drawn and dove out of the way of her attack, and that left the doorway wide open.

As Thea neared the door, she felt a sharp pain scraping into her left shoulder and let out a piercing scream. Morrigan had finally hit her mark, digging her talons into the soft part of Thea's shoulder. Thea's right arm flew up to protect her face from the bird's pecking beak, but she felt the contact it made with her skin and the rush of warm blood.

"No! She needs to be alive!" the king yelled, sounding closer than Thea liked. A set of small, stiff hands wrapped around her wrists, and Thea turned her head to face her sister as she tugged her arms behind her back. Both physical pain and emotional distress overwhelmed her as she saw the hope of her escape fading away. She needed to get to that door. She'd even thought she had a chance. For a moment, she'd had hope, but now, as Amara pinned her hands and the bird screeched in her ear, all she could feel was hope fading away.

"Alive for what!?" Her voice was not her own; it was violent and pained. She thought of everyone she'd just failed, everyone who was counting on her to stop this madness. "Amara, release me!"

She glared at her half-sister, but realized then that something had shifted in her eyes. She looked less frightening when she was terrified of her father. It made Thea feel sorry for her, despite the tight grip she had.

"Just do what he says," Amara whispered in a way that Thea was sure no one else heard. Morrigan finally retracted her talons from Thea's shoulder, and blood pooled onto the floor around them. Thea felt dizzy, although she was unsure if that was from the loss of blood or the magic she'd used. The bracelet had stopped glowing, and Thea knew its magic was gone too. It had given her the moment of strength she'd needed, but she had still not been strong enough to escape. Just like she hadn't been strong enough to save Marcus, and would not be strong enough to save the rest of her people.

The door closed in front of Thea, her only chance at freedom disappearing with the click of a lock. The Faerie guards remained on the inside of the doors now, looking slightly worse for wear than they had before Thea hit them with the tornado. Amara turned Thea toward their father once more, leaving the door to freedom behind them. The king clenched his hands into fists and stared at both his daughters with the same hatred, as if Amara too had just struck him with magic and tried to escape. Amara shuddered under the gaze. Thea's limbs weighed her down as she slumped slightly against Amara. Every breath that she took felt like fire seared her lungs. She feared her broken rib had punctured something inside of her, as she spit bloodied saliva onto the ground beside her.

"I am done with your games," the king said. He reached a hand up, running it through his graying hair. "I have an offer for you."

His eyes met Thea's now, a smirk sparkling within his gaze. He motioned to the guards behind Thea, and suddenly Amara was also being held in custody. She let out a scream of surprise and turned her hateful eyes on the Faerie, but there was no way she could fight them off with her hands pinned behind her, so instead she returned her questioning gaze to her father.

"You want your boyfriend back, right? The human one?" He tapped his fingers against the wood of the chair. Thea's back straightened, her vision refocusing on the world around her. She knew Marcus was dead, but her father speaking of him brought the darkness back to the surface. She could kill them all. She knew she could. If she just let herself taste that power again. Maybe she could even control it, she tried to convince herself, now that she knew the risks. "What if I told you I could bring him back to you?"

"That's impossible," Thea said, although her voice betrayed her as she wondered if it really was. The king smiled, knowing he'd captured her attention, and motioned toward the raven who had settled back upon his shoulder. Thea's blood dripped from her talons.

"Not for us, it isn't." He glanced at Amara with a nearly apologetic smile. "It will cost us, though."

Amara looked between King Malachi and Thea with a terrified gaze. Thea didn't want to meet her eyes. She continued to stare at the king, observing his expression.

"Cost *us* what?" she asked carefully.

"Morrigan can give me the power to bring him back, but you will need to agree to bring her back first. For that, I would need your blood." He held up his hands when Thea protested. "Just a small amount, given by your own will."

"I don't see how this costs you anything," Thea said with a raised eyebrow. Her arms ached from being pinned behind her back. All she wanted was to lie down and sleep, but she couldn't show that weakness, not when she was about to find out why she was really here. She glanced at Amara, who was still being held against her will, and at all the other curious faces in the room. A few humans had returned, now that the commotion had settled down. Morrigan rested with thoughtful eyes on the king's shoulder, and the king himself kept his distance from both his daughters, hiding behind two more Faerie guards who had arrived while Thea had been busy fighting off the raven. Thea saw his cowardice for what it was. He knew Thea was powerful but not powerful enough to take on an army by herself. Still, he played his role from a safe distance.

"Life is delicate. I cannot just restore one life without taking another." He looked at Amara directly. "And with this spell, dark magic took a life. Therefore, we would exchange the slayer for the slain."

"Father, you can't be serious!"

Even Thea was surprised by how easily the king offered to exchange his daughter's life, especially the only daughter who cared about him, to achieve his aim.

"It's for the greater good, Amara. I cannot bring Morrigan back without your sister's blood, which is why I had you kill the boy to begin with."

Thea couldn't believe her ears. Her father, *their* father, had set Amara up like a lamb to the slaughter. By the look on her sister's face, Amara was just as stunned. Her hands shook behind her and tears swelled in her eyes. For the first time, Thea saw that she had crystal-blue eyes beyond that red rim of darkness. The blue glistened when she cried.

"Don't waste your tears. Faerie will honor your sacrifice. You'll be a legend!"

Faerie, Thea thought. *Not him... he didn't care if she died.*

Thea's fingers tightened into fists as she thought of what the king was proposing. He wanted Thea to kill Amara just to bring Marcus back. She wondered if her decision would have been different on the day Amara murdered Marcus, but she didn't even contemplate the choice now. Thea's eyes settled on Amara, who suddenly was the spitting image of her mother, and asked herself how she'd even missed it before. Iris trusted Thea to protect her daughter, and Thea planned to keep her promise.

"I won't do it," she said calmly, her gaze finding her sister's. For a moment, Amara looked panicked, but her panic faded as they looked at each other. "I forgive you, Amara."

The words were like a foreign language on her tongue, because in all honesty, how could she forgive someone who had murdered her first love? She didn't know how to explain the logic behind it, but she knew it was the right thing to do.

Tears spilled down Amara's cheeks, and Thea felt like her eyes were growing wet as well. She wanted to reach for her sister and tell her that things would be okay, that she would protect her, but it was unlikely with her arms bound and energy depleted. Amara's lips opened to say something, but the king let out an angry scream, throwing the chair he'd been gripping across the floor. Everyone in the room, including Thea and Amara, winced at the sudden movement. Morrigan soared back toward the ceiling, no longer safe on the king's arm.

"Stupid children," the king growled, striding toward them. Amara looked terrified, but Thea held herself upright and dared not look away from him.

"Thea, he has Kieran," Amara whispered just loud enough for Thea to hear before the king got close enough. The guards surely heard, but they didn't dare get in the middle of the royal mess Thea had started. Thea turned to look at her sister in surprise, the words hardly registering. She saw her father's angry body coming toward them both, shadows flailing out around him. He was out of control. Perhaps he'd kill her now and they would never have to worry about Morrigan's release.

"How?" Thea asked Amara.

"Morrigan is the one who gave your seer the vision. It was her idea to give Kieran the potion in the first place—so that Father could use him as leverage. He has spies everywhere, Thea. T-that's why I took you to the village... to stall you so that they could bring Kieran in. I'm so—"

"Silence!"

Thea's heart was racing. King Malachi had reached them and his hand now gripped Amara's throat. The guard who had been holding her released her immediately, stepping backwards, and the king lifted his daughter into the air. Her feet flailed as she gasped for breath, the shadows engulfing her.

"Let her go!" Thea screamed, and the king turned his gaze on her, dropping Amara to the ground, where she did not move.

"I tried to give you what you wanted. I tried to save your human toy. You are as ungrateful as your mother ever was."

"My mother was the queen, as will I be. You are an imposter in a land that doesn't belong to you. You curse it with darkness, and you're dooming it to the hands of death herself!" Thea spit at him, her fingers twitching behind her back. Seeing Amara's limp form on the ground made her angry, but not nearly as angry as the fact that the king had Kieran.

The king's smile returned, although with a new sense of wickedness to it. He strode to stand in front of her, his breath smelling like spoiled wine. He nodded for his guard to let go of Thea, seeing the exhaustion on her face.

"Guards, bring me the unconscious fool. My daughter is ready to lose another man in her life. Soon, all she will have left is her dear old father." He laughed, and a few of the guards left the room. Thea's heart pounded against her chest. She needed a weapon. She needed something, because her magic could not get her through this fight alone.

If ever I needed you, it would be now, Thea prayed, wishing desperately for a response from Ainé, but none came. Thea counted the guards in the room. There were six Faeries, three of which had wings, and all of which had swords. Two armed centaurs stood outside the double doors; Thea had seen them before being pulled away from her freedom. Most importantly, though, she noted at least a dozen humans who came from the kitchens throughout her time in the dining hall. She realized they bore no weapons, but she thought of Elizabeth's words to her earlier, hoping they would stand by her side if the moment came. Thea knew she couldn't count on everyone to fight with her, but she couldn't give up hope that they had a chance to survive this. She glanced at Amara's unconscious body for only a moment, because the sound of the doors opening again behind her made her entire body stiffen.

The sweet scent of nature and sweat tickled her nose familiarly as the wind brushed against her skin. Without even seeing him, Thea knew without a doubt that Amara had not been lying. She controlled her reaction to his presence, but as the guards dragged his limp body to the king and tossed him on the floor in front of Thea, her eyes gave her away. His dark hair stuck up in strange places, like it did sometimes when he returned from the skies. His wings, which were bent uncomfortably around him, seemed lifeless. His face was at peace, though, more so than Thea had ever seen it. She wanted to go to him, to pull him into her lap and tell him how stupid and sorry she was, but she didn't have time. The king drew his sword and pressed the tip to the left side of Kieran's chest.

"No!" Thea's scream echoed through the dining hall. Her eyes widened as she looked at Kieran's helpless body at the end of her father's weapon. She lunged but the guard at her side's steel grip around her arm stopped her.

"Give me your blood, and he lives." The king smiled, pressing his sword down against Kieran's chest until the fabric of his shirt tore and a slight trickle of red liquid dripped to the floor. Kieran did not move, even at the touch of the sword. Thea, on the other hand, cried out, her entire body trembling as she fought against the guard whose hold she could not break.

"Let him go or I will kill you!" Thea said, her voice low and dangerous. *Ainé, please,* she basically screamed in her head. Tears stung at the back of her eyes but didn't fall, and despite the exhaustion she felt, darkness was threatening to claw its way out of her. The image of Kieran lying lifeless in front of her the way Marcus had flashed through her mind, and as the king pressed the sword deeper into Kieran's flesh, she flinched. She begged and begged Ainé for help, but if the Goddess would not show herself now, she had no choice left.

"Give me your blood, or you both die tonight." The king's voice was calm, and the raven that was the Goddess of Death herself landed on Kieran's abdomen with taunting eyes, pecking at his clothing, uncaring of whether she was shredding his flesh along with it. More blood spilled.

"I'll do it," Thea blurted out, still fighting against the Faerie guard. The king retracted his sword, just slightly, with a look that made Thea want to fall to her knees and bawl. She couldn't lose Kieran the way she'd lost Marcus, no matter what the cost was. She thought of Iris and Ethel, wondering what they would have done in this situation. They would have known Kieran would rather die than be the reason Morrigan returned, but Thea couldn't let him go. She curled her fingers into fists as the king motioned to a human to bring him a golden goblet from a serving table across the room. Thea watched as the human child, no older than Ethel, walked toward them with shaking hands. He looked at Thea with eyes that asked what her plan was, eyes that trusted her to do the right thing. Shame settled over her.

Whatever happens, we will stop Morrigan—together. Thea knew Kieran couldn't hear her, but the reassurance was just as much for herself as the boy handed the goblet to her father and hurried out of the room. Thea felt all eyes on her the guard released his grip and handed her a dagger—the weapon she had been hoping for—but the sword still threatened her mate's life. *I will always choose you, no matter the cost, no matter the consequence. I am yours, and you are mine, forever.*

The words rang through her head as the blade slid painfully across the soft part of her palm. Blood dripped into the goblet, slowly at first, and then more quickly. King Malachi watched with an anxious gaze, Morrigan resting perfectly still on his shoulder, and as soon as enough blood was in the cup, he snatched it from her, pushing her down to the floor beside Kieran.

Thea crawled to him, ignoring the betrayed gazes from the kitchen doorway, and felt the tears streaking her face. The king whispered something to his guards, and Thea pressed her bloody hand into Kieran's.

"I'm so sorry," she whispered, pressing her lips to Kieran's cheek as her head fell against his chest in a sob.

She had failed everyone. When she looked back toward the king, the weight of that failure felt unbearable. He was whispering something into the goblet using a language Thea didn't understand. It sounded Gaelic, but not quite like anything she'd ever heard before, possibly an older version.

Engrossed in whatever spell he was casting, Thea did not immediately realize that Kieran's wings twitched.

CHAPTER 21

KIERAN DIDN'T OPEN HIS EYES IMMEDIATELY. HE FELT THE STICKY, warm fluid between his hand and Thea's, but he didn't dare let King Malachi know he was awake. Ainé had warned him that this might happen, but now that Thea had woken him, he couldn't blow the only chance they had.

"I'm so sorry," he heard her say, and wanted to say something back. He wanted to tell her how ridiculously foolish she was not to confide in him or trust him. He wanted to be angry with her for nearly getting herself killed. Most of all, though, he wanted to pull her into his arms and take her away to safety. Their lives were in danger at this very moment, and if Ainé was right, the lives of everyone in Faerie were at risk too.

"Thea," he said in the lowest whisper he could manage. His wings shifted, just slightly, and he tightened his fingers around hers. He noticed the second it took her to react, as if she couldn't believe what she felt, but she reacted. Her hand, which had been holding his tightly, loosened just in the slightest. He squeezed again and dared to open his eyes. The light took him a moment to adjust to, but he soon saw her gray gaze staring back at him full of tears. He did his best to communicate the importance of silence to her, but she seemed too shocked to say anything anyway. Her mouth fell open, just slightly, her bottom lip sticking out farther than her top lip. She brushed her thumb across the back of his hand, and he knew she understood exactly how quiet she needed to be.

"Kieran," she mouthed his name, but it had the same effect on him as if she'd said it aloud. It said everything he needed to hear and more, but right now, they needed a plan. Slowly, he examined as much of the room as he physically could without moving a muscle. He saw the high window and chandelier and knew the exact room they were in. Despite the many years away, he'd grown up in this castle and knew it backwards and forwards. He even knew that if one were to go through the kitchens, there would be an exit which led to the gardens, which were only a brief run to the stables. This was his best plan of escape.

However, the look of absolute dread on Thea's face told him he'd missed something very important. She glanced over to his left, and he dared to follow her gaze. He saw Amara, crumpled onto the floor, and then looked back at Thea.

"We can't leave her," she whispered, and Kieran held his breath hoping no one heard. He agreed with Thea; they couldn't leave Iris' daughter behind—no matter what she'd done. However, he didn't know how he was supposed to get an unconscious teenager and a weakened Thea out of there alone.

"There's a way out through the kitchens," he said back as quietly as possible. He heard the guards by the door shift uncomfortably, but they said nothing. Thea nodded her head, just slightly, and he waited until the guards focused back on Malachi before making his move. Kieran exhaled the breath he'd been holding, letting the air bring life back into his burning lungs and reached for Thea's hand. They were on their feet in the span of one swift movement, facing King Malachi.

"Get Amara and go," he told Thea before anyone could react

to their movement. Thankfully, she listened and ran straight for Amara, pulling her small, limp form up against her side. It was clear carrying Amara's weight was a struggle, but she'd have to manage. The king had spun around, a golden goblet in his hand, and now stared at them with wide, angry eyes. The guards behind him moved, and Kieran observed it all in slow motion, focusing his senses. He'd trained for this. He'd prepared. And yet, it all felt more real with Thea in danger too. She stared at him with wide, questioning eyes, and he knew she didn't want to run.

"Remember your promise."

"I'm coming back for you." Thea said the words just as the guards reached them. Kieran turned, spreading his wings wide to block Thea from their oncoming attacks, and saw her beginning to drag Amara toward the kitchens, where a few curious human eyes watched. Kieran faced the two winged Faeries with a small smile, relieved Thea was leaving, but knowing full well that she'd return.

"Kill them all," he heard the king command. Kieran had no weapons, but a small dagger glistened on the ground, bloody and forgotten. He snatched it up and tucked his wings, rolling to the side just as the first guard lunged at him with his sword drawn. A loud screeching noise filled the room as a raven soared into the air, and meeting its eyes, Kieran knew that Morrigan was with them in her imprisoned form. He put the pieces together quickly enough to realize the ritual had already begun, but the most important thing he could do now was get Thea and Amara out of here safely.

The second guard lunged at him, but he dodged again, sticking his dagger in the soft crease of the guard's armor. The guard let out a cry of pain as blood spurted from the open wound, and backed away from Kieran, gripping his side. The other guard lunged, catching Kieran's arm with his sword, but the cut was only a scratch. Kieran spun on his heels to see that

Thea was safely out of the room and then launched himself into the air, the guard close behind him.

The king screamed furiously as Morrigan dove back toward him. Kieran sensed he needed to keep the raven away from the goblet, but he didn't know how, as more guards entered the dining hall. He dodged attack after attack, finally acquiring a sword from one guard, but the exhaustion was overwhelming. He'd been asleep for days, but his body felt stiff. He used magic as little as possible until the ogres and centaurs flooded the room. He prayed Thea got away.

ELIZABETH AND MILLIE met Thea in the kitchens as soon as she stumbled through the doors. She didn't dare glance behind her to see if she was being followed. Now that the king had her blood, he had no use for her or Amara; they were expendable, and his focus would center on completing the ritual, not stopping them. Thea needed to get Amara to safety so that she could return to Kieran's side. She thought of Mirielle's prophecy, dread filling her stomach. Amara's unconscious form weighed her down, but she knew exactly what she needed to do.

"Where are the stables?" she demanded. The sound of swords clashing and screams filled her ears, taunting and torturing her. Kieran was back there, fighting alone to give her time to leave, but she refused to leave him alone. It was her fault they were in this situation, and if anything happened to him, that would be her fault too. Elizabeth glared at Amara. "I made a promise that I intend to keep. I assure you I will punish her for what she has done, but for now, she is under my protection. Now, will you help us or not?"

Despite Thea's exhaustion, she raised her head higher, hearing the note of authority in her voice. Millie glanced at her grandmother with wide eyes, and Elizabeth bowed her head slightly. Thea's anger outweighed her apology for the harshness of her words. Her father had threatened too many people she loved, and she was ready to put an end to it, no matter how defeated she felt. She owed it to everyone she loved to stop him, or die trying.

"I'll take you to the stables," Millie finally said, bringing a sigh of relief to Thea's lips.

"You two." Thea looked at two young men who had stopped kneading bread to stare at the commotion happening in their kitchen. "Do you know how to fight?"

They looked unsure of their answer.

"Don't let anyone follow us," Elizabeth finished Thea's thoughts, and the two nodded in agreement, grabbing kitchen utensils that would apparently be their weapons. One held a kitchen knife, while the other picked up a large pan. Both looked fearful, but Thea didn't have time to worry about the innocent lives she was putting at risk. She needed to command whatever army she had and put a stop to this, or else they'd all be dead.

"Show me the stables."

Thea, Elizabeth, and Millie hurried out of a side door, thankfully unfollowed by anyone. They shifted Amara's weight between them, and she stirred.

"What's happening?" she asked in a mumble. Her eyes blinked open slowly, but she did not shift her weight away from Thea's arms. "Where are you taking me?" A note of fear echoed behind her words.

"You're going to go for help," Thea told her without meeting her eyes. She noticed the looks of disbelief on both Elizabeth and Millie's faces. "You're going to your mother."

"I can't..." Amara started to say, trying to get out of Thea's arms as they neared the stables. Outside was quieter without the sounds of battle, but it made Thea uneasy. If there were no soldiers out here, that meant they'd all gone into the castle, and Kieran was in trouble.

"You can, and you will." Thea grabbed Amara's face, turning her to look at her directly, and stopped walking. "This is how you redeem yourself, do you understand? Your mother asked me to protect you. I'm doing that. But I need you to go to her and tell her that we are in trouble. Kieran and I might die tonight, but if the rest of the resistance comes after us, maybe a difference can be made before it's too late."

"You expect to die?" Amara asked with wide eyes. Thea could see the tiredness behind her eyes, but for once, she saw the girl there. The child who felt abandoned and unloved. She saw the evil she'd committed, but like Ainé had said, she saw hope too. "Run with me."

"I won't leave Kieran behind. This is my fault." Thea opened the stable doors, releasing Amara, and then paused with a curious tilt of her head at the familiar tingle that crept up her spine.

"Faylon?" she called into the darkness of the stable.

As soon as she said his name a door burst open and the large black unicorn came pounding out against the cries of the three stable boys who stood tending to other horses. Apparently Faylon wasn't *required* to follow her orders. She didn't think he'd ever even left Ivandor, but she was grateful to see him now.

"You're a fool on a suicide mission. Once Morrigan returns she will kill us all. We need to run." Amara's voice was almost begging now, but her eyes stared at Faylon with awe.

"I'm prepared die, but I have to do everything I can to stop Morrigan. If I don't, then what kind of queen am I?"

"An alive one…" Amara mumbled, and Faylon gave a snort.

"Take her to Iris," Thea told the stallion, petting his mane gently and kissing his warm nose. She felt the tears swelling in her eyes, knowing she would likely never see her familiar again, and saw a similar glint to his own. "And this time, actually go. They'll know she isn't lying when they see you."

Faylon rested his forehead against Thea's and no one spoke. Even the stable boys stood staring with their mouths agape as Thea closed her eyes.

I wish we had more time together, but I am forever grateful for your friendship and loyalty, Thea thought, knowing he would hear. A single tear shed from Faylon's eyes.

You are brave. You are strong. You are our queen.

Thea pulled her head back to look into Faylon's eyes once more, wiped her eyes, and stood straight.

"Millie, go with them," Elizabeth said suddenly. "Death is coming to Ivandor, and I promised your mother I would keep you safe." She wrapped her arms around her granddaughter.

"No—"

"Yes. Ethan, get her a horse." She waved at one of the stable boys, who immediately went to fetch a horse for Millie. Thea nodded her understanding and helped Amara onto Faylon.

"Ride quickly and silently—you are this land's last hope."

"I'm sorry for my part in this," Amara said, twisting her fingers into Faylon's mane. "And I'm sorry for your friend."

Thea didn't reply. She'd already told Amara she forgave her for Marcus, but that didn't mean she was ready to talk about it. Especially since there were much more important things to deal with right now. She gave Faylon a small pat and he lunged out of the stable, nearly leaving Amara behind. She gripped him tightly just before they disappeared into the dusk.

"Goodbye, sister," Thea whispered, turning her attention back to Millie, who had just mounted another horse. "Go to my friends. They'll keep you safe."

Millie nodded, looking fearful.

"I need to go." Thea looked back toward the castle. "Elizabeth—"

"I'll gather as many as I can. We will stand by you."

Thea nodded her thanks and, with one last look at Millie, she left the stable and ran toward the castle. As she neared the door to the kitchens, the fighting grew louder and she knew the guards had made it to the kitchens. She took a deep breath, trying to recover her strength, and then entered the fray, ready to die for those she loved.

CHAPTER 22

THE SHEER NUMBER OF GUARDS BECAME OVERWHELMING AS Kieran fought off one soldier after another. He lifted the sword he'd taken from a centaur guarding the double doors and blocked the attack of a bloodied ogre advancing on him. The clash of metal on metal echoed through the dining hall like an off-key symphony, but Kieran did not falter. Sweat glistened on his brow and soaked his shirt as he spun to face each incoming enemy. Ogres, centaurs, Faeries, and dark magic backed him as far away from King Malachi as they could. He could see the king, chanting over the golden goblet on the far side of the room, with Morrigan perched upon his shoulder, but no matter how hard he tried, he could not get any closer. Kieran thought about trying to knock the goblet out of his hands, as if that might solve all their problems, but dark magic protected the king. It vibrated around him like an impenetrable wall. That meant that a distanced attack just wouldn't do the trick. He or Thea needed to get closer.

Kieran groaned and gave up on flying in the small space, knowing he had more of a physical advantage on his feet. After all, he'd trained for this nearly his entire life.

A sharp pain across his left bicep and sudden stinging warmth pulled his attention away from the bloodied ogre. He cursed seeing the injury his fellow Faerie had left on him and ducked to dodge a blow from the ogre behind him. He tossed his injured arm back, palm up, and a burst of wind and magic sent the ogre flying into the splintered dining-room table. He hit it with a groan, and Kieran returned his attention to the Faerie who'd injured him just in time to raise his sword and block another swing. His hair stuck uncomfortably to his face and neck, and his muscles ached with each swing of the sword, but there was no turning back now. Kieran knew he would die here tonight; he only hoped that he could take down enough of the king's guards to make a difference for when the others arrived.

"Kieran!" he heard her beautiful voice call above the chaos. Despite the room's size, Thea remained out of his reach. She stood just outside the kitchen doors. She no longer cradled Amara at her side, which he hoped meant she had gotten the younger girl to safety. Her hair had fallen around her shoulders and her eyes were wild but exhausted. Her chest rose and fell in quick movements while she scanned the room for him. She was his warrior princess.

"You have to stop him," Kieran cried out to her, hoping his voice would carry, as his sword sliced cleanly through the stomach of his Faerie foe. He felt the familiar wrongness of striking down a Fae kin, but then reminded himself that this was war. "He's going to bring her back!"

Kieran tried to fight his way past the line of soldiers that stood between him and Thea, but she seemed so far away. Her position by the kitchens put her closer to the king and Morrigan, though, which Thea seemed to realize as she glanced in their direction. Her eyes conveyed the same message that he felt deeply in his own heart: they both expected to die tonight. He mouthed the words she needed to hear and then returned his sword to the fight, taking down as many enemies as he could to save her.

Exhaustive magic coupled with physical fighting was wearing on him as the bodies dropped. He had many injuries, though thankfully none of them had stopped him from continuing on, but he couldn't fight forever. As his sword grew heavier and the clang of metal buzzed through his ears, a new group joined the fray, brandishing weapons of different varieties.

Humans.

Some had daggers or swords, but most carried kitchen knives or staffs. They fought well against the Faeries, as if they'd been training for this moment for years, and Kieran thought that perhaps they had been. Perhaps all they had been waiting for was someone to come and spark the fuse that would light the fire. He saw Thea, his beautiful warrior princess, strike down many creatures in her path, but she never stood alone. Beside her were humans, fighting to get her exactly where she needed to be. This made Kieran's heart race with hope. A dangerous hope that perhaps there was a way out of this.

It didn't take long before the humans joined him as well, taking off some of the pressure. One confronted him about his wounds, telling him he needed to treat his arm, but he shook his head in refusal, looking toward his princess, his queen. The human seemed to understand and remained at his side, a right-hand soldier as they made their way across the dining hall.

"Can you keep them from shooting me down?" Kieran asked.

"I will do my best," he replied. Kieran handed him his sword. "Won't you need this?"

"This is a war of ancient magic," Kieran said as his only explanation before soaring into the air. The room had limited space to fly, but he did not need to get far. He felt a sharp pang along his foot where something had caught him, but he flapped his wings harder to get to Thea. The clang of swords below told him that his new companions were doing as promised. It did not take more than a moment for him to land at Thea's side.

"You have to stop this," she was saying. Her hands trembled at her side, and Kieran knew the magic she wielded was tearing her apart at the seams. Morrigan soared in and out, trying to hook her claws into Thea, but Kieran's hands flew up, creating a barrier between their bodies and the raven. Thea glanced at him with relieved surprise, realizing he'd arrived.

"This will save us," King Malachi said, adding another ingredient to his goblet. The smile on his face told Kieran they were in deep trouble. "You'll see. She's going to bring peace and balance to our world."

"Peace and balance come from coexistence and equality, not from subordination and classism!"

Kieran didn't know how Thea knew this, but something in the way she spoke made him believe she knew exactly the kind of evil threatening Faerie.

"Growing up with humans made you soft, girl."

Kieran stood beside Thea as her right-hand soldier, her protector; and took her hand.

"Growing up with humans is what will make her a queen," he said. The king's men outnumbered them, even with the help of the humans, but if he was going to die, he'd do it by her side, defending her. He stretched his wings out wide behind him and extended his other arm out, palm up.

"You think you're stronger than me?" King Malachi smirked, shadows growing around him. His pride was the flaw that Kieran was counting on, as Malachi took his eyes away from the goblet. Kieran focused, sending a blast of energy toward the king. Thea squeezed his hand tightly as the attack was easily blocked.

"Maybe not alone," Kieran said.

Thea raised her free hand then, copying his movements with

a ragged breath. Kieran saw the strain behind her gaze as she summoned the strength to perform the magic.

The king laughed, but his defense faltered, and their combined attack made him stumble back a step. Morrigan made an angry sound as she landed beside the goblet, dipping her beak into it.

Kieran and Thea moved forward in unison, never lowering their hands as a shield of air guarded them from the shadows. Kieran noticed Thea's eyes close as he guided her, and soon the ground trembled, making the king stumble and spilling part of the goblet's scarlet liquid.

"Focus," Kieran told Thea between breaths. He flapped his wings, sending a stronger gust of wind toward Morrigan, who had landed to inspect the liquid spill. She rolled backwards, her wings twisting at odd angles as she did.

"I'm trying," Thea groaned. Her hand trembled in his, but as he glanced at her something knocked him square in the chest. He looked up just in time to see an ogre break through the line of humans. Bodies lay limp or cowering on the floor as he swung what looked like a giant wooden bat. Kieran had to release Thea's hand to avoid falling backwards. The ogre had struck him with the bat and Kieran's chest ached from the impact.

Thea's eyes darted to his, but they were separated once more. The ogre swung again, and Kieran tried to get himself airborne in time to avoid the second impact. He wished desperately for his sword as the space closed in around him and the bat collided with his right wing, giving a deafening crack.

Thea screamed, but searing white pain blinded him. He fell to the ground, his shattered wing crumpling beside him. His body trembled in agony as he tried to push himself up, but the ugly creature roared behind him. Another sickening crack split the air, and his vision blurred into scarlet blood. He couldn't stop the guttural scream that escaped his lips as he pressed his slick palms into the ground in front of him for support. Both wings stuck out at odd angles, and a pulsing sound in his ears told him his heart was racing, but he had no control over his limbs anymore. He heard Thea screaming for him, but shadows clouded his vision as wispy dark tentacles tightened around his arms and legs. When they twisted icily around his neck he clawed at them, trying to break free, and felt them slip between his fingers—it was like trying to clutch air. His vision blurred from lack of oxygen as he thrashed painfully on the floor. His wings felt limp on his back and his eyes bulged; he tasted death on his tongue, metallic and sweet.

"No!" Thea's voice was distinct in the chaos. He clung to her delicate tone, remembering how it had sounded when she'd whispered his name. His nails dug into the wood flooring, and he coughed against the shadows, trying desperately to get the breath of air his lungs craved. The burning in his chest was nearly unbearable, though, and he knew he would not last much longer.

A final whispered wish to see Thea one last time through the darkness was all Kieran thought as the wind picked up around him. It stung his face and eyes almost as much as the darkness did, and it nearly blew him sideways as it hit him. It was as if a tornado had gusted through the dining hall, and by the screams surrounding him, he realized he was not the only one feeling it. The suffocating shadows around him loosened, and Kieran's body reacted instinctively as he drew in deep breaths to fill his burning lungs. His eyes squinted into the wind as the shadows disappeared, and he saw the ogre that had attacked him thrown clear across the room. The humans were not faring well against the unnatural tornado either. Many clung to each other for help, while others fled back toward the kitchens, trying not to get knocked off their feet in the process. As the wind cleared away those left standing, the casualties spread out in front of them in mangled heaps of lifeless gazes. Most were human.

Kieran placed his palms on the ground and pushed himself behind the half of the dining room table that remained. A human with a swollen, bloody lip and half-closed eyes stared at him as if he was unsure whether he was friend or foe.

"What's happening?" Kieran asked, trying to sound calm. The pain on his back was nearly debilitating, and he knew his body was shaking beyond his control. "Who's doing this?"

"The princess," the human mumbled in return, trying to peek over the table. He looked only a few years older than Mica and scared for his life. Kieran tried to look over the table to see Thea, but the wind had only picked up harder and pushed the table, as well as Kieran and the human, a few feet farther back.

"That's impossible," Kieran said more to himself. He looked back at the young man and frowned, seeing that his hands were not the only ones shaking. "I need you to take a deep breath. You're going to be okay," he said, immediately recognizing the panic in the boy's eyes.

"My brother... I saw him..."

The body of a centaur flew as light as a rag-doll past them, screaming, and Kieran wondered what type of magic Thea had stumbled onto. For a moment, he feared she had tapped into dark magic once more but it did not seem likely since it wasn't darkness tossing things through the air. Furniture and people were flying around him. It was no longer just the humans fleeing the room, but also the soldiers.

"Come back, you filthy traitors!" Kieran heard King Malachi scream. His voice was hoarse from the wind.

"When I say run, you run. Do you understand?"

"Your wings, though—"

"I have to get to the princess, but you're going to run to the kitchens. It's the closest exit."

The boy nodded, unable to say anything else, and Kieran pulled himself into a squatting position. Pain engulfed every inch of his body with every move he made, but he did not wince. He thought of Thea, knowing he needed to protect her, and then he counted down for the boy before tossing the table aside with every ounce of energy he had left.

Kieran didn't look back to see if the boy had followed his instructions. Instead, he headed straight for the eye of the tornado that had engulfed the room, limping slightly and dragging his wings behind him one agonizing step after another. An abandoned sword became his weapon as he found the source of the commotion. She was high above the place where the king now stood looking panicked over the fallen goblet. Mysterious liquid bubbled across the floorboards and Morrigan was nowhere to be seen, but Kieran's eyes looked amazed toward the ceiling.

There, flying as if she'd been born to do it, was Thea, and she had magnificent burnt umber wings.

CHAPTER 23

THE BLINDING PAIN OF HAVING ENORMOUS WINGS SPROUT FROM
her back was enough to make Thea's stomach turn into knots,
but she knew there was no time for puking up the inconsider-
able amount of food left in it now. As soon as the pain stopped,
Thea took the surprise of the king as a chance to teach herself
how to fly. It felt as natural as riding Faylon, if she was being
honest, but she wondered if most of that was adrenaline. Seeing
Kieran's broken form suffocating beneath the waves of darkness
sent Thea over the edge. Something broke within her that she
didn't know if she would ever get back, or would ever want
back. She could taste blood on her lips and feel the swelling in
her limbs where the fight had worn her down, but she ignored
the pain, stretching her arms out around her. She'd seen Kieran
do this a million times, and yet, the actual act of doing it herself
was exhausting.

The wings felt heavy on her back, but she could nearly touch
the ceiling now. She stared down at the man who called himself
her father and then at her love as he stumbled into the clearing
below her. His wings did not move behind him. Instead, the
feathers stuck out at odd angles and their core bent unnaturally

in different directions. Thea saw the pain on his face as he tried to stand straight and face the king, but she didn't have time to go to him—Morrigan had returned. She headed straight for Thea, whose distraction cost her the balance she'd fought to establish. She dropped a few feet in the air, fighting to keep herself airborne as she dodged the raven.

Below her, a soft glow traced the edges of the spilt bubbling liquid. It sent a blinding light into the air, throwing Thea painfully against the wall. She heard nothing break, but her body ached from the impact as she fell to the bloodied ground and attempted a clumsy roll back onto her feet. The tornado of wind stopped as soon as she lost her focus, and she found herself surrounded by dead bodies, mostly humans who had died fighting for her.

Thea raised herself up and found Kieran, who now stood staring at the strange place where the goblet had spilled. Her father was on his hands and knees beside the glowing crack in the floor board. Thea pictured the crack in the hillside that Kieran had come through with dread.

The king wore a smile of triumph even as blood oozed from a gash in his side. The shadows had deserted him, leaving him defenseless in his weakened state, but Thea knew it wasn't over yet.

"What's happening?" Thea asked. Kieran also didn't stand in his usually erect form. Many humans and Fae had fled the dining hall when Thea's tornado hit, and none returned now. Thea imagined they were not far away, though.

"I think it's a portal," Kieran said. His voice cracked and blood dripped from his lips. Thea saw the paleness of his skin and the way his sweat-soaked hair clung to him. He appeared to be going into shock.

"A portal to where?"

Kieran was about to reply when the ground began to shake and the king's laughter filled the air. Morrigan had landed at the portal's edge, and with one triumphant look at Thea, she stepped into the liquid, disappearing through it.

"What—" Thea took a step forward, but Kieran collapsed beside her. "Kieran!"

"She will rise, despite this silly game you two have played," the king said with amusement. "And he will die, because you are too weak to save him."

Thea pulled Kieran into her arms, staring at the place where Morrigan had disappeared and then down at Kieran's barely breathing body. Ainé had given her these gifts, all of these powers, and she still couldn't save the one she loved. She'd come here to stop her father, and yet he was about to win. As she tried to think of what to do, movement came from behind them, soldiers trying to get back into the room. She turned just as the doors were opening and screamed, her hand flying up and flames shooting toward the incoming crowd. It felt like her world might explode with the intensity of that fire.

She was going to die here with Kieran, because no one was coming to save them.

The flames she'd conjured engulfed the doors of the dining hall. Untamed, they climbed the walls and blazed dangerously toward the three of them. The shaking of the ground had stopped as soon as Morrigan had disappeared into the portal, but now the heat of the fire brought a sweat to both Thea and her father's brows. She laid Kieran's unconscious form gently onto the floor, kissing his forehead one last time, and then stood between him and the portal as a hand reached out, covered in a black slime.

The hand was hardly a hand at all. It looked more like bones with translucent skin attached to them. The nails were long and curled, and it clawed at the ground to pull whatever body was attached to it out of the portal. Thea clutched the two daggers she'd secured during the fight, squaring herself for whatever would come, and the king crawled closer to the mangled hand.

He stared at it, transfixed and adoring. It made Thea feel sick to her stomach to see his devotion.

"My queen," he cooed, reaching for the grossest excuse for a hand Thea had ever seen. However, just as his hand reached out to her, another rose from the small portal. Thea jumped a little in surprise upon seeing it. It was clean, almost human-looking, aside from the fact that it was emerging from a magical portal. It wrapped tightly around the wrist of the mangled hand, and what sounded like a scream erupted from the portal. The sound was deafening. It shook the air in the room and made Thea's hands fly up to cover her ears. The king, standing so close to the portal, fell to his side with a cry of pain. Blood spilled from the corners of his eyes and ears as his eyes bulged with agony. As soon as he was writhing and distracted, the first hand reached out to grab the king's shaking body, and before Thea could even move from the shock of what was happening, something dragged her father into the portal with a cry of despair.

Only seconds later, another body rose, climbing its way out.

This body wore no clothing, but the same black goo that had coated its hand covered the rest of it. Thea could tell it was a woman. The tips of pointed ears were visible beneath the hair that reached to the lower part of her back and covered her breasts. Her red eyes glowed beneath the liquid on her pale skin, and she smiled, showing a row of pointed, razor-sharp teeth.

"Morrigan," Thea said, trying not to recoil from the sight of the Goddess of Death. "What have you done to Ainé and my father?"

Thea's eyes flickered to the portal, whose light was dying now. She knew it had been Ainé's hand who had tried to hold Morrigan back, but something had happened when Malachi went into the portal. The smile on Morrigan's face told her that something had not been a good thing.

"They are dead," Morrigan said, slowly, like she was trying to remember the muscles used to speak. She laughed, a high-pitched laugh that twisted Thea's stomach into knots. She continued to stare at the Goddess of Death, her wings twitching behind her and folding against her back. She didn't know if she believed Morrigan about the death of Ainé, but her father's death seemed probable by the amount of blood on the floor where he had moments ago lain crumpled in pain. A small part of her grieved his disappearance, while a larger part felt a relief fill her body. He was gone, which meant he couldn't hurt her or anyone else anymore. However, the threat that now stood in front of her seemed far worse.

Morrigan took two unstable steps toward Thea, her eyes sparkling, but Thea did not move away. She saw the effort it took Morrigan to move and wondered just how strong she was now. There was no way of telling, but if she was going to die anyway, she had nothing to lose. She held up her daggers, digging her heels into the ground so that she would not stumble from the impact. She glanced at Kieran one last time, wishing he was awake to say goodbye to.

Morrigan slashed out with her long, talon-like nails, and Thea dodged. It was all the energy she had left. She struck her dagger out at Morrigan and missed, but Morrigan clicked her tongue against her teeth with a mocking smile. Thea kept herself between Morrigan and Kieran, never letting her eyes leave the Goddess'. As they danced and blocked, Thea controlled her breathing the way Kieran had taught her to. She desperately wished for his help now, but there was nothing that could be done for that.

Thea choked on smoke as it saturated the room. She heard fighting through the kitchens, where the humans held off any of the king's remaining army, and knew she had one shot at this. With a deep, steadying breath, she threw herself at Morrigan, lifting the dagger into the air, and grazed the Goddess' shoulder. Both she and the Goddess let out a yelp of surprise at the contact. Thea glanced at her own shoulder and saw a thick trickle of blood dripping down her arm. It took her a moment to register it before her eyes met Morrigan's, and she saw the surprised look reflected on her face.

"Interesting..." The Goddess spoke mostly to herself. She smiled, but no longer looked triumphant as her hands lowered to her side.

"How is that possible?" A loud bang sounded behind Thea as the door crumbled beneath the fire she had started. Thea spun to see the mob of creatures charging through the smoke. She readied herself for them, knowing her chance had ended. She crouched beside Kieran and looked them in the eyes as they came.

"Enough!" called a voice from behind her. She'd turned her back on the Goddess who now strode forward holding her hands up to the oncoming army. They stopped instantly, every single one of them kneeling to the ground. "She is now under my protection."

Thea looked at Morrigan in disbelief, her breathing heavy and uneven. Blood coated her body and clothes, tears stung her eyes from the smoke, and her entire being felt like it was on fire from an overexertion of magic, but nothing compared to the confusion she now felt. Every enemy had stopped in their tracks looking just as confused and anxious. Thea pushed herself up into a standing position and felt a wave of dizziness threatening to end her consciousness. She fought it with great effort.

"But, my queen—" The centaur who'd fought Kieran earlier was bleeding from his brow, but his voice was cut short by an outstretched shadow wrapping around his throat. It had come from Morrigan's fingertips and sent a chill down Thea's spine. The centaur coughed thick crimson liquid, sputtering and begging, until his eyes bulged nearly completely out of their sockets and he fell limp to the floor. Everyone else's eyes lowered.

"Until we meet again, child," Morrigan said, her tongue

clicking again as she glanced over her shoulder at Thea. The hair on Thea's neck rose, and she raised her dagger. "Don't be stupid, or I'll take him." She looked at Kieran. Thea stepped to block her view and glared.

"Why are you doing this?" she demanded, but Morrigan was already halfway out of the room. Thea, panicked and unsure of what might happen next, threw her dagger as hard as she could at the Goddess' back. She knew it was cowardly to fight an enemy from behind, but they had taken so much from her that she didn't care. Morrigan needed to die, and if Ainé was gone, then Thea was the only one with the power to do any damage. The dagger stuck into Morrigan's back and Thea fell to her knees in pain.

There was a sharp pain in her back, as if someone had stabbed her as well.

Thea heard Morrigan mutter a few insults as she jerked the dagger out of her own flesh, but Thea could hardly see past the blinding pain. A soft buzz vibrated against her eardrums and her vision blurred as she crumpled onto the floor. She heard the distant sound of voices in the hall but could not distinguish friend from foe—all she saw was darkness.

CHAPTER 24

THEA AWOKE IN HER BEDROOM IN IVANDOR. SHE SAT UP QUICKLY, wincing with every inch of movement her body made, and found her arm in a sling. Her wings were twisted uncomfortably beneath her and felt the same way an arm did when she slept on it incorrectly. She tried to stretch, but every move she made hurt worse than the last.

"Sleeping with wings is difficult. It took Kieran quite a while to figure it out," a familiar voice said from the corner of the room. Thea turned her head, a bit too quickly, to see Ethel. Her cheeks were rosy, and her eyes looked painfully red.

"Ethel!" Thea nearly fell out of the bed trying to get to her. Her legs tangled into the blanket, and she grimaced, wrapping her free arm around Ethel's small frame. "Thank the Goddess you're okay, and here, and—"

"I can't breathe, Thea," Ethel said through a laugh that didn't really touch her eyes. Thea looked at her, kissing her forehead and brushing her curly hair back.

"Is Iris here as well? Did Amara find you?"

At the mention of Amara's name, Ethel's eyes darkened and Thea felt a familiar dizziness taking over. Ethel must have noticed because she hastened Thea back to bed, insisting she stay seated.

"Yes, Amara found us, and yes, Iris is here as well."

Thea studied Ethel's face, trying to understand the conflicting emotions showing there. She grabbed her hand, squeezing it tightly in her own, and breathed in her familiar scent, enhancing her own senses in the process. Despite her soreness, Thea felt rejuvenated. The magic she'd used during the battle had drained her. In fact, she'd thought it would kill her, but somehow it hadn't.

"Morrigan—"

"Has disappeared and taken the king's army with her, although none of us knows why," Ethel said quietly. "Your father is gone too."

Thea hesitated a moment. No one besides herself had heard Morrigan say that her father and Ainé were dead. She didn't know if it was true, but if she was thinking logically, her father *had* disappeared into a magical portal and could be dead. She had no proof of either death though, and didn't feel ready to discuss what her father's death might actually mean to her, so she just looked down.

"I should have been strong enough to stop her."

"You were alone, and you expected to defeat a king far more experienced than you in magic, an army of dark magical creatures, and a Goddess of Death? Alone?" Thea didn't miss the anger in Ethel's voice and winced at what she knew was coming next. "You practically got yourself killed because you didn't think to talk to us first!"

"I was just—"

"Being selfish? Stupid? Arrogant? Naïve?"

"Okay, okay." Thea let go of Ethel's hand and looked away, tears stinging her eyes. She'd nearly died and didn't feel like being scolded. She'd lost another father. Despite how much of an evil bastard he was, it still hurt. She wanted Ethel to hug her and tell her she was glad she'd survived, but maybe that made her naïve. "Where's Kieran?" Thea asked, suddenly needing his reassurance that she was not a complete idiot once more.

A knock sounded on the door and Iris poked her head inside before Ethel could answer, but that didn't keep Thea from noticing how the younger girl would no longer look at her. A heavy weight settled in the pit of her stomach as Iris entered the room, looking worn and sleep-deprived.

"Oh good, you're finally up," was all she said.

"Nice to see you too," Thea mumbled, causing Iris to roll her eyes. "Sorry, I might be a little grumpy."

"Understandable for a girl who's been through what you have. How's your arm?" Thea, momentarily forgetting her endless list of questions, remembered the pain in her shoulder that had made her pass out. She still felt a dull ache there, but nothing like the pain she'd felt before.

"It seems okay."

"Mirielle worked her magic on you." Iris smiled, but like Ethel's, it did not touch her eyes.

"Mirielle is here too? Is Mica here, then?"

Iris nodded and sat beside Thea on the bed. Ethel shifted from one foot to the other and glanced toward the door. No one said anything else. Instead, they stared uncomfortably at each other until finally Iris wrapped her arms around Thea and pulled her into a tight hug. She rubbed Thea's back, careful of her bandages, as all the emotions bubbled to the surface.

"You saved her," was all Iris said as she stared at Thea with tear-filled eyes. She didn't need to say anything else; Thea could see the gratefulness and the way the worry had lifted off her shoulders. She could see the unconditional love of a mother who hadn't even known her own daughter still shining brightly within. It made her heart ache for her own mother, or mothers.

"Where is she?"

Thea wanted to talk to her half-sister. She didn't trust her in the slightest, and the closer she stayed, the more comfortable Thea would be. However, the aversion of both Iris and Ethel's gazes made Thea sit up a little straighter. She looked between them both without a word, trying her best to summon all the "queen-like" features she could, but this was Iris and Ethel—this was her family. She could not be a queen with them. She could only be Thea. The silence was deafening between the three of them, though, making Thea's heart thump a little faster and the twisted knot return to her stomach.

"What aren't you telling me?"

"Amara is with Kieran," Ethel said finally. Thea felt a little of the weight lift off her shoulders. Of course Amara was with Kieran. Kieran would never have let Amara anywhere near Thea while she was not at full strength. He had no idea what had happened, besides whatever Amara had told them, so, of course, Kieran would make sure Amara was watched. Thea smiled a little, but then faltered because Iris was not meeting her eyes. Instead, she'd taken a small folded-up piece of paper from her cloak and was shifting it between her fingers. Ethel suddenly burst into a sob and ran from the room without another word.

"What is that?" Thea asked in a small voice. The door slammed behind Ethel loud enough that Thea's arm ached from the vibration. "Iris, what *is* it?"

"Kieran is gone, Thea. King Aragon asked for volunteers to reach out to our neighboring kingdoms, and Kieran volunteered."

Thea looked up at Iris, confused as the first three words repeated over and over in her head. She reached her hand slowly forward, holding her palm out for the letter.

"He left without saying goodbye... with Amara?" She refused to allow the anger she felt turn into tears, but her voice sounded completely hollow. "But, why?"

"He explained it all in this," Iris said, placing the note onto

Thea's palm. "I'll give you some time to read it, but we need you to come to the council hall within the hour."

"We?" Thea asked, her fingers closing around the thin piece of paper. She blinked up at Iris in confusion as the older woman stood up. Iris looked more withdrawn than usual, but Thea couldn't make herself understand why. All she could think about was what this note might say, what Kieran could possibly have said to make leaving okay when he'd promised to remain by her side.

"With King Malachi missing, we've formed a council with King Aragon's help. It comprises the few surviving elders from Ivandor. Not all of them escaped into hiding when your mother was murdered, but we summoned those who were left to meet their future queen."

The word queen reminded Thea of the reason she'd done all of this. She'd come here to protect her people. She'd come here to stop a cruel ruler from terrorizing the innocent. She'd come here to be a queen, and yet, all she was thinking about now was why her boyfriend, if that was what he'd been, had just up and left her after she almost died to save his life. Her heart, broken and aching in her chest, was not the most important thing right now, but her people were. She closed her eyes, inhaling, and then set the letter on her nightstand. Iris watched her with a curious gaze.

"You're not going to read it," she said without a tone of question. Thea stood, her body hurting with every movement.

"He decided without me. We are…" Thea fought control over the trembling in her voice. "I thought we were soulmates, but if that were true—"

A single tear fell down Thea's cheek, and Iris wiped it with her thumb. She cradled Thea's chin in her palm, tilting her head up so that they looked at each other directly, but it seemed to take her a minute to find her words.

"I love Kieran with all of my heart, but sometimes he can be a little hard-headed. You need to do what you feel is right here. Just know that I love you too, and you are never alone." Iris kissed Thea's forehead before releasing her. "And, for what it's worth, I'm sorry he's doing this to you."

Thea couldn't answer. She just nodded in response and glanced at her reflection in the mirror. She was bandaged and bruised all over. One of her eyes had turned an ugly shade of purple, and dried blood clumped the hairs of her eyebrows. It all looked like a horror-film scene.

"Will you help me prepare to meet the elders?" she asked Iris, turning herself fully away from the note from Kieran. It felt like a piece of her soul remained on that nightstand, but she could not force herself to read the letter. Whatever he'd written could break her completely, and she could no longer afford to break. If Aíné really was dead and Morrigan had returned, then Thea could not be a brokenhearted princess; she needed to be a queen. Whatever excuse or reasoning Kieran had for breaking her heart could not take her away from that, not after she'd come this far.

"I'll have Ethel run you a bath, but there is one more thing..." Iris looked at Thea with a look so broken that Thea's dread returned. "It's about Faylon."

"I can't handle any more bad news, Iris." Thea's voice was unsteady and her eyes watered once more, despite how much she fought the tears.

"Kieran was practically dead when we arrived, Thea. His heart hardly had a beat, and..." her voice faded away. She could not meet Thea's eyes.

A unicorn's horn is said to be one of the purest sources of magic in our realm, but that magic is their life source. Thea's heart, which she'd thought couldn't be broken any further, shattered.

"No!" Thea glared at Iris. This was the cruelest thing she'd said yet. Kieran leaving had been devastating, but this? This was unbelievable.

"Faylon knew you couldn't survive in a world without your soulmate," she said quietly.

"My soulmate left me!" Thea's anger exploded and she crumbled to pieces, because despite the argument she was having with herself, she knew that what Iris had said was true. If Kieran had been dying, Faylon would have done everything in his power to save him.

Someone else had died for her.

"Where is he?" she choked out through the terrible burning in her chest. "I need to say goodbye."

"I buried him in the gardens," Iris replied quietly, as if waiting for another explosion from Thea.

Thea controlled herself, trying to remember the last words she'd said to her familiar, wishing she'd said more. She'd expected to never see him again because of her own death, not because of his.

"I'm going to give you time to process, but Ethel will come draw you a bath in a few minutes." Iris squeezed her hand again before leaving the room. Thea wasn't sure if Ethel would actually do that. It was clear she was extremely upset with Thea, yet again, for the pain she'd caused. However unbearable the death of her familiar felt, nothing but stopping Morrigan mattered now. She needed to do what Ainé had asked her and unite the four kingdoms. That was her fate.

Thea went to her nightstand while Iris was gone and picked up the letter. She walked to the fireplace, tears filling her eyes, and stared at the flickering flames that warmed her bedroom. They danced and crackled while Thea's hands shook around the small piece of paper.

"I will not be one of those girls who lets a man break her," Thea said, tossing the paper into the fire. She knew the words were as much of a lie as saying she and Kieran were not soulmates, but it was a lie she needed to tell herself. She needed to know that she was going to get through this. She needed to remind herself that she could.

I will never leave your side. The broken promise echoed in her thoughts as the paper burned beyond her blurred vision, but a weight lifted from her shoulders all the same. Kieran had made his choice to leave; now she needed to make her own. She heard the door open and turned to find Ethel waiting.

"I'm sorry," she said quietly, looking at the floor.

"I'm sorry, too," Thea replied, and they hugged. "I'm sorry that I'm the reason he left." It was the first time she'd spoken the thought aloud, but the truth of it made her broken heart ache a little deeper.

"He's an idiot," Ethel said as her only response, but both girls smiled just a little. "Come on, you have a bunch of old people to meet soon."

Thea couldn't help herself; she laughed despite her broken heart. Ethel took her hand and led her away from the words Thea longed for, now burning away to ashes. Thea knew she needed to stop thinking about the letter, but the unread explanation would haunt her until the day she saw Kieran again—if she ever did. She embraced it, though. She embraced herself as Queen Thea without her right-hand soldier. Despite his pledge to always be by her side, she embraced the new life she would choose to live. Her wings stretched behind her and her eyes cleared of their tears.

"You know what, Ethel? I actually need to do one thing before I get ready to meet the elders. Can you do me a favor and send Mica to meet me in the gardens? I'm going to say goodbye to Faylon, but I need to speak with him about something."

"Okay, but don't be too long. Your bath will be cold." The two girls stared at each other for a moment longer, and Thea gave her an encouraging smile before she turned and walked out of the bedroom. She headed in what she hoped was the right direction to the dining room, but when she reached it, she didn't stop to see the disaster she'd caused within its four walls. Thea walked past the scorch marks and the broken furniture, ignored the dried blood and shattered windows, and bee-lined straight through the empty kitchens. Although she figured the humans were likely recovering, the castle walls felt creepier without their presence.

With a pang of guilt and regret, she glanced toward the stables where she'd last seen Faylon. She imagined him standing and grazing on some fresh hay outside, knowing he hated to be confined, but all that did was remind her of his now-lifeless body suffocating beneath the soil.

Thea had come outside to say goodbye to him, but more than that, she felt the fresh air on her face. Kieran had told her once that flying was the most amazing feeling in the world, and right now, she needed to feel that freedom. She needed to let go of the emotions that threatened to explode from her. So she turned away from the ghosts that broke her heart and ran as fast as she could away from the stables.

Kieran had said flying was difficult, that it took time to learn, but nothing about it felt difficult to her. She soared into the sky with ease, her muscles aching but reacting by instinct to what she wanted to do. Even with an injured arm, she could keep herself moving. The wind dried her tears, and she warmed the surrounding air with magic. She soared into the clouds, allowing the moisture of them to soak her skin, sticking her hair to her face, and then she shot higher to look out over the entire kingdom of Ivandor.

People crowded the streets of the crumbling village, cheering and laughing below. No one saw the heartbroken princess above; they only felt the joy of freedom and the power of hope—something *she* had brought to them, despite the cost. She knew that more people would come. They would return home. They would thank her for getting rid of her evil father. The truth was, though, that she had no idea what she was doing.

She should be dead, but for some reason, Morrigan had let her live. She remembered the way her own injuries had mirrored the Goddess', but she still did not understand it. She didn't understand how that connection had formed between them, but it was the only clue she had about the reason she lived and how she would stop the Goddess of Death. Nothing but that mattered anymore.

Diving toward the ground, Thea landed in the castle gardens uneasily, and saw Mica stood waiting for her. He said nothing, but he bowed his head as she approached.

"I have a job for you," Thea said, and despite all the arguments she'd had with herself about this since burning the note, she knew it was what needed to happen. Mica's face lit up, just like Thea had known it would. "I need you to find Kieran."

"Find Kieran?" he repeated, a look of confusion crossing his face.

"Yes," Thea replied, shivering as a breeze of icy air wrapped around her. "And report back to me that he's safe."

"You want to know he is safe?"

"I need to know that he's okay." Thea's voice grew tight. "Can I count on you to be discreet?"

Mica straightened up, his eyes meeting Thea's. He stood like a soldier, just as Kieran would have done, and then nodded his head.

"Of course, Princess Thea."

Thea wanted to reach out and hug him, but she didn't. Instead, she kept the posture of a queen and nodded her approval with a small smile of thanks. She knew she was taking advantage of Mica's good intentions to serve her, but she needed to know that Kieran was okay. She was also curious why Amara was with him, but he'd probably explained that in the letter she'd just burned to ashes.

Thea didn't want to know why Kieran had left, because if she knew why, then she might break into the million pieces that were being held together by a single thread. However, that didn't mean she would just forget he existed. His safety mattered to her more than anything.

"I need to get ready to meet the elders," Thea said.

"I won't let you down," Mica replied. They looked at each other one last time before Thea headed back into the castle.

As she walked, she saw the smallest daisy poking out from the deathly looking earth around her. She sighed, kneeling down to look at the beauty trying to withstand the darkness surrounding it, and promised herself that no matter what happened next, she would stop Morrigan and she would bring peace to the land of Faerie.

DID YOU ENJOY "WINGS OF FATE"?

If you enjoyed this book, please leave an honest review on Amazon and/or Goodreads.

Reviews and ratings are extremely important to indie authors because they not only give readers an idea of what to expect, but they also give me, the author, valuable feedback.

I look forward to reading your thoughts and opinions, but most of all, I thank you for taking the time to read this story!

ALSO BY SKYE HORN

Don't miss out on more magic, myth, and legend in Book 2

WINGS OF DECEPTION IS

AVAILABLE NOW ON AMAZON

Interested in more information about the Kingdoms of Faerie Series, upcoming books, or the author?

VISIT SKYEHORN.COM AND RECEIVE A FREE PREQUEL TO THE *KINGDOMS OF FAERIE* SERIES WHEN YOU SIGN UP FOR THE AUTHOR MAILING LIST.

ACKNOWLEDGMENTS

I need to start by thanking my incredible, patient husband, Robert. From reading early drafts to listening to me rant about plot lines to making me coffee so that I could stay awake to work—I couldn't have done it without you, babe.

Second, I'd like to thank my family and friends for their constant love and support. If I could, I'd list you all by name, but I hope that you know who you are because you've kept me sane during this entire process by listening to me rant and reminding me that I'm doing what I love.

Last, I'd like to thank the Self-Publishing School coaches and community. They were there for me through each and every question; through cover design; and through launching my debut novel. I honestly would have been lost without you all being there to answer my questions and support my journey. So, thank you.

ABOUT THE AUTHOR

SKYE LIVES IN THE SAN BERNARDINO MOUNTAINS WITH HER HUSBAND AND TWO FUR-BABIES. SHE ENJOYS THE BEAUTIFUL AND QUIET MOUNTAIN LIFE, MORNING WRITING SESSIONS WITH A CUP OF COFFEE ON HER HOME'S LARGE DECK, AND DANCING IN HER LIVING ROOM TO HELP HER CREATIVE JUICES FLOW. SHE HOPES TO INSPIRE A NEW GENERATION OF YOUNG WRITERS TO ALWAYS FOLLOW THEIR DREAMS BY TELLING THE STORIES THAT CONSTANTLY DISTRACT THEM FROM REALITY.

f facebook.com/skyehorn.author
🐦 twitter.com/skyehorn_author
📷 instagram.com/skyehorn_author